HOC GF

1 9 NOV 2019		

Please return this book on or before the date shown above. To renew go to www.essex.gov.uk/libraries, ring 0845 603 7628 or go to any Essex library.

D1375522

30130505765680

Discover us online:
www.crookedcatbooks.com

Join us on facebook:
www.facebook.com/crookedcat

Tweet a photo of yourself holding
this book to **@crookedcatbooks**
and something nice will happen.

With love to my witty, talented,
supportive and vivacious
school mum friends:
Mitch, Jackie, Liz, Holly,
Helen, Emma *and Lou.*

*You can bring sunshine
from the rain.*

About the Author

Award-winning inventor and author, Lizzie Chantree, started her own business at the age of 18 and became one of Fair Play London and The Patent Office's British Female Inventors of the Year in 2000. She discovered her love of writing fiction when her children were little and now runs networking hours on social media, where creative businesses, writers, photographers and designers can offer advice and support to each other. She lives with her family on the coast in Essex. Visit her website at **www.lizziechantree.com** or follow her on Twitter **www.twitter.com/Lizzie_Chantree**

Acknowledgements

Thank you to Crooked Cat Books, for being supportive and having confidence in me. Thanks to Alice Cullerne-Brown for being a completely brilliant editor and for all of your hard work. You are not only a talented editor, but also one of the kindest people I've met.

A big hug is sent to my amazing family and friends, especially, Martin, Mia and Ella. You've kept me writing and smiling and believed in me, which means everything.

Finally, a really big thank you to my readers. You inspire me every day and without you I wouldn't be on this incredible journey. You are stars that shine brightly and I appreciate all that you do.

Ninja
School Mum

Chapter One

Skye tapped her feet impatiently as she looked at the ominous grey clouds hovering above the playground and tried to rein in the anger she could feel blazing in her chest. She had learned the skill of outwardly controlling her emotions and appearing like she hadn't a care in the world long ago, but if her son came out of school crying because a more boisterous kid had poured water on his head, or scribbled all over his carefully written work again, then she would struggle not to pick the culprit up by his leg and throw him into the neatly manicured flowerbeds that surrounded the glossy green windowsills of the school building.

She noticed the quiet red-haired woman who was sitting on a nearby bench, glancing longingly at the same group of school mums again. They were all huddled together like a rugby scrum, chatting busily about their day. Skye wondered why the redhead didn't get up and join them if she wanted to be part of the group so badly, but she could tell from the woman's body language that it was never going to happen. She obviously lacked the confidence or courage to break into such a tight-knit group of friends.

A movement to Skye's left caught her eye and she noticed the woman with the mop of curly hair and inquisitive eyes watching her again. She was frowning in concentration before realising that she had been spotted and seamlessly blended back into the throng of people waiting for their children to appear.

The sound of the school bell jolted Skye out of her reverie and she joined the other parents and carers craning their necks to catch a glimpse of their children. Skye's son had only recently joined this school, as they were new to the area, and it was taking Leo a while to settle in. A particularly annoying boy in his class had quickly realised that he was an easy target because of his quietly spoken ways and polite manner. Leo had only been at the school for a couple of weeks and most of the other children were a friendly bunch, but Skye's patience with this particular child was rapidly diminishing.

Suddenly the reception classroom doors flew open and a sea of children surged forth, all with rucksacks slung over their shoulders and water bottles grasped in their hands. Skye scanned the crowd and immediately spotted Leo, angrily brushing tears from his eyes as the annoying brat, Miles, followed closely behind, pulling her son's backpack and attempting to push him over. As they drew near to where she was standing, thunder grumbled overhead and Skye pulled Leo to her side, angling the tip of the long umbrella she was holding towards the ground slightly. Seconds later, Miles' foot connected with it and he started to fall. His hands flailed around and he let go of Leo's bag as he fell forward.

As if in slow motion, Skye reached out and caught Miles' own backpack, which was securely strapped to his back. Just before his nose touched the ground, she quickly braced her legs, swung him away from the floor and turned to put him back on his feet. Supporting his weight, she crouched down in front of him and brushed his coat to make sure he hadn't collected any dust from being near the floor. She made soothing noises at his near miss and he gave a shaky smile to his saviour. He was totally unhurt and it was all over so quickly that he didn't seem sure what had happened. She bet he was thinking that the weedy Leo boy was lucky he had managed to escape this time though. He'd soon learn not to mess with her son.

Looking directly into Miles' eyes, Skye gave him her warmest smile. 'Are you okay, Miles?' she asked sweetly, making him start in surprise that she knew his name. Miles' mouth hung open as his gaze roamed back and forth between Leo, who was by now standing quietly looking at his feet as if they were the most interesting feet in the world, and the lady with the piercing eyes who was staring him straight in the eye.

4

Leo dared to peek up, then moved behind his mum's waist as Miles' mum rushed over and grabbed her son's hand, while squawking at him for being clumsy and making her late, totally ignoring Skye and Leo. As she dragged him away, Miles looked over his shoulder at Skye with a frown of confusion, and she happily waved at him as he left.

'Mum!' hissed Leo frantically. 'You shouldn't do that here.'

Skye bent to retrieve the school bag that had been pulled from her son's back. She noted in disgust, that the bag was now torn. Standing up, Skye noticed that she had attracted the interest of the same woman who had been watching her earlier.

'Who is that?' she asked, inclining her head towards the woman who had just turned to greet a young girl with her hair in jaunty pigtails.

Leo looked over his shoulder to see who his mum was talking about and shrugged. 'Oh, that's Allie and her aunt. Allie's in my class. She told me that Miles tried to steal her backpack yesterday.'

Thoughtfully, Skye watched the retreating backs of the woman and child as they walked through the school gates, the woman pushing a shiny new black pram. Something was troubling her about the woman, but Skye couldn't quite decide what it was. Accepting defeat for the minute, and remembering that she didn't have to view every other human being as a threat any more, Skye held out her hand for Leo to take and they followed the steady stream of people out of the school gates and along the main road towards home.

Chapter Two

The following day, Thea peered out of the changing room of the little boutique she'd found down a side road. It was away from the main shopping streets but near her favourite coffee shop, in the small town where she lived. What had she been thinking, trying on a size 14 dress? She'd ballooned when she was pregnant and her misery had been compounded when she found she had developed a severe addiction to marshmallows during her first trimester. Thea peered morosely at her reflection in the badly lit, incredibly small mirror, and wondered how the hell she was going to be able to get the dress off again.

In desperation, she grabbed hold of the green curtain that was supposed to shield the interior of the cubicle from the outside world but, in reality, only marginally managed it if you put your bag on one corner of the floor and then used one hand to hold the other edge to the wall. The thought of letting anyone see her looking like a writhing mess in a too-tight party dress made her want to wail and sob in dismay.

She had felt like crying literally from the moment she had discovered she was pregnant to the first glimpse she had of her beautiful daughter. If it hadn't been for her sister telling her about the little estate cottages that had just come up for rent at the big manor house down the road from her, Thea might actually have gone completely mad. The prospect of being near her family again, after so many years apart, had gone a long way to healing a tiny part of her broken heart and offering a smidgen of comfort for the otherwise pretty solitary life she found herself living. She desperately tried again to unzip the back of the dress, but it seemed to have her in some sort of death grip. She stamped her foot in frustration and hot tears threatened to cascade down her rosy cheeks. A whimper from outside the cubicle made her gasp and she quickly took a furtive glance outside, from behind the edge of the curtain, keeping the bottom of it firmly wedged closed with her backside. Her gorgeous baby girl, saviour of her sanity, was still slumbering peacefully and was probably dreaming about her next feed. Almost falling backwards as the dress seemed to get tighter, Thea fought to take a proper breath in before she noticed the woman who had tripped up that horrendous boy, Miles, at the school. She was sucking her thumb and cursing, after stabbing herself with a particularly vicious, faux diamond cluster brooch she had been admiring, while the snotty-nosed assistant watched her over the rim of her tortoiseshell glasses.

'Pssst...' hissed Thea, almost hysterical at this point, thinking she might pass out from lack of oxygen as the dress was cutting off her circulation.

Skye jumped in surprise and Thea sighed, relieved, as the woman noticed the shiny new pram she had seen at the school the day before. Thea had left it in front of one of the two changing rooms at the rear of the shop, but the lighting was so bad that the woman couldn't really see who it was that was hissing at her.

The cubicle was rocking slightly from side to side as Thea frantically tried to release herself from the monstrous garment. It felt like it was literally sucking the life out of her and she slipped to the floor in a heap of limbs, just as the curtain flew back.

The woman seemed to assess the situation quickly, then stepped into the cubicle, which wasn't easy as Thea was rolling around on the floor, and closed the curtain behind her. Thea looked up helplessly as Skye gently reached behind her and released the zip at the back of the offending dress.

'Thank you!' Thea panted, when she could breathe properly again. Skye offered her a hand and helped Thea to her feet, as she was bright red and sweating profusely.

'I'm Skye,' she said politely, introducing herself, when Thea would rather she disappeared and forgot this ever happened. Her face flamed in embarrassment and she grasped the front of the dress to her ample bosom before it slithered to the floor into a seemingly innocent looking pool of silk and evilness. She couldn't quite pluck up the courage to meet Skye's eye, but she knew the inquisitive woman would be taking in every detail of her abundant curves and sweaty countenance. Thea wished she could crawl into the pram with her slumbering child and hide until the woman did the decent thing and left her alone in her humiliation.

Skye coughed gently and stepped out of the cubicle, pulling the curtain firmly closed behind her. Thea could have kissed her when she raised her arm and nonchalantly leant onto the side of the changing room to stop the nosey shop assistant, who was busily hurrying in their direction, from pushing her way in and discovering the poor woman inside.

Thea dared to peek out of the curtains, but she held her breath. 'Can I be of assistance?' asked the shop assistant, who seemed to have a very short nose, but still managed to be looking down it at Skye. Skye gave her a most disarming smile and the woman faltered a little in confusion.

'My friend is trying on a dress,' said Skye conspiratorially, 'which means I will need to look knockout too. Could you be a gem and grab me the red dress from the rail by the window?' The assistant heard muffled noises from the cubicle as Thea tried to smother a giggle, and looked suspiciously at the booth where Thea had been trying on the dress for an age now. Thea had been to this boutique before though and heard the assistant being reprimanded. She must have decided that her manager would tear a strip off her if she had yet another argument with a customer, as she paused for a moment, then turned and grumpily stomped back in the direction of the door, where the party dresses were displayed. 'I know there's only one size 10 left in that particular style and colour, and I thought I saw you pick it up and admire it when you first stepped into the shop,' she called over her shoulder to Skye, which made Thea gasp, as she was basically calling Skye a thief.

As soon as the girl's back was turned, Skye grabbed the red dress she had, indeed, picked up before Thea called her over. Thea realised that she had dumped it behind the dark blue velvet chair next to the changing rooms, as soon as she had seen poor Thea's plight. Skye hastily brushed the dress down and hung it up on a garment rail with a line of rejected dresses that were ready to go back to the shop floor and gladly sank into the chair to catch her breath, just as Thea shamefacedly pulled back the curtain and hung the tight dress next to the red one.

The shop assistant came rushing back, about to accuse Skye of stealing, when she spotted the offending dress hanging neatly on the rail. 'This might be the right size,' she said, picking it up and looking at the label sewn into the back, squinting her eyes suspiciously at Skye who was sitting innocently in the chair and cooing at the sleepy baby in the pram. She seemed sure something was wrong here, but couldn't quite work out what it was.

'Oh. I've just noticed what time it is!' exclaimed Skye, jumping gracefully up and moving the pram in front of Thea. 'My friend and I have to go and feed her baby before she wakes up and screams the place down. Isn't that right?' she asked a surprised and confused Thea as everyone turned their eyes to the peacefully slumbering child. Evidently the thought of the brat waking up and disturbing the peace with her squawking made the shop assistant turn puce in horror and she ushered them out to the front of the shop, holding the door wide open so that they could exit the building. 'I already have a headache,' she spluttered, 'the last thing I need is more noise!'

Skye and Thea reached the pavement outside, walked a few paces past the shop and then doubled over in laughter. 'Did you see her face?' gasped Thea. 'She looked like she was sucking lemons when she looked at us.' She held out her hand to Skye. 'I'm Thea, by the way.'

Skye held her ribs as if she was trying to stem her laughter and just managed to thrust a hand into Thea's before she was taken over by uncontrollable giggles again.

It felt so good to laugh. It had been such a long time since she had enjoyed herself so much, thought Thea. 'Coffee?' she asked, admiring how the other woman was so selflessly having fun. 'At least one good thing has come out of my predicament in that blasted cubicle. Shall we find cake?'

'You bet!' laughed Skye.

Chapter Three

The town had many bustling side roads off the main shopping area, but Thea chose a pretty little coffee shop a few doors down that had delicately decorated cupcakes and huge slabs of coffee and walnut cake in the window, as these were her favourites. Skye helped Thea lift the pram over the slightly raised threshold of the shop and they stepped inside the bustling seating area.

'I love this place,' whispered Thea reverently, as if she shouldn't really be there. She lifted her face up and breathed in the heavenly smell of cupcakes and coffee. 'Can you tell?' she asked holding a handful of her waistline in exasperation at her own weakness for light and fluffy frosted icing.

'You've just had a baby!' exclaimed Skye, quickly finding them a table that the pram, containing the still slumbering baby, could fit next to. 'Give yourself a break. The first months are exhausting and the least you can do is treat yourself to the odd slice of cake.'

Thea smiled at Skye's kindness, but knew she needed to curb her sugar craving and stop using it as a crutch for the misery she found herself in. She would go for brisk walks with her daughter and she would get fit!

'Were you much smaller before you got pregnant, then?' asked Skye candidly.

'No!' laughed Thea. 'I've always been curvy, but I now use the fact I've had a baby as an excuse for my fat bum.'

Skye giggled at her new friend's self-deprecating humour. 'People who get too thin can look years older,' she said conversationally. Thea eyed Skye's striking face and size 10 frame suspiciously and raised an eyebrow in question.

Skye held her hands up in defeat, but before she went to the counter to order two huge slabs of coffee cake with enormous frothy coffees on the side, she lent forward and whispered in Thea's ear, 'If you really want to lose weight, then I'll help you, but not until you've finished breastfeeding that gorgeous baby of yours.'

Returning with the fragrant coffees and cakes on a little black tray, Thea's eyes lit up, before she noticed Skye had spotted her reaction. She blushed to the roots of her hair.

The baby woke up and began to sniffle, so Thea expertly scooped her up and cuddled her to her chest, making soothing noises as she gently rocked her. Gazing down, she noticed the milk stain on her top and raged in exasperation. 'What the hell is the matter with me? I'm lusting after a slice of cake while my breasts have a mind of their own and are ready to combust with enough milk to flood this shop. This is Florence, by the way.' She held up the now wide-awake child who batted her lashes at her mother and decided she was really hungry now that she could smell her breakfast.

Thea darted a look around to see if anyone was going to start screaming the place down if she fed her child in public and sighed in relief that no one was taking the slightest bit of interest. Thea hastily unlatched her nursing bra, settling Flo to her nipple with minimal fuss. Once she was organised, Skye slid a plate across in front of Thea and she grabbed a fork with her free hand and stabbed a piece of cake, stuffing it into her mouth and sighing in sheer ecstasy.

Skye followed suit and they both shared a conspiratorial smile at how delicious and disgustingly naughty the combination of coffee and sugar was. 'Bliss!' sighed Skye, looking fondly at the happy baby before grimacing. 'I remember how many times I tried to feed my own son this way. I sweated it out for so many weeks, but failed miserably and had to give up in the end. My nipples felt like razor blades and there never seemed to be enough milk for Leo,' she berated herself, 'but the midwife assured me I was latching him on correctly, so I had to accept that and stop moaning.'

Thea noticed that Skye had gone quiet and was gazing off into the distance so she gently turned Flo round to wind her, while hoisting her top back into place.

'Thanks for helping me out,' she said.

'You're welcome,' smiled Skye. Thea could see she was trying to brighten her mood and not let the tears that were glistening in her eyes show. Thea frowned as Skye was pressing her unpainted nails into her palms, hard. It looked like the trick worked, as she winced and straightened her back before the tears fell.

'What would you have done if I hadn't come along?' asked Skye.

'I would have stayed all night rather than tell that snotty-nosed cow that the dress was too tight,' said Thea, trying not to laugh out loud as the vision of the rocking cubicle came to mind.

'She was watching my every move,' said Skye. 'She saw me pick up the red dress.'

'You managed to hide it from her pretty quickly though,' said Thea. 'Remarkably fast reflexes!'

'I move like a panther,' joked Skye in a sexy French accent, before stuffing another huge forkful of cake into her mouth and rolling her eyes theatrically.

I bet you do! thought Thea. There was something strange about Skye. Years of doing her job had taught her about the nuances of a person's personality. The woman sitting opposite her was outwardly relaxed, but the way she had scoped the room when they entered the coffee shop and managed to grab the table they were sitting at, right under the noses of a group of boisterous teenagers, roused her suspicions. When Skye had arrived at the school, Thea had put her name into an internet search engine. Everyone had photos online these days, but until two years ago, Skye and Leo didn't seem to have existed. Either she was mightily private and kept off social media, or something had changed for her then.

13

Chapter Four

Skye pushed open the door to her little cottage and grinned to herself at the sight of the comfortable furniture and the few trinkets she had started to put around the place. The owner of the cottage had great taste and had picked the style that Skye would have chosen herself. The kitchen was modern, with sleek surfaces, but the couches were squidgy and comfortable. There were no frills and flowers, which you might expect from a period building. The mood inside was warm and welcoming, but functional, and the owner had made efficient use of space too. Skye particularly loved the hidden ironing board, which slid gracefully from a drawer in the kitchen, and the American style fridge, which was tucked under a beam next to the oven. She would have to decide soon if this was the place for them to put down roots. Renting a cottage on the edge of the village was okay for now, but she was already starting to like this place and she was fully aware that she couldn't put off making a permanent base forever. It wasn't fair on Leo and it was a pretty solitary life for her too.

Though there were many areas of her life that she controlled seamlessly, once her little bundle of joy had arrived, he obliterated her defences and managed to drive her insane trying to do the right thing by him. She thought back to her earlier conversation with Thea about breastfeeding. In the end, the midwife had put a stop to it and arrived with a bag full of formula tins before Skye wore herself out any more. Leo only had to get so much as a sniffle and Skye blamed herself for not feeding him correctly when he was a newborn. For a normally strong, sane female, she could be pretty daft about some things. She knew it was irrational and that millions of children survived perfectly well on formula milk. She had fed him herself for the first two months, so he had got some immunity from her, and she'd just lost her husband so she had been a complete mental and physical wreck. Maybe she should cut herself some slack, she decided finally.

Skye loved her son, but she was sure she had been a saner person with more brain cells before he erupted into her life. He was just like his father, a bundle of excitable energy. Leo's birth had been a difficult one, not the calm division of labour she had planned, with Reece taking some of the responsibility by feeding her sweets and massaging her back and feet. She had decided to forgo pain relief in the belief that she would push once or twice and a perfectly behaved baby would emerge. Then she would sit up, she had thought, have a sugary tea, lovingly prepared by her husband, and go back to work.

As it turned out, the birth had been emotionally draining for all of them. It had been a breech position until the last minute when, typically of strong-willed Leo, he changed his mind and decided he would turn round and come out. The problem was that, in turning, he caught the umbilical cord around his neck and the assisted birth that followed included two epidurals and a ventouse hose thingy. When Leo finally arrived, twenty-four hours later, every surface of the birthing room had been splattered with blood as the ventouse slipped from his head with a resounding crack and Skye had screamed, thinking everyone was dead! By the time she had come round after passing out, and saw her son sleeping peacefully in her husband's arms, the previous day of hell was immediately forgotten as she fell head over heels in love again.

The day Leo was born had made Skye quake in her boots, but if it meant another Leo in the world, then she would do it all over again in a heartbeat. She had never met anyone so astute, loving and sensitive. Not since his dad anyway. They were like two peas snuggled up together in a little green pod and she missed him terribly.

Walking into the kitchen with a tired sigh, Skye reminisced about that day's events and how poor Thea had been struggling to get out of that hideous dress. It wasn't really that the dress was the wrong size either, she decided; it was completely the wrong shape for a new mum with mammoth breasts that were like armed missiles ready to explode with milk at any moment. If Thea gave it a few months and lots of brisk walks with that stylish pram of hers, then Skye thought that she would more than fit into the pretty purple dress Skye had seen in the boutique window. The colour complemented Thea's eyes and the neckline scooped down across the chest in soft layers of silk and tapered beautifully at the waist into an A-line skirt.

Skye hadn't discovered that much about Thea over coffee, other than her daughter's name and the fact that she looked after her very bossy sister's daughter during the day. She had a feeling that Thea's heart had been broken. She didn't wear a wedding or engagement ring, not that it meant as much these days. People often got married and didn't wear rings, or lived together without wanting to get married.

Studying the simple gold band on her own finger, Skye felt tears scratch the back of her eyes. She hastily brushed them away and walked into the kitchen to unpack the shopping she'd collected from the little supermarket at the end of the lane on her way home. The cottage was only a short walk from the village, but tucked far enough away from the main roads to give some privacy and avoid the gossip she assumed went with living in a small town. A woman like her arriving on her own with a young son was bound to create all sorts of rumours sooner or later. Thea seemed to be on her own and Skye hadn't heard any gossip about her, although Skye didn't exactly ingratiate herself with the other school mums by standing on her own and scowling at the pavement most of the time. Maybe she should make more of an effort if she did decide to stay here. No one was looking for her and the parents at the school probably had better things to worry about than the lanky woman who always dressed in dark colours and looked like she had been slapped in the face by a wet fish.

Skye began to unpack the shopping and frowned when she saw movement in the fields behind the cottage. Her body immediately tensed and her eyes strained to see what was hiding behind the tree she had singled out. She picked up a sharp knife, kept in a locked box above the kitchen cabinet, that she had brought down to clean before she went out. The handle felt familiar and she released it slightly so that it was resting perfectly in her palm, ready to throw. She moved adeptly to the side of the window, never taking her eyes from the tree, then sighed in frustration at her own paranoia as a broad-shouldered man stepped into the daylight and bent to pick up something from the forest floor. A flutter of... she didn't really know what, began in her stomach. It was totally inappropriate to stare, but the man was half-naked! His arm and chest muscles shone in the morning sunlight and the taut backside, lovingly encased in jeans, made her mouth go dry and her pulse start to race. Moving to the draining board, Skye grabbed a glass to fill up from the sink. She turned the tap to cold and, as the water burst from the pipes, she felt compelled to check if the man might need any assistance. She found herself scanning the field to find him again.

When Skye had spoken to the owner of the huge estate that included her cottage, he had assured her that she would have complete privacy here. He'd said the cottage had been recently refurbished and backed onto the estate wood and fields, which it did, but he'd also said that no one used the fields behind her garden, as you could go via the village road to get to the main house. He had also mentioned that the cottage was fairly isolated from other people, except for those who occupied the main house. Skye had explained to the owner that she was a reclusive author who couldn't concentrate with everyday distractions and that this suited her perfectly. He'd seemed happy enough with this and she hadn't enlightened him further. Her references checked out, they always did, and as she had paid six months' rent in advance, the owner had probably decided to take the money and quit while he was ahead. He'd obviously popped over to check on her and Leo the previous week, but fortunately they had been out. Skye knew someone had been in the cottage the minute she stepped over the threshold, but a neatly scrawled note stuck to the fridge explained that he had stopped by to introduce himself and to make sure everything was sufficient for them and that he was sorry to have missed her. He also apologised for letting himself in, but he had needed to check that the fire alarms were in order, which they were.

Skye really didn't like the idea of someone else having a key to her house but, until she decided to buy somewhere, there was not much she could do about it. It was his property, but she trusted that he wouldn't come in uninvited again. She hoped not, as she might mistake him for a burglar and accidentally break his neck.

She had assumed from his voice when they had spoken on the phone that the owner was of retirement age and a bit of a toff, as he was well spoken and lived in the huge estate they had passed on the road to the cottage. From her old job she knew that wealth could come from anywhere, but the house looked like a family home that had been passed down through the generations. She berated herself for not looking into it. That was slapdash of her. She usually checked every last detail, but had missed that vital one. She had been exhausted from months of meticulously planning her next move, and had then changed her mind completely at the last minute, on a whim. She knew she could never go back to her old life, after what it had done to her. She just needed to accept that and start being a bit more responsible.

She wondered idly who the mystery man in the wood was. His body language had been completely relaxed, so he didn't know he was being watched and wasn't looking for her. Maybe he was a groundsman or a grandchild of Mr Travis, the owner of the estate? Skye sipped her water thoughtfully and her body felt heavy, suddenly, as sadness engulfed her. She hadn't reacted physically to a man for such a long time. She could certainly pretend to be attracted to someone and it used to come in very handy for her old job, but the real thing? She had thought that part of her had died with Reece.

Eventually, Skye began to open cupboards and stack her groceries away with her usual efficiency, all food types together and nothing that would go to waste. She was used to packing up and leaving at a moment's notice and the habits were ingrained. Leo sometimes complained that they never had piles of snacks in the 'goodie' drawer she kept in the kitchen, just a few bags of crisps and some biscuits. That was enough for one child as far as she was concerned, but if they did stay here, maybe she would relax her routine a little.

She quickly finished cleaning her knife and locked it away again. She would have to learn to chill out a bit and be a little outrageous once in a while, instead of letting her training control her life. Skye used to have so much fun with her friends and family when she was growing up, and felt guilty that she had stayed away from them for so long, but she had felt it was safer that way. She vowed to leave her knives alone and take a leaf out of Thea's book. Maybe she should buy a dress like the red one and go to a party or two?

Skye's usual attire consisted of skinny black jeans, black T-shirts and clumpy boots. It wasn't because of her line of work either, as she had worn all sorts of outfits there and had often added a splash of colour before, but since Reece had gone, she wore black to symbolise her loss. No one else would realise what it was for, but she mourned him every day. Perhaps it was time to let a bit of colour back into her life, let down her guard a little and make some new friends, like Thea? She could always launch herself into the rugby scrum of mums and shock the hell out of them. That probably wasn't the best way to make a good impression though. She didn't really think they were her kind of people either. For a start, they all dressed the same; secondly, they were too groomed and expensive-looking for her. She was lanky and messy, and not glossy enough to fit in. Perhaps if she bothered to slap on some make-up and brushed her hair every day it would help?

Skye thought back to all the times she had been draped in expensive silk and dripping in diamonds for work, and the memory was like a thousand knives in her heart. She had loved her job and her husband, but she couldn't keep dwelling on the past. Life was here to enjoy and her precious son was starting to crave some stability. She couldn't keep dragging him all over the world any more while she ran from her demons. Leo's happiness was her priority, and it was about time she started to live again.

Chapter Five

Thea sat on the low wall, which ran around the school entrance and up to the playground, rocking Flo in her pram. The baby grumbled slightly before falling into a dreamless sleep. Thea wished that she could get some sleep herself but, between coping with a baby on her own, and the recurring nightmare she had about her boyfriend and his boss, Laura, in bed together, she felt that her eyelids were sprinkled with sawdust and her nose was the colour of a very ripe beetroot from crying herself to sleep at night. She really should pull herself together; after all, she practically used to run the lives of thirty-five people in her team. She was as efficient as a machine, her old boss used to joke, when she organised yet another sting operation or embedded three new people into someone else's life. That was before Laura took over and ruined everything.

How had she become such a loser? Thea berated herself, kicking a helpless pebble hard so that it ricocheted off the main school wall and flew up into the air. Thea cringed, waiting for the inevitable angry cry when it struck someone, but Skye reached across with lightening reflexes from where she had been leaning against the rain shelter and caught the pebble mid-air before it could do any damage. Everyone else was busy nattering away and completely missed the incident. Thea rubbed her tired eyes and wondered if she was hallucinating and imagined what had just happened.

Skye pocketed the stone and casually walked over to join Thea, sitting on the wall. 'Bad day?' she asked, peering into the pram and running her fingers over Flo's soft face. 'Does she ever wake up and cry?' Skye joked, obviously trying to lighten the atmosphere.

Thea smiled gratefully at the change in subject, but then decided to tough it out. She would not be a wuss and avoid confrontation like she used to. If she had learned anything from her last job, it was that she didn't need to pretend to be someone she wasn't. If people didn't like her, then it was their loss. She just had to keep telling herself that.

'Thanks for catching the stone,' Thea said bravely, watching Skye carefully.

Skye hesitated for a second, then smiled and laughed it off. 'I thought you had something against that redhead,' she looked towards the shy lady, sitting on her own once more, staring at the other groups of mums who were happily chatting to each other. 'Thought I'd better head you off before you took someone's eye out,' she giggled, nudging Thea's shoulder with her own.

'Great reflexes,' said Thea, determined not to drop the subject. Skye made her think of her old life and Thea suddenly felt her lunch rise up in her stomach in protest.

'I used to be a gymnast at school,' answered Skye when she realised that Thea wasn't going to let it go. 'It's great for co-ordination. I could have been a champion if I hadn't been so lanky... all arms and legs.' She shook out her arms, stretched her legs out and wiggled her toes to make her point. 'I got to a stage where, instead of being graceful, I began to fall over my own limbs,' she joked. 'I was so clumsy and hormonal that my parents despaired. The flips and twists did give me good balance though. I do like to do the odd cartwheel as well, but Leo gets so embarrassed that I've had to stop doing them in public,' she said solemnly.

Thea giggled at the mental picture she now had of Skye cartwheeling down the high street. 'It's nothing really,' she said finally. 'Just too many sleepless nights.'

'Allie told Leo that Flo had started sleeping through the night?'

'Ah...' mumbled Thea. 'Well, she has really, but sometimes she does wake up and last night was one of those times.' Skye arched her eyebrow at such an obvious lie and Thea's shoulders sagged in defeat. She felt like she was under the spotlight with Skye's piercing eyes scanning her face every few seconds. This felt like a job interview.

At that moment, the school bell rang and children seemed to flow from every direction, like the evening tide reaching for the shore. Thea jumped up as Allie ran towards her and grasped hold of her legs, sobbing into Thea's jeans. Leo came rushing closely behind, carrying her broken backpack. Skye shot him a questioning glance as Thea bent down to comfort her niece.

'Miles?' asked Skye. Leo nodded and carefully placed the backpack under the pram, out of sight of Allie where it might upset her further.

'He grabbed Allie's bag and tried to run off with it while it was strapped to her back,' he explained angrily. 'It snapped the strap and pulled her over. She's scraped her knee.'

'Right!' said Thea, jumping up, having checked over Allie's rather red and slightly bloody leg. 'I've had just about enough of that boy. I'm going to have a word with his mother.'

'No!' wailed Allie, grabbing at her aunt's leg as if the world was ending. 'You can't. He'll make my life hell if you say anything.'

'What else am I supposed to do?' asked Thea, trying to shake Allie from the death grip she had on her leg. She was remarkably strong for such a small child.

Skye gently disengaged Allie's arms to release Thea. 'He can't keep getting away with such bad behaviour.'

'Mum,' said Leo with an edge to his voice.

'It's okay,' she soothed, crouching down to whisper in his ear. 'It doesn't mean I'm going to hang him upside down by his ankles. I might just shake him up a little…' she winked, making him wince and roll his eyes at her. Thea was waiting expectantly, as if Skye had all the answers. Skye seemed to be making a quick evaluation of the motley group in front of her. 'Come to our house for dinner after school,' she said to Thea and Allie.

Thea frowned at the sudden invitation and wondered what the hell that could have to do with dealing with Miles, but Allie had brightened up considerably at the thought of visiting her friend's house for the first time.

'I'll have to check with her mum,' said Thea, 'but as she doesn't get home from work until six-thirty, it shouldn't be a problem. Where do you live?' Skye reeled off her address, then looked slightly shocked, as though she was surprised she had actually invited people into her home. Thea wondered if she had always tried to keep them at a distance before. That way they couldn't get hurt – or end up hurting her!

'We live in one of the estate cottages, just around the corner,' said Thea. 'There are four in a terrace by the main entrance from the road. You must be in one of the other two nestling into the wilderness. Don't they back onto fields or something?'

'Yes, that's us,' said Skye, as the children happily chatted. 'We can walk home together then, if we're almost neighbours. Let's go!'

Thea quickly pulled her phone from the depths of her messy handbag, the latest model. Thea knew she didn't look much like a tech geek and hoped Skye didn't realise that this particular phone had only just been released in the States. Otherwise she might wonder how on earth Thea had got hold of one or if she had exotic friends abroad with good connections.

Looking away, and obviously trying not to pry as Thea shoved some baby wipes back into her bag, Skye grabbed the pram and walked ahead, giving her friend privacy to make the call. Thea felt uneasy about someone else pushing Flo in her pram and tried to wipe her hand down her top, as the thought of calling her sister had made her hands start to sweat. She was annoyed at herself for letting her personal life get so muddled. She used to be so organised but, since Flo, everything was sliding into oblivion.

Thea dialled her sister's office number and held her breath, waiting for the inevitable disapproving tone when she answered. She haltingly explained that Allie had been invited to tea, when her sister finally stopped telling her off for phoning during office hours, then had to listen to several sharp questions about where they were going, before she managed to ring off with a sigh of relief. She couldn't win! She was moaned at for calling the office, but would get even worse condemnation if she had taken Allie anywhere without telling her sister first. The woman was a menace.

'Problem?' enquired Skye, who seemed to be hoping that she wasn't going to have to disappoint the children.

'Ongoing,' sighed Thea, smiling tiredly at Allie, who took that as a signal for assent and whooped with joy. She grabbed Leo's hand, who blushed profusely, and pulled him towards their homes.

'How that little angel has such a sweet temperament when she lives with my sister, is beyond me.'

'Is she hard work?'

'She's a royal pain in my backside,' laughed Thea, letting go of some of the tension that had been building in her chest. She took a calming breath and, after taking the pram back from Skye, released the brake and followed the children home. 'She works for a legal office and all she ever does is bark orders at me. I had a responsible job of my own before I came here, but to hear her talk, I'm a complete imbecile. I know Allie is seven and I've just had my first baby, but that doesn't mean I require two lists a day on how to look after her daughter and twenty phone calls to check up on me.'

Skye grinned. 'Maybe she's just really uptight and hates being away from her child?'

'Nope,' said Thea simply, grinning too now. Skye's smile was infectious and it had been a long time since she had had a real girlfriend to confide in. The last one had been a complete bitch and stolen her man. 'She's married to her work. Before I came along she had three nannies and a live-in childcare assistant, whatever that is. She managed to annoy the hell out of all of them. She's a control freak. Allie is so lovely and easy-going, but that's probably due to her dad, who's amazing. He's in advertising or something, so he can be home for weeks on end or away travelling. When he's around, my sister is actually nice, too. Well, sometimes anyway.'

'Good job Allie has you then,' Skye said simply, her dark hair flowing behind her in the breeze. She was dressed in dark colours and had angular shoulders and a graceful walk. Her look was effortless, like she had just grabbed the first thing out of the wardrobe, which would be easy as Thea hadn't seen her dress in anything but various shades of black. She wasn't what you would call stunning, but there was something about the way she moved that made you stop and stare. Thea couldn't quite work out what it was about Skye that made her interesting, but it was probably the fact that she didn't seem to care what anyone else thought and dressed for comfort not style. The understated look worked for her, though, and the slim fitting jeans and plain T-shirt under her open bomber jacket showed off a pretty spectacular figure, whether that was her intention or not.

Thea's chin wobbled slightly and she thought she might cry when she remembered that Allie had hurt herself. Her sister would throw a barrage of abuse her way for the small scab that was forming on her niece's knee. Skye dropped her arm around Thea's shoulder and squeezed surprisingly hard for such a slight woman. Thea gulped in some air and smiled gratefully, brushing a few stray tears across her nose with the back of her hand.

'Come on. Let's crack open a bottle of wine while I warm up the spaghetti Bolognese I spent ages pouring from a jar earlier. Can you drink while you're feeding Flo?'

Thea sighed heavily again. 'My sister says I'm a terrible mother if I so much as sniff a pressed grape. I will have a sip of yours, though.'

'You seem like a great mum to me,' countered Skye, walking towards home, 'although an emotional one,' she joked, seeing Thea's eyes fill with tears. She squeezed her shoulder even harder, making Thea cringe in pain. 'Let's forget the wine. I'll make some amazing non-alcoholic cocktails. You won't believe they don't pack a punch as they're so sour, but they're delicious nonetheless.'

Thea was a bit in awe of how Skye seemed to be able to make her feel happy and calm with a few words. That was a skill she wished she had.

'I was so worried about being a lousy mum myself, that I

banned alcohol for two years,' said Skye conversationally. 'Luckily, I didn't have friends to see me sink to such depths of despair.' Thea tried to hide her shocked expression at the thought of Skye having no friends. 'With my old job, I couldn't drink more than the odd glass of wine for years, so it wasn't that much of an adjustment. The pressures we put on ourselves are ridiculous,' Skye continued, then quickly tried to change the subject, looking upset that she had mentioned her old job and staring at Thea as if she was some sort of voodoo princess who got people to tell them their innermost secrets. She seemed wary, suddenly, and the light in her eyes dimmed as they reached the cottage and went into the tiny lounge.

Thea noted the mention of a job, but her years of training told her to drop the subject for now, from the way Skye had started to twitch slightly. She was just glad Skye had opened up to her, although she didn't believe the bit about her having no friends at all. Who wouldn't want to know this slightly eccentric woman who kept to herself, always dressed in dark colours and scowled at everyone? Thea giggled, making Skye look up from where she had started to make the cocktails in the kitchen. From the way she stood back and observed the friendship groups in the school playground, rather than trying to muscle in and ingratiate herself, Thea got the impression that Skye chose her friends carefully.

Skye began whistling out of tune as she turned the hob on to warm up the meal and Thea bent down to scoop Flo up into her arms for a cuddle as she watched the children playing in the vast garden behind the cottage, her bruised heart melting at the sight. Thea could see why Skye had chosen this place; it was heavenly. The row of cottages where she lived was much smaller overall. The actual houses were pretty similar with compact, but functional, kitchens and two bedrooms upstairs, but the garden here was glorious. It was edged with deep green, leafy shrubs and an abundance of flowering plants, which also smelt wonderful from inside the house. There was a big expanse of lawn in the centre which, for some reason, was laid out with four long tree trunks lying parallel to each other. Thea's cottage had a tiny garden, as you would expect from a building of its period. It was perfect for her, though. She was too exhausted from looking after Flo and Allie, and listening to her sister's endless lists of complaints each day, to have the energy to prune a hedge or drag a mower out of a decrepit shed. Not that her shed was old or falling apart, but the thought of even opening the door made her feel rather faint.

Thea realised now why her old job had suited her so well. She had freedom from her family's endless demands on her, she had discovered that she wasn't useless and she'd mastered some marketable skills along the way. She thought back to when she had been recruited, joining a small firm and organising them efficiently within a year. Then, on one particular day, a client had arrived, which was most unusual. They never had clients come into the office. For the very shy Thea, this was perfect. When her boss had summoned her, she had been told she was requested for the meeting and she had almost fainted on the spot. No one had really asked her opinion before, even at work. They just handed her the task with a nod and she got on with it. Thea had no idea what to say to a client, although she knew her own role inside out. She had discovered she had an affinity with computers and ran all their systems and calendars. She had even taken a college course at night and became qualified. It was at this point Thea wished that she hadn't lied on her application and said she had more skills than she did, but she was resourceful and wanted so desperately to prove to her family that they were wrong about her stupidity. As it turned out, they weren't, as the certificate she so proudly collected for her course had a made-up name and address on it and could never be presented to her family. She was such an idiot!

Thea had walked shakily into the meeting, assuming that her number was up and she was going to be shamed and fired. She felt even worse when her boss nodded for her to sit across from the client and then left the room, quietly closing the door of the sterile room behind him, leaving her scared out of her wits and completely tongue-tied. She valiantly tried to raise a smile for the serious-looking woman who faced her and gulped a mouthful of water from the glass on the table in front of her, to try and get some liquid into her parched throat. Thea took a deep breath and waited to see what the client wanted. It seemed she was destined to be one of those people whom others walked all over and took advantage of.

Everything changed for her that day. The woman had noted her unease, rested her arms on the table, removed her glasses to rub between her tired eyes and smiled at Thea reassuringly. Thea had been so shocked by that smile that she had almost fallen off her chair. She was gripping the water glass so hard that she thought it might burst into a thousand shards and put her out of this endless misery. Her fingers eased their grip a little, but she wasn't willing to put the glass down just yet. As the woman spoke, she explained where she had come from and what would be required of Thea. A smile had suddenly spread on Thea's face and she rested the glass back on the table. They wanted to poach her. Her! She didn't really care who 'they' were at that time, she just understood that, for the first time, she was being told she had done an amazing job and they were offering her a chance to turn a corner and start again. No more of the endless chores and infighting at home, or the invisibility she seemed to have at work, even though she practically ran the place. They had picked the perfect time to recruit her, although she now knew it had all been carefully orchestrated. She had been an easy mark. She was a sponge who soaked up information and was willing to learn more. Her skill set was quite valuable to them and she had proved them right time and time again over the years… until recently, she supposed.

There had been no banners or leaving party when she left that job, not that Thea really cared. They hadn't even known her real name. She was escaping her life and inventing a new Thea, well, for a second time anyway. She hadn't confided in her new bosses about her real identity and they hadn't queried it; she had a sneaking suspicion that they wouldn't have cared a jot anyway. It was probably an added bonus that the person they were recruiting was used to lying as it was an asset in her new career. There had been no going back.

What scared Thea, looking at the sleeping baby in her arms

and the excitable children playing outside, was that things had now come full circle and she was back where she had started. Getting shouted at by her family and doing a job for her sister that was neither appreciated nor that welcome. Her sister had asked her to come home and offered her a job because no one else would work for the narcissistic control freak. Thea had needed to get away from work when she found out she was pregnant and this was the only place she could think of to hide where Flo's dad wouldn't come looking for her. Not that he knew Flo existed. He didn't deserve to know about this precious baby girl after the way he treated her mother, the cheating scumbag!

Skye's whistling was coming to a crescendo and it was hurting Thea's ears, but she smiled when she turned round and saw that Skye was doing it to snap her out of her reverie. She gently placed Flo onto the soft rug by the fireplace so that she could kick her legs out for a while and took the tall, brightly coloured glass of bubbly drink that Skye held out towards her. She sniffed the drink cautiously, took a tentative sip and cringed in disgust as her toes curled up in protest at the flavour. After the first sour punch, she tasted a sweet hit of sugar syrup and a mouthful of strawberries that was blissful. Her eyes went wide in shock and, rather than spitting the drink out, which had admittedly been her instant reaction, she took another sip.

Skye giggled at Thea's reaction. 'Good after the first hit, isn't it?'

'Where the hell did you learn to make that?' asked Thea, not sure what to do with the glass as another mouthful might knock her sideways. 'That must be alcoholic?'

'Not at all,' said Skye, tapping the side of her nose. 'It is a trade secret though.'

Thea gave up looking for somewhere to place the drink and took a big mouthful of the heavenly concoction instead. 'Right,' she said, giving up on finding out what she was drinking and savouring the burst of tartness instead. 'So what's your plan for keeping the kids away from Miles the Manipulator?'

Chapter Six

Zack kicked the doorframe in frustration, and then wished he hadn't as a lump of wood flew off. Blasted woodworm! He would have to get Mike to treat it before the whole thing crumbled to dust. He had been neglecting the upkeep of the house while finding his feet with his tree climbing business, CloudClimb. Zack was quite surprised at how much he was enjoying being in the land of the living again, instead of shutting himself away from the world and staring at his computer screen all day. He knew the apps he designed paid for all this, but Zack was discovering that he liked working outdoors with a team of friendly and easy-going people. He'd chosen his staff carefully and made sure they were competent enough to get the job done without him, but under his guidance. He had also poached a couple of people from a similar site in the next county, but the rest were all locals. He had an onsite office, and one in the main house where he could hide away from everyone when the noise of all their chatter and gossip got too much.

Zack picked up the small piece of wood and placed it onto his work desk. He loved his new app-designed workroom, in the old library. Other than walls of books and a few items of furniture, it was completely empty. He had a huge leather lounge chair, an indecently-sized flat screen television which could be hidden behind a sliding panel on the only blank wall, and three computer screens which were linked up on one side of his solid oak desk. He didn't need fancy art or vases bursting with oversized flowers, as the room was on the right of the manor house and had huge picture windows on both sides. The stunning views of the gardens and fields beyond were nature's paintings and the sight lifted his black mood slightly.

His daughter was crying again and Zack couldn't seem to soothe her tears this time. Her mum had walked out of their lives when Emmie was two and he hadn't been able to refuse his daughter anything since then. He knew he was an idiot who spoilt her and she was turning into a demon child, but she could be so sweet and a complete angel when she wanted to be. Attending the local school had helped to ease her violent tantrums somewhat. She was perfectly well behaved with other adults and children, she just directed her anger towards him, shouting and generally using him as a verbal punch bag. Zack threw his arms wide in frustration before hunching down in front of his daughter and enveloping her in a warm hug, which was not gratefully received. She looked at him mutinously.

'Look, Emmie,' he explained carefully. 'We can't get another puppy.' Zack looked over to where their two dogs were flopped out on the floor in exhaustion after two hours of playing with Emmie in the extensive grounds that encompassed their sixty-acre estate. 'I don't think even a puppy would have enough energy to play for this long. Buzz and Poppy might be a bit old...' he gestured towards the panting dogs which they had inherited when they moved there. He knew they would need dogs with a property this size, but didn't have the energy to train puppies as well as Emmie, so it had worked out okay in the end. 'But they do run around with you as soon as you get in from school. They're so excited to see you when you arrive home. How come you aren't tired after a long day at school anyway? I'm exhausted,' he sighed, rubbing his sore back from where he had helped Mike build a new lower walkway for the tree business that morning. Zack's muscles had certainly developed since they had moved there, but boy, did he ache all over. Emmie wiped away her tears and hugged her dad fiercely, making him rock back in shock at the sudden burst of emotion.

'Is there anything else bothering you?' he asked, pulling away slightly, but loath to break the contact completely and dreading the 'M' word.

31

'It's Miles,' she sniffed, wiping her nose on his arm, as he tried desperately not to scold her for being so disgusting or to stamp his feet at the mention of Miles. 'He says that my dogs are old and useless and that his puppy, Roseby, wins rosettes at the Puppy Club.' Emmie raised watery eyes to his and Zack's heart melted. He pulled her in for another hug and she snuggled into his arms. Maybe he should be thanking Miles for making his daughter want to hug him, but he couldn't quite be that gracious to the little horror.

'Well,' Zack said carefully, trying not to squeeze the life out of his daughter, grinding his teeth and wishing that Miles would stop bragging and go and find other friends. 'Miles doesn't know everything and his dog has a stupid name.' He saw Emmie smile at this and Zack laid his head onto her soft hair for a proper cuddle. Miles was probably only being friends with Emmie because her dad ran the local tree climbing centre.

The centre was situated in the wood surrounding their home, on the side of the main road. The back of the house had a formal kitchen garden with an abundance of vegetables, if Zack ever had time to pick them. To the right were fields, which ran across to the last two cottages on the estate. Zack had never invited Miles round, as the boy was a menace, but his mum kept booking him onto the training sessions that Zack ran up in the trees and she insisted on standing underneath and taking surreptitious photos of her son, but only when Zack was working.

Zack was a workaholic who always ran the safety checks personally before any paying guests were allowed onto the site, so he was often around. He really didn't like people sticking their noses into his business, which was why he restricted the site to one side of the estate, where the cottages were. Only one of the more isolated cottages was rented out at the moment, by a reclusive author and her family, although all of those on the main road were full. The last cottage by the fields was still a bit of a mess, as Zack hadn't had time to refurbish it yet.

To access the estate, you had to travel via a grand driveway to the house; the cottages acted as a barrier to the estate and then the tree climbing business nestled in the trees along the drive. It meant that Zack could see the hustle and bustle of people, but not get involved if he didn't want to, and Emmie had kids to play with occasionally. Zack didn't have time to be lonely with this place and Emmie, but he wondered if his ex, Kay, would come crawling back if she realised how well things had turned out.

The problem he was finding was that Emmie was old enough now to start asking him for sleepovers and friends to tea. He was quite domesticated, through necessity, but he would rather pull teeth than have a house full of gossiping women and their messy brats. He bet they would love to find out he had been dumped by supermodel Kay Idol, as she self-deprecatingly called herself. Dumped with a baby and left for another man with a bigger wallet. Not that they had lived here then. He bet she would have hung around if they had. She left him for the guy who had hired her to model his diamond jewellery collection. The enticement of the material things he could offer her, draping sparkling stones around her wrist and throat, was too much to turn down and she hadn't looked back, not even for her child. The family had lived in a small flat at the time. Kay was just becoming well known and Zack was struggling to get his first phone app working. She lost her patience with him and the responsibilities of having a child, leaving Zack devastated and Emmie distraught. She was such a selfish witch. He tried to think what he had ever seen in her, then he remembered her soft skin and her taut muscles. Zack had been so besotted by Kay that when she had decided her career wasn't taking off and they should have a child, he had been sceptical, but happy. After despairing of him ever making a success of things, and tired of a squawking baby, Kay had landed herself a job abroad, met the diamond dude and called him to say she was never coming back.

Zack had struggled to make ends meet and look after a demanding child, but he had done it, and just look at them now. He couldn't quite believe his life had turned out like this, but he was glad that it had. His grandfather was well known in affluent circles and had owned this estate, but had let it pretty much run into the ground. He had tried to offload it on his son, Peter, but Zack's dad was swanning around the Med and ignored his old man. It was just another crazy whim as far as he was concerned. Peter had saved carefully to be able to spend his retirement travelling with Zack's mum. Although the family had good bloodlines, Zack's grandfather was on a mission to spend all their money. Zack's parents had become proficient at being frugal, even though his granddad was sometimes quite wealthy. He could be at rock bottom, then some bond or deal would work for him and he'd be rolling in cash again.

Peter had grown up on large estates like this one, but seeing his dad fritter away the family money on his latest fads was soul destroying. He'd distanced himself from him, even though he loved him dearly, and let him get on with whatever interest currently held his attention, learning the hard way not to get involved, when his own trust fund had dwindled to nothing through constantly bailing his father out. Zack had a similar view of his granddad, although he did admire his free spirit and joie de vivre. Zack had not had any money for his granddad to ask for until recently and, even now, he kept his newfound wealth close to his chest.

This time, though, Zack had grudgingly taken the opportunity to help out. Gramps was incorrigible and Zack didn't want to be asked to extricate him from mountains of debt, but Gramps had finally abandoned somewhere that had potential as an investment and Zack had some money to pay the creditors and could keep the building. The main house on the estate was a bit of a mess, but five of the cottages had been easy enough to renovate and rent out to pay for themselves. The woods had been turned into a valuable business with the tree-walking and adventure trails, which Gramps had started and got bored with, or ran out of money for. Apparently, his previous inamorata loved nature and wanted him to make a business out of the trees, but she hadn't accounted for his short attention span and had to be practically dragged out of the wood when Gramps had swanned off to Italy with a darling woman he met while walking his miniature pet pig. Zack had found a new home for that before Emmie had a chance to fall in love with it. Apparently, 'miniature' pigs could grow to the size of a house.

The new business was easily accessible from the main house, but far enough away for Zack to have privacy from prying eyes. The house would cost hundreds of thousands to renovate and keep up, but Emmie loved it here. They had found a great local school and she had a nice group of friends, Miles notwithstanding. With the basic business model Zack had implemented for the tree climbing, and by selling off the horrendous antiques Gramps had amassed then dumped all over the house, he was able to turn a profit fairly quickly. He hired a firm of specialists to come in and complete the trails in the woods, and finish securing the tree-walking ropes and walkways and, before he knew it, word of mouth had got round that the old man had moved on and his grandson had started a new place for kids and adults to blow off steam. It had been an almost overnight success. Zack couldn't add to the place fast enough.

The shock of losing his wife and bringing up a toddler on his own had been enough to turn a fun-loving guy into a virtual recluse. His own business had been in its infancy then and he had buried his bitterness and broken heart in long hours at home with his little daughter, praying that her mum would return. Zack had tried calling her endlessly, and left humiliatingly awful pleading messages saying how much they both missed her, but she ignored them all. Kay sent a quick note to say that she was sorry, but she wouldn't be back. Zack's heart broke for Emmie and he dreaded the day she asked him more about her mum. The few tentative questions Emmie had asked had been stilted, as if she was frightened to cause him pain. Zack didn't know if Emmie remembered her mum but, as she grew older, he was sure she would want to know more. He sometimes wondered if this was the trigger for her tantrums. How could he tell a child her mum had abandoned her? The thought made him shatter inside and burn with uncontrollable rage.

Zack knew that they were better off without Kay, who was now regularly featured in magazines. Luckily, she lived abroad, but a tiny part of him knew Emmie would crave a woman's guidance one day. Better his influence than a woman like her mother, Zack thought bitterly, as he released Emmie to go and sit on the floor with the dogs now that she was calmer. He smiled as he watched her lay her head on Poppy's chest while the dog didn't budge an inch, she was so tired.

Zack thought how lucky he was that the endless hours of hard work, in the flat where they had lived previously, had paid off. He designed colourful applications for phones and computers from the library in the main house now, although he did occasionally like to wander over to the separate office he had built by the side of the CloudClimb reception building. The phone app he'd designed wasn't meant for children as, although he was a dad himself, he couldn't stand most other people's kids, but he had been totally astounded when the bestsellers' list came out and his game was top of the rankings. Kids had told their friends and everyone was playing his game. No one outside the industry would know Zack had designed it, but he found that he had a talent for connecting with children through play. Who could have guessed?

Zack now had enough money to rebuild the house and grounds and, if his programs kept selling the way they were, he would never have to worry about paying for anything again. He had originally thought that he would dump the tree climbing business, as it would be too much trouble, but he had decided to see if it could work, for Emmie's sake really. Having a business that brought children to the estate, and didn't leave her as isolated as his app design business did, could only be a good thing. Also, it meant he wasn't a sad loser who sat in a big house on his own all day with just a small child and two old dogs for company. Zack wouldn't have minded this, but he knew Emmie would. He didn't want to be compared to her vivacious mother and come out lacking. He tried his best not to hate Kay, but it was an ongoing daily battle that he was losing. It was exhausting, carrying so much hatred around after all these years, but he couldn't seem to shake the resounding sense of failure that followed him everywhere, however much he tried to build something new for them and paper over the cracks in their family life.

He might be a bit grumpy and have taken time to establish himself, but Zack always knew he had skills in design and could maximise an opportunity when it fell into his lap. CloudClimb paid for the estate grounds to be kept in order and the app business sated his craving for technology and meant he could easily afford to update even a house this size. He had been looking into ways to bring the two businesses together and was actually quite excited about the possibility of using his latest app design outdoors. He was planning interactive games that began the moment a child, or adult, stepped onto the adventure trail, which wound its way through the woods and ended back at the entrance to the tree-walking site. The app would work via people's phones and he was excited at the thought of installing video cameras on all of the safety helmets for the tree walkers, so that they could livestream their adventure to friends or parents on the ground.

While he had been drifting off and dreaming of his expansion plans, Emmie had wandered somewhere. Zack assumed she had gone upstairs, but seeing the tail of one of the dogs disappearing behind a tree leading to the fields, he got up and started after her. Emmie was allowed to play in the fields, but now that someone was occupying one of the cottages beyond the farthest field, Zack quickened his pace. He hadn't met the tenant yet and didn't like the idea of his daughter coming across a stranger without her dad being by her side.

Chapter Seven

'Right,' said Skye to her two new pupils as she crouched down in front of them and beckoned conspiratorially for them to lean in, much to the amusement of Thea who looked on from her vantage point at the little garden table by the back door.

The children had scoffed down two huge bowls of spaghetti Bolognese, a whole loaf of garlic bread, plus almost half a bowl of grated cheese. Thea and Skye had managed to eat a small bowl each too, but the children had vacuumed the food up as if they had never been fed in their lives before. Thea had woefully said that her sister would berate her when they got home, as Allie had a beautiful splotch of tomato sauce right down the front of her pristine school blouse. Maybe next time, she should bring a change of clothes? Skye thought fleetingly, before forgetting it, as any pain Thea's sister gave her over the stain must be worth it for the amount of fun they were having.

'Okay, you two,' Skye whispered theatrically. 'You are now part of a very secret and elite team. Do you understand?' Both children giggled into their hands and nodded solemnly. Skye placed her palm on her chest and the children followed suit. 'Do you swear to keep our club a secret from people whose names begin with the letter 'M' and all other grumpy children?' Allie and Leo fell about laughing until Skye gave them a hard stare and they got up and held their hands to their chests again, still offering muffled giggles, making both Skye and Thea exchange grins. Skye raised her eyebrows at Thea who promptly stood up and put her hand on her chest too, noticing another milk stain on her top the same time as Skye did and openly cringing at Skye, who smothered a laugh.

'Right then,' Skye said, loudly now as there was no one else for miles around, 'you are all part of Project Ninja!'

Thea gasped. 'Project Ninja?'

Skye laughed at her friend's alarmed face. She supposed she secretly enjoyed shocking people. She had got used to having the element of surprise in her last job and it had stuck with her. 'Isn't that what they call people who stand on their heads and jump off high buildings?'

Skye gestured to the climbing apparatus she had built with planks of wood and rope bought from the local DIY shop. The children had been climbing up and jumping off onto the yoga mats placed on the other side, which she and Leo had bought to try and find some Zen-like calm but had just used for dozing sleepily on the lawn. 'They will learn to balance five spinning circles on their arms,' she nodded towards the heap of hula hoops that would help with balance and timing. 'These,' she winked at Thea, 'are ninja skills.'

Leo rolled his eyes at his mum but seemed to be enjoying himself and kept quiet. Skye knew he was used to his mum's theatrics and wacky behaviour but wouldn't want her to scare his new friend away. 'The way to beat the more forceful kids,' continued Skye, as if she hadn't just seen Leo's response to her little speech, 'is to avoid them, have no reaction and not care about their actions. Once a week at Project Ninja, we will learn skills to get out of the way when a naughty child approaches, have quick responses when they launch something at us and outsmart them at every turn. Are we all in?' she asked, looking earnestly at the group. She was interested to see what Thea's reaction would be, although she seemed to have been stunned into silence. Skye had only just finished building the course earlier today and had thought that only she and Leo would ever see it.

'How do you know what to teach us?' asked Allie as Skye noted the look of determination appear on Thea's face.

'I'd like that point explained to me too,' said Thea.

'I used to be a gymnast,' joked Skye, swishing her arms about theatrically. 'I had to learn to move quickly, listen and have great balance. I was good at cartwheels,' she sighed dramatically as Leo was about to butt in, 'but I was rubbish at everything else. I should have been a ninja,' she laughed at their shocked faces. 'I'm joking!' she said quickly. 'I was a professional rock climber in a former life, but had a fall, so I decided to hibernate here and write a book for climbers like me. I had to settle for being an author and dreaming it all up in my head instead of scaling great mountains and jumping off them.' She pretended to climb up an imaginary mountain and drop off the side, falling to the floor and spluttering as if she'd just been shot dead. Both kids howled with laughter as she picked herself up. 'I can certainly teach you both the tricks I practised during my training, though. It might help you plant your feet on the ground when Miles tries to push you over, or dodge out of the way before he gets there. Plus, I went to a self-defence course for fun before I had Leo. I have enough skills to take a man down and make him cry,' she joked, making them all giggle again at the thought.

The children looked at each other with glee and appeared to love the idea of thwarting Miles. 'We're in!' they chorused, looking towards Thea.

'I give up,' Thea said, throwing her arms up in exasperation as she walked towards the house, wiping her hands down her fraying jeans. 'I'm in too,' she called out behind her as the other three whooped with joy and danced around the garden.

Skye noted that Thea didn't bother to turn round and see what silliness they were up to now but walked through the open door and crouched down in front of Flo, who had dozed off and was dribbling slightly. Thea scooped her up to place her gently back into her pram, setting it just outside the door so the baby could sleep outdoors and Thea could see her if she woke up, which made sense to Skye. She bet Thea was wondering what the hell she had she let herself in for.

After an hour of assisting the children as they balanced carefully on the logs she had found piled along the back wall of the garden and had arranged across the lawn, Skye started to fire soft tennis balls in their direction for them to dodge. She had bought them when she'd decided it was time to take up tennis, but had been bored within an hour, even though the instructor had been fit and gorgeous. Next, it was time for them to run in circles around the garden, before they all collapsed into an exhausted heap of arms and legs, panting heavily.

Skye regarded their sweaty faces and thought maybe she had got a bit carried away with the drill sergeant act. She had quite enjoyed bossing them around and they hadn't complained once. Maybe this was how she should parent in the future? Although she had a feeling that Leo would give her one of his death stares if she tried it when they were alone. Skye, very kindly she thought, told them that there was ice cream in the fridge. Suddenly, in a burst of energy, the children jumped up and ran inside before Skye changed her mind and asked them to do the plank, which involved balancing their bodies on their arms and holding themselves as flat as planks of wood for minutes at a time. Maybe she could introduce that next week? she mused.

Skye looked at the brick wall at the end of the garden, just in time to see the little face appear again. Within a few strides, she had reached the back wall and placed her toes into the two grooves she had made earlier in the week. You would have thought they were part of the old wall's natural aging, if you happened to take a closer look. Skye picked up speed as she moved closer and she was standing on top of the wall before the head had time to bob back down again and out of sight. It wasn't a high wall, as the view to the fields beyond was too beautiful to block out and there were no neighbours other than the manor house and one other cottage nearby.

Skye glanced at the house and saw Thea dish up the ice cream through the kitchen window. She looked up as if to ask Skye if she wanted any of the lemony treat, then got distracted and licked a drop of ice cream that slipped from the spoon sighing in pleasure, obviously deciding she should have a small cone too, which made Skye smile. So much for the diet she had harped on about.

Thea scanned the garden and Skye hoped she hadn't seen her practically parallel climb the back wall, as she jumped down the other side. It wasn't a huge wall, but it would have looked like Skye was walking on air.

Skye could imagine Thea frowning and rubbing her eyes, which were already sore with exhaustion through lack of sleep. She would probably think that some of the sponge balls had flown over the wall and Skye had gone to collect them. Either way, thought Skye, Thea would sneakily make a cone for herself and leave Skye to do her own when she came back.

Chapter Eight

Emmie gasped as Skye appeared on the wall, almost stumbling off the pile of logs she had built up behind it so that she could see what all the laughter was about. Skye jumped down on the other side and held Emmie up so that she didn't fall, then gently helped her step back down onto solid ground. Emmie wiped hands dirty from carrying logs on her deep blue leggings and left a big grimy mark, before looking around to see if there was somewhere to run to. As the woman was smiling at her kindly and didn't look too cross, Emmie stayed where she was. The woman was wearing skinny black jeans and a worn-out black T-shirt with a faded grey motif on the front and she was standing patiently, not saying anything, but looking at Emmie with a question in her eyes as to why she had been peering over her wall. Emmie had only been there for ten minutes and had tried really hard to keep her head down and not be seen. She had heard laughter as she played with Buzz in the fields. Some guard dog he was, as he was currently rubbing his face all over the woman's arms in welcome as she crouched down and made a fuss of him.

She had been surprised to see the new boy and that irritating girl, Allie, playing in the cottage garden. It looked like they were having such a brilliant time running around that Emmie couldn't seem to stop herself from watching. It hadn't been easy lugging the logs over, but she had been desperately bored and there was no one around to stop her. It was her property, after all, so surely she could do whatever she liked.

'Emmie!' shouted a harassed voice, which was growing closer. Skye looked up at Emmie, who was rooted to the spot at the sound.

Skye stood up slowly, which Emmie assumed was to show

her she wasn't so scary. 'I'm Leo's mum, Skye. I think someone's looking for you?' she said gently, still smiling, which told the very astute Emmie that she wasn't cross with her and about to yell like her dad. Emmie knew that she was pretty as a picture, with shoulder length dark, silky hair and what her grandma called a striking pair of inquisitive green eyes, which adults always went soppy over, but her mouth was set and her stance was defiant. She was fed up with having no one to play with and didn't really care if her dad was mad.

'Are you allowed out here on your own?' Skye asked conversationally.

'It's my house!' said Emmie haughtily.

'Oh,' replied Skye looking surprised. 'I assumed the owner would be of retirement age, but maybe you're his granddaughter?'

'Emmie!' came another cry from just beyond the edge of the field, as her dad vaulted, rather impressively, over a small hedge and landed firmly on his feet. Her dog, Poppy, was close at his heels, although she squeezed through a hole in the hedge which had been made by a badger, almost getting her backside jammed on the way through, which made Emmie snicker into her hand.

Skye waved her arms to get his attention, then whistled an ear-splitting noise into the air, which made him stop and turn their way. He started towards them with a purposeful stride. It was clear he was cross, from his tautly bunched arm muscles and the way he was gripping his own hands, as if to control his anger. Emmie looked at her father's face and cringed theatrically. 'Oh man. My dad is going to kill me!'

'Why?' asked Skye. 'Have you wandered too far from home?' Emmie could see she was trying not to stare at the hunk of man who was heading her way. She made a retching sound, as she'd overheard Mile's mum describe her dad this way the other day and it sounded revolting.

'I was bored, so I ran off,' Emmie said simply, as if that explained everything.

'Running off is never a good idea,' said Skye solemnly, peering into the worried eyes of the child in front of her.

Emmie was trying to look confident, but her bottom lip had started to quiver and her skin was prickled with sweat.

Emmie had no idea that the woman beside her was practiced in interpreting nuances of behaviour and could feel that this meeting wasn't going to be pleasant, from the Emmie's reaction to her dad.

'Why not?' asked Emmie, moving over to hold Skye's hand. Skye seemed surprised, but smiled as she recognised Emmie's tactic to outwit her angry-looking father, by letting him think she had been with another adult all along, and didn't say anything. 'It's more fun than sitting around bored on my own,' continued Emmie, straightening her back and gritting her teeth as her dad drew nearer.

Skye kept hold of the child's hand, then leant down and picked a daisy from the ground by their feet, before handing it to Emmie. 'Because if you ever were really lost,' said Skye in an even tone, 'people might think you were still playing and not look for you.'

'Oh,' was all Emmie said, a little grumpily, hanging her head and staring intently at the daisy in her other hand as her father's feet came into view and she knew she would have to look up and face the music.

Zack stared at Skye, taking in her skin-tight jeans and an old black T-shirt, which moulded her curves. He saw she was holding his daughter's small hand in her own, and looked like he might combust in anger. Emmie braced herself, as she was sure he was about to tear a strip off her for running away, although if he was going to be as mean and moody as he looked now, Skye probably wouldn't blame her.

'What are you doing here?' he asked accusingly to Skye.

She looked into stormy grey eyes, taken aback. 'I guessed you would be angry with your daughter for wandering off, but had thought you would politely thank me for finding her, not treat me like some sort of criminal. I live here,' she said simply with an inclination of her head towards the cottage wall. It was clear from her tone that she was trying to keep calm and not knock him to the floor.

His mouth dropped open and his shoulders sagged, as he

obviously realised she wasn't some random weirdo. 'You're the mysterious new tenant?'

'Emmie here heard my son and his friend playing in the garden, then I said the magic words, 'ice cream', and she couldn't resist peeping over the wall,' Skye explained. Emmie sent her a grateful glance for the omission that she had been spying on them.

He looked at the small pile of logs that had been dragged up to the garden wall. 'Do you live in one of the estate cottages as well?' Skye asked, visibly trying to control her anger at his rudeness but not wanting to tear a strip off him in front of his daughter. 'Emmie says she lives here too?'

'She does,' was all he said, before crouching down in front of his daughter and calmly but firmly explaining that she was not allowed this far onto the estate without a responsible... he glared at Skye, adult. 'I apologise if she disturbed you,' he ground out before grasping his daughter's hand and whistling for the dogs. Emmie's bottom lip wobbled but she wordlessly followed her dad as he strode away, her little legs racing to keep up.

'What an obnoxious man!' fumed Skye, as Zack strode off in a casual shirt that showed off his pecs and was rolled up to reveal impressive forearms. She stared at him for a few seconds too long for Emmie's liking.

As they strode away, Emmie turned and offered an apologetic glance her way and Skye summoned a reassuring smile in return, then did a quick somersault behind his back to release some tension, making the little girl's eyes go wide in shock, then a big grin appear on her face. She hadn't seen an adult do that before, other than acrobats on the TV.

Emmie's dad was getting impatient with her dragging behind and gently pulled her along, so that she was forced to turn towards home and speed up to match his pace. She chanced a peek up at him, but he was looking mighty angry, so she kept her gaze on the ground and wordlessly followed him. She hadn't really seen her dad get cross before, and it made her tummy hurt a bit. She could usually get whatever she wanted out of her dad, but this time she knew she had pushed

46

him too far by disappearing without letting on where she was.

The dogs, knowing something was wrong and that their master was upset, hung their heads too and the morose group strode back to the house, waiting for the telling off they knew they would receive for wandering too far from the main house. Buzz pushed his wet nose into Emmie's quivering hand in reassurance and she stroked his soft fur in thanks. Maybe dogs weren't so bad after all she thought. At least they were going to be put on the naughty step with her, she almost giggled, as she recalled a programme her dad had tried to show her once where the parents disciplined their children by shoving them onto the stairs. He had never actually used the technique and she hoped he didn't try it now. The stair carpet was full of dog hairs! A stupid puppy like the one Miles had would be too small to run in the fields with her, like Buzz and Poppy did. She made a mental note to remember to tell that to Miles tomorrow at school, while she regaled him with her adventure in the woods.

Chapter Nine

Skye walked into the kitchen, just as Thea had finished washing up after dinner. 'Wow! You are a total domestic goddess,' she said admiringly. 'I would have left that until the morning, then been annoyed that I was too lazy to do it the night before.' Thea looked around Skye's immaculate and fairly sparse kitchen and frowned slightly.

'It's always more fun to tidy up someone else's kitchen. I hate cleaning up my own mess. Where did you disappear to?' she asked, changing the subject and looking too tired to argue the point.

'I saw someone watching the children over the wall.' Seeing Thea's horrified look, she held up a hand to stop that train of thought. 'It was a child. Seems she'd wandered off from her parent. He showed up hollering the place down and I might add, he was pretty mad with her… and me for that matter!'

'What on earth would a child be doing on their own all the way out here?' asked Thea in an angry voice. 'What was the dad thinking of, letting her wander around the woods and fields here? It's so secluded. Anyone might have come across her.'

'He called her Emmie,' said Skye, recalling the frantic way he had been calling her name and softening slightly at his plight. Then she remembered how rude he had been and her guard rose again.

'Emmie! Oh, that explains it. Well, almost,' said Thea, frown lines appearing on her rosy forehead, which was flushed from all that washing up as Skye had used every pan in the house to reheat one spaghetti Bolognese. 'Why was he mad at you, for heaven's sake?' Thea already sounded protective of her new friend.

'You know her, then?' asked Skye, not waiting for an answer. 'I think he was cross at her for wandering off, but felt that I had somehow coerced her into it, even though I've never set eyes on her before in my life. I was very kindly checking that she wasn't lost. Talk about a caveman with no manners. However worried he was, he could have said thanks for my not leaving her on her own.'

'Emmie is Zack's daughter,' said Thea as if that explained everything.

'Zack?'

'He owns the estate.' Thea leant back onto the kitchen counter and blatantly enjoyed the look of shock on her friend's face. Skye frowned as she tried to match the deep phone voice with the hot angry guy she had just had an altercation with. Seeing Skye's confusion, Thea chipped in. 'His daughter Emmie is in Allie and Leo's class at school. She's best friends with …' Thea looked furtively around for the children, but they had got bored and gone back outside to finish their ice cream in the last of the day's sunshine. 'Miles!' she hissed theatrically, grinning from ear-to-ear.

'Miles! What is a sweet little girl like that doing hanging around with a bossyboots like Miles?'

'Well,' said Thea, drawing out the story, as though she hadn't had a good gossip for ages. 'She can be a bit of a handful, so Allie tells me. She's great with the teachers, but not so much with the other kids. Allie says it's because she tries to be like Miles. He pretty much controls her and tells her who she can be friendly with. No one else will play with her because Miles gets jealous of any other friendships. We invited her to our house for tea last week, as Allie said Emmie was trying to find new friends, but Miles kicked her and she didn't come.'

Anger burned in Skye's chest for the little girl she had just seen marched away. She hitched her bottom onto one of the four bar stools in her compact kitchen and listened enthralled. It was like a story out of a soap opera, except the story involved kids, for goodness' sake. Surely one child couldn't have that much influence?

49

'What's his mum like?' asked Skye, remembering the miserable woman who had dragged her son away without checking he hadn't hurt himself at school.

'That's the point,' explained Thea, resting one buttock on a stool before shuffling her whole body up onto the chair. 'His mum is really controlling. She's always scowling, but she's a major player in the best mates' club.'

'Best mates' club? Oh, you mean the mum scrum?'

'Mum scrum?' laughed Thea, almost toppling off the chair, which was too high for her short legs. She tried to stop herself wobbling and almost landed a kick to Skye's shin, before she swung her stool round and out of harm's way. The problem was that she was now facing the wrong way and Skye enjoyed the fact that Thea had no clue how to get down and now both of her buttocks seemed to be welded to the shiny surface. Skye grinned and swung her friend back round to face her. 'I love that thought,' said Thea who was flushed and still giggling, making Skye laugh too at the sight of her. She looked like a Rubenesque artist's muse. 'I will never look at that impenetrable huddle the same way again. I'll picture them all in grubby rugby kits and wonder who is going to score!' She held her sides to stop them hurting from laughing so much.

'You don't want to mess with Miles' mum, apparently,' Thea continued in a slightly more serious tone. 'Even my sister, who is a hard-nosed cow, wouldn't want to get on the wrong side of her, although they both seem to be in a similar friendship group. Apparently, she can make or break a woman's spirit.'

Skye scoffed disbelievingly.

'You may mock,' said Thea, poking Skye in the ribs, 'but she's a gossip queen and my sister says she's got the hots for Zack. It's why she's told Miles he has to befriend Emmie and keep her close. Miles doesn't really like her, as he wants to be the top kid and have the best of everything. Emmie, living in a place like she does, must niggle at him like nettle rash.'

Skye leant her arm on the kitchen counter and rested her head on her hand, staring at Thea in awe. This place was becoming more exciting by the minute. Who needed her old job, when this little village had enough drama to keep her busy for years?

'Miles' mum, Mirabelle,' continued Thea, oblivious to her rapt audience, 'thinks that if the kids are friends, then the parents will be friendlier. Miles spends half his life stuck up a tree because his mum fancies the local tree man. I could almost feel sorry for him, if he wasn't such a nasty little troublemaker.'

'She's called Mirror Ball?' asked Skye with a gasp. Thea laughed and stuck out her tongue.

'She's called Mirabelle, but demands that everyone addresses her as Belle as she thinks she's so damn beautiful.'

Skye spluttered and bit her lip to control her giggles. 'What about the tree man?' she asked, giving Thea a lewd wink and licking her lips. 'How did he get his name? Has he got a secret weapon we should all know about?' When Thea just raised her eyes to heaven and ignored her, Skye sighed and tried another route. 'How on earth did you find all that out? I thought you'd only been here a couple of months longer than me?'

'My sister,' said Thea simply. She appeared to be trying hard to shake the mental image of what might be inside Zack's shorts, now that Skye had mentioned it. 'She hates Belle with a passion, but has to pretend to be best friends with her, apparently, to keep her social standing. Doesn't stop her from slagging Mirabelle off to anyone who will listen, though. Not really that smart a move in a little town. One of these days 'Mirror Ball' Belle will hear something and come round and wallop her one. Luckily, people are just as terrified of my sister and wouldn't dare rat her out in case she started slagging them off too,' Thea said cheerfully, making Skye smile.

It was great to see Thea properly relax and enjoy herself. She seemed like quite an uptight person who worried about what everyone else thought, rather than not giving a damn, like Skye. Who cared what the stuck-up bitches of the world thought, when you had lost the love of your life?

'Hang on,' said Skye, backtracking slightly in her mind. 'Did you say Miles spends half his life up a tree?'

Thea giggled and tried to disengage her bottom from the

sticky furniture, which seemed to want to come with her. Skye jumped down from her stool and gently helped Thea from the seat, trying all the while not to tip her off, which was her first instinct to show how daft this all was. She hadn't had this much fun in ages, angry hot man aside.

'Zack runs a tree-walking centre on the grounds of the estate. It's just off the road, near my cottage. They say the previous owner set it up for his hippie lover, then got bored and ran off with a barmaid or something. No one really knows Zack's story as he keeps to himself, but I don't think he's been here that much longer than you or me. Maybe we should start up a newbie mum scrum and throw Zack into the middle? It can be a dad-mum scrumptious scrum!' Now she sent Skye a wink, which looked more like she had something in her eye, and Skye burst out laughing, although the thought of rolling around with Zack did make her skin flush. She quickly brushed her hair round her face to hide her embarrassment and hoped Thea hadn't realised. 'He is pretty easy on the eye though, you have to admit,' said Thea, as Skye's face flushed interestingly.

'I hadn't noticed,' lied Skye, nonchalantly, realising that Thea was staring at her with that dratted raised eyebrow in silent question again.

'He's not one for conversation,' said Thea checking on Flo and flopping into one of the cool grey armchairs in the lounge. 'No one knows where his wife is as they've never seen her, although Belle started a rumour that she's dead, evil cow! Allie asked Emmie once, but she just said her mum was incredibly busy and important and didn't have time to visit. What a bitch!'

'I've not seen him at the school before,' said Skye, drawing the conversation back to Zack, seething inside that a woman could abandon her child. Although, to be fair, she might be the best mum in the world and just have been turned into a complete harridan by the rumour mill.

'Zack does go to collect Emmie from school, but he avoids other parents like the plague. He tends to stand at the back behind the rain shelter and occasionally chats to one of the

52

other dads, Mike. He's a carpenter, but seems to be working more and more for Zack at CloudClimb. Personally, I think he's hiding from 'Mirror Ball' Belle.'

'Well, if Zack is as grumpy with her as he was to me today, she's welcome to him. Such a waste of a good body,' she sighed theatrically, making Thea almost choke on the first sip of the fresh soft drink Skye had just got for her. Skye smiled, innocently taking a sip of her own drink, then pulling Thea up so that they could go into the garden and see what the children were up to. They'd been awfully quiet out there for the last ten minutes.

Chapter Ten

Miles growled at Allie and Leo as they walked past his desk and swiped his hand across the surface and into the walkway between the desks. Allie managed to swerve her body to the right and avoided colliding with it. Leo speeded up and swung his body into his chair at the back of the room and sent Allie a conspiratorial smile.

From the desk behind Miles, Emmie watched them with interest. She didn't know what was going on, but those two had a secret and she was determined to find out what it was. Allie and Leo had been whispering in corners ever since she had witnessed them playing in the cottage garden. Her dad had been watching her for every moment of every day, and even the dogs had refused to co-operate and explore the fields again. Her dad had been mad at her and had lectured her for ages about not going that far alone, but Leo's mum fascinated her and she was sure they were having lots of fun at his house.

They had almost always managed to avoid Miles since that day, too. If there was a secret to that, then she wanted to know what it was. Miles was as bossy as her dad. He wouldn't let her have friends to play with, and was really boring to be around. Her dad tried his best to spend time with her, but the new business made him distracted and, instead of making friends with some adults so she could invite their children to tea, he rudely blanked most of them and then insulted others like Leo's mum. Emmie had been excruciatingly embarrassed by her dad and that had never happened before. She loved living where they did now, but sometimes she thought things had been easier when it was just her and her dad in their little flat. At least he had mostly worked at night then.

Leo's mum often sent her a wink when she saw her outside

school and Emmie would beam at her in return, hoping she would invite her round, but it hadn't happened. Leo and Allie didn't want other friends, although she had noticed more children wanting to play with them lately. Well, ones that had the courage to wind up Miles, anyway.

The end-of-day bell rang and Allie and Leo were the first up, swiftly and methodically packing their school bags and saying goodbye to their friends before Miles had a chance to stand up. He stamped his foot in frustration, as Emmie knew he enjoyed winding up the new kids, but he couldn't get near them these days. Maybe he would start arriving at school earlier and surprise them on their way in, she grimaced. A gleam of menace lit his eyes as he must have had the same idea and he smiled manically at Emmie, who was trying to stuff the day's belongings quickly into her bag and go home. She offered him a weak smile, and hoped he decided to leave soon, as he kept patting her on the head like a puppy and it was beginning to drive her mad.

Her dad's patience with Miles and his pushy mum was really starting to irritate her. He kept saying he was going to give 'that boy' and his mother a piece of his mind, which sounded disgusting, but yet he hadn't done it. He often said it when he thought she couldn't hear him, but he was quite loud mid-rant, even if he was whispering. He always seemed to be muttering to himself these days. Emmie hoped that he wasn't going senile, as she'd heard that was a really bad thing. She thought the word must mean he couldn't see things properly, but he climbed the trees most days and hadn't fallen off yet. Maybe she should ask him if he needed glasses? Anyway, she couldn't pretend she didn't hear what her dad said, especially if it was about Miles. Emmie wished that, if he was going to do something, he would hurry up and do it, so she could have some proper friends. She'd tried so hard to fit in at her new school, but it was harder to find someone to like her than she'd thought. Her dad always told her she was amazing, so she couldn't understand why the other children didn't think so too.

Emmie knew she could be pretty hard on her dad, but she was having a difficult time getting away from Miles and she was too scared of him to ask a teacher or her dad for real help. He would go bananas and the teachers would tell Miles' mum, who would also go bananas, which would make Miles even meaner to her. She was supposed to be his friend, so she felt even sorrier for Leo and Allie and the other kids; Miles really hated them.

Chapter Eleven

Allie and Leo ran up to Skye. She'd offered to walk them home and give them some dinner so that Thea could take a nap when Flo did, and then come and collect Allie later, although Skye was curious to see what her cottage looked like. They always ended up at Skye's house, as this was where they 'trained', but every time Skye offered to drop her home, Thea would breezily say she was coming that way anyway. Skye assumed that Thea's place was a mess and she didn't want them to see it, but curiosity was beginning to get the better of her and she would have to push the matter soon.

Visiting Skye's cottage had become a routine over the last few weeks and she had used the time to teach the children new skills at the ninja club. The first week had been child's play, but she had raised the stakes after Miles pushed Allie over and cut her knee again. Thea had wanted to complain to the school, but Allie had pleaded with her not to, as Miles would make her life so difficult. Against Thea's better judgement they had let it go for now, but if Miles didn't back off, then she would pull out the big guns and tell her sister how it had really happened. Allie's mum may have wanted to keep on Mirabelle's good side, but if it involved her daughter being hurt, then the gloves would be off and there would be a power struggle, which would probably involve a lot of hair pulling and name calling... from the adults, Skye grinned to herself.

Skye walked the children out through the school gates towards home and then noticed Zack, the rude man from the estate, watching her behind the rain shelter. He was wearing black jeans and a brown T-shirt and, if he hadn't so many muscles in his arms, he would have almost blended in with the wood of the shelter. Skye smiled at the thought of the chameleon dad, trying to hide from everyone. She looked him straight in the eye until he looked away. She frowned at the sudden surge of butterflies that had appeared in her stomach. She quickly surmised that she must be hungry as she'd skipped lunch because she was too busy setting up the garden. That must be it. She chastised her own silliness.

Skye glanced back over her shoulder just in time to see a miserable-looking Emmie appear, with a boisterous Miles tagging along behind her, hopping from foot to foot. One look from Zack, and Miles about-turned and with a weak wave went off to meet his mum, who had stopped chatting for once and was craning her neck for a better look at Zack. Catching his eye again, Skye sent him a sympathetic smile and he started in surprise, then sent her a self-deprecating grin back, which made those butterflies resurface.

Skye carried on walking with a spring in her step. She was still mightily cross with him for being such a rude, hot guy, but there needed to be some solidarity in the battle to overcome the reign of Miles and 'Mirror Ball' Belle.

Reaching out and unlocking the door to the cottage, stepping aside for the children to precede her inside, she revelled in the squeals of happiness they made when they saw the gigantic cookies she had attempted to make earlier that day. She had forgotten that they spread to twice their size in the oven and maybe she shouldn't have covered them in Smarties, which had melted and made multi-coloured swirls everywhere, instead of the professional-looking confectionary she had hoped for.

The children grabbed a slab of baked cookie, looked in the fridge for a drink, then shouted with glee when they opened the back door to the garden. Over the last few weeks Skye had, through play, taught the children to balance, with endless repetitions along the beams she had laid out on the grass. She had also sawn some of the beams at various heights and held the children's hands while they learned to traverse them without falling off. Seeing the children sprint to the end of the garden and hop onto the first one with ease was so satisfying to watch. The number of times she had to catch them as they fell, it was a good job she had natural agility of her own, or they would have literally pulled her arm out of its socket.

Today, Skye had set up a mini obstacle course. She had laid out piles of books for the kids to balance on their heads as they walked over the beams, hula hoops in various sizes and colours for them to throw in the air and catch, and the basket of softballs she had used weeks earlier. The softball basket was sitting beside a ball launcher, which was set to move around and would send balls spiralling across the garden for them to dodge. The garden table was set out with trays of small objects to play a memory game. She would remove one item each time to see if the children had memorised everything, to help them remember to pick up all their belongings from their school desks before Miles could grab things and hide them. His favourite trick at the moment was to stuff things down the back of the class radiator, where they got covered in cobwebs and sticky spilt drinks.

Skye had set this club up to distract the kids from worrying about Miles but, to her astonishment, it really worked. Leo had reported that, even after a mere few weeks of ninja training, they had pretty much managed to avoid Miles' kicks and punches by working together and keeping out of his way.

Skye had noticed the red-haired mum looking longingly at Belle and her group again today and, although it wasn't Skye's thing, she felt bad for the other woman because she so wanted to be part of that gang. Mulling over an idea she had had a few days previously, Skye clapped her hands to catch the children's attention and began to explain a great technique to warm up their muscles and get the blood flowing into their brains, making them more alert and able to concentrate. They would have to be paying attention to what she said to keep their balance, not drop the apparatus and co-ordinate their senses to complete the course without having to start again.

'Mum,' called Leo, in a voice that Skye immediately knew meant he was going to ask something she might not like. She looked up expectantly, almost doing the Thea eyebrow thing, but he hesitantly looked at Allie for support, and she wondered what was going on.

59

'What is it?' Skye asked, a little impatiently. Leo was such a good boy, but he was an individual and sometimes threw her a curveball by asking her something outlandish. It was her own fault for travelling so much with him when he was small and not hiding her true self from him. He was only a child, but he was all she had and he'd had to know about her old life, for his own protection. She had been very careful not to scare him, but had told him the bare minimum to keep him safe. He had been fascinated originally, but after a while got bored and moved on. He accepted that she was a little eccentric and he had inherited some of those traits.

'Well…' he began, slowly. 'A few of the boys from school are getting really upset about Miles.'

'Then their parents should speak to the school,' Skye said carefully, sensing where this was going.

'You didn't call the school,' he said innocently.

'Yes, but…' he had her there. What could she say?

'It would just be Tammy and Z.'

'Z?'

'Yeah, his name's Barry, but he hates it, so we call him Z. It's cool!'

'Oh,' said Skye in confusion. She assumed this was Leo's plan. She bet Barry had been perfectly happy with his name before today and Leo had encouraged him to change it to get into the ninja club. Skye looked at Allie who was studiously gazing at the floor and twisting one foot behind the other.

'Allie?' she asked.

'Well… I kind of said to Maisy and Alice that I would ask you about them coming over too…'

Skye threw her hands up into the air in exasperation. 'Did you not swear an oath of secrecy?'

'We didn't tell them about the club, honest!' they both chorused. 'They've just noticed how we manage to avoid Miles now. We only told them we had worked out how to keep out of his way.' Skye slapped her hand on her forehead in frustration as Leo continued, 'Plus, Allie said she likes to come for dinner and now they all want to come.'

'Oh, for goodness' sake! I'm not running a childcare club. It was supposed to be a bit of fun.'

'It will be even more fun if we help our friends too,' pleaded Leo dramatically, grabbing Allie's hand as they both stared at Skye. 'I'm really popular now I'm not so scared of Miles. How can you ignore other children when you've helped us?' Allie looked at Leo in awe of his manipulation skills.

Knowing her son, Skye guessed that they had written down what to say at lunchtime. She was supposed to be strong but Leo would know he had won the minute his mother's shoulders sagged in defeat. 'Okay,' Skye conceded. 'Just those four children and then absolutely no more after that. I don't even like children,' she joked, grabbing Leo and Allie into a playful joint hug. The children ran around the garden whooping with joy and Skye could have kicked herself for being such a pushover.

Emotionally blackmailed by a pair of junior school children. She would be forever ruined! Why could she manage to function perfectly well for many years, making critical decisions that affected people's lives without a second's hesitation, yet one pleading gaze from her son's baby blue eyes and she was a goner? What a mug.

'What will we tell them?' she asked the complicit duo. 'We can't say we're pretend ninjas. They'll laugh us out of town. A Miles avoidance club?'

'We can say they're coming here to play, but you sometimes teach us climbing skills and gymnastics,' said Leo proudly, obviously deciding he had found a solution. Allie was nodding enthusiastically at his idea, her silky bunches bobbing up and down as she agreed.

'I'm not a climbing instructor or gymnastics teacher.'

'But you told Auntie Thea you were a gymnastics champion,' said Allie innocently. 'That would be enough for most mums I know.' Skye bit her lip and looked very shifty for a moment. She had known that that lie would come back to bite her on the bum. Leo sighed in exasperation and stared straight into his mum's eyes.

'Oh, okay,' she acquiesced, 'but I may have exaggerated my abilities slightly to your aunt, Allie.' She hated the shocked look on Allie's face and the knowing smile from Leo. 'The only gymnastics medal I ever won, was when I was about four. I was rather good though,' she said dreamily, before Leo coughed and she had to snap back to the matter in hand.

Allie started giggling and stared sternly at Skye. 'The moral of this tale is not to tell lies,' she admonished before she fell onto the floor laughing. Leo smiled too, but still looked cross at her for making stuff up again.

Skye gazed at her son thoughtfully and then pretended to hang her head in shame. 'Lesson learned. Your friends can join you tomorrow, but I am not cooking them dinner. They can come round for a play and fill their stomachs at home.'

'Mum's not the best cook,' said Leo solemnly, a twinkle appearing in his eyes now he had got his own way.

'The spaghetti Bolognese we had in our first week was delicious,' said Allie loyally, earning another hug and a kiss on the top of her head from Skye as she stuck her tongue out at her son.

'The sauce came out of a jar,' Leo said helpfully.

'You eat loads of fruit and salad,' said Skye defensively.

'It's safer that way,' joked Leo, as Skye swatted his backside with a newspaper she picked up from the little table under the windowsill.

'Right, you two,' she commanded, suddenly serious. 'Let's get back to work.'

Chapter Twelve

Zack tried to control his temper as Miles kicked the vending machine again and swore at the beeping noise it began to make as soon as he tried to shake it from side to side.

'Can I help you?' Zack asked through gritted teeth, making the boy jump and blush at being caught in the act.

'This stupid machine ate my money again,' Miles whined, not meeting Zack's eyes as he checked the digital readout.

'What were you trying to buy?'

'Crisps,' said Miles, dragging his dirty hands through his sandy coloured hair and making it stand up on end, as if he'd had an electric shock.

'You haven't put enough money in,' said Zack evenly. 'You need to check the cost first, which is written clearly here,' he pointed to the prices printed in big red numbers in front of each product, 'and then put the correct money in here,' he continued, pointing to the money slot as if he was talking to a five- year-old. He was aware that he was being rude, but he had just had to put up with Miles' mum taking videos of his backside while he was setting up some equipment again. It was all so embarrassing. What on earth did she do with them anyway? Watch them at night when she was all alone? Gross.

When she had noticed that he was looking directly at her camera, she had hastily turned and said she was filming the sun streaming through the trees. What a load of crap. The woman was becoming obsessed. Mirabelle turned up at CloudClimb with Miles at least once a week now for tree climbing sessions and had enrolled him for an adventure course Zack had set up, until she found out that Mike was running it for him and did an about-turn.

She might as well come up and lick his face, the amount of

subtlety she showed. He was sure she thought it was funny to keep complimenting him on his physique and how manly he was. Maybe she thought it would turn him on? She couldn't have been further from the truth, as his is ex-wife had put him off women for life… almost. He did have occasional dates, but he didn't have anyone to help him with childcare, so it was more trouble than it was worth. He had tried one local babysitting service, but Emmie had cried from the moment he left the house and he had been called home within thirty minutes. In the end, he'd just given up.

Mirabelle had taken to wearing tighter and tighter clothing, which was not flattering when it was still fairly cold outside and her designer shirt was two sizes too small! He was only human and had glanced her way, but she was starting to distract his staff. Many of them didn't know where to look when she was around.

Delving into the pockets of his jeans, he handed Miles a twenty pence coin and the boy grabbed it without a word of gratitude and rammed it into the machine. When the crisps appeared in the bottom window, he pulled them out and ran out of the refreshment building that had just been added to the site, without thanking Zack or offering to repay him.

It had taken a small investment to create this area, but Zack had designed it so that the seats looked out over the tree climbing sessions and the chairs were really comfy, with dark green padded seats and soft backs. Parents flocked here already. Zack abhorred poor coffee, so the fancy machine he'd bought churned out perfectly frothy cups at a premium price. He had even designed an app that parents or carers could tap their coffee preferences into; the drinks machine would rustle them up while the app told them what their choice said about their personality. It was a bit of fun and brought them back to try new combinations each time. He had been thinking of expanding this idea to inform customers who their best coffee match was from everyone taking part, but didn't want people to start getting jealous if their match wasn't the person they had arrived with! He was rushing way ahead of himself on that one, anyway. It would all come together with time, though.

With the phenomenal rate his latest apps were being downloaded, he could afford to develop pretty much any idea he wanted to. Zack quite liked the thought of integrating life experiences with technology, although it did mean he had to be rather more hands-on than he would like to be. CloudClimb had come with the property and he had been hoping he could ignore it, as he hadn't wanted to have more hassle in his life. Plus, he had absolutely no experience in running a business like this. Luckily, he had been on several climbing holidays and had loved outdoor sports when he was younger, but that had been cliffs and walls, not trees.

Emmie had pleaded with him to give the business a try, as he had taken her climbing a few times over the years and she had the bug for heights and adventure. Zack just couldn't seem to be able to say no to his vivacious daughter. As it turned out, after a year of extreme research and development, and a complete revamp, they literally hadn't looked back in their second year. There was still so much to do and learn, as the business model they had opened with had been quite basic, and he had thought the whole thing might be a waste of time and fail, but it had been almost an instant hit and Zack's head was still spinning at its incredible growth.

It might have been a complete nightmare at the start but, with Kay leaving, he had finally got fed up with wallowing in self-pity and been ready for a new challenge. The final decision had been made because the flat they were living in reminded him of the time when it wasn't just him and his daughter. Emmie needed this real home, though it was huge, with the two slobbery dogs making up their new family unit while his granddad was off gallivanting somewhere in the Caribbean with a twenty-something model. His own parents tried to visit when they could.

His dad had run a very successful business and Zack had enjoyed a few holidays a year and a comfortable home, but they were retired now and were flitting around before finding a new place to call home. Zack secretly hoped that Emmie would be enough to entice them to this corner of the country, with its lush woods and picturesque villages, but he knew they enjoyed city life and would probably end up back near his dad's golf club, where Zack had grown up, just outside London. Even though they both said they wanted to jet about and see the world, Zack knew that his parents would miss their friends if they were too far away. His mother was a social butterfly who took centre stage wherever they were. Zack loved this about her, as no one could say she was boring, but he had sometimes wished, as he was growing up, that she was a bit more conventional, more like his friends' mums, who wore jeans every day and walked the dog. His dinners had often been colourful, eclectic collections of ingredients his mother had discovered in the endless magazines she read to keep up with the latest trends, which was probably why she got along so well with his badly behaved granddad. Zack sometimes wondered if it was why he kept his emotions hidden. Who wouldn't, when they were always hiding under a bed with embarrassment while their granddad arrived with yet another tall tale, or a girl young enough to be his daughter, while his son's wife found the whole set-up hilarious?

Peeking out of the refreshment building, he scanned the heads of his customers for Belle's distinctive, sleek, highlighted haircut. When he saw that the coast was clear, he breathed a sigh of relief and stepped outside but, as he did, an arm reached out and stopped him in his tracks. He almost jumped out of his skin in fright.

Belle giggled coquettishly, but didn't drop the death grip she had on his arm. He pointedly stared at her hand, before she had the good grace to blush and let go. 'Miles just told me you bought him a snack,' she said seductively, running her tongue over her lips in what he guessed she thought was a suggestive manner, but which just looked ridiculous. He wondered fleetingly if she'd had Botox.

'Well…' he began.

'You must let me repay you,' Belle purred. He assumed she was going to give him the twenty pence back, but that turned out to be wishful thinking. 'Let me buy you a drink one night?' Zack's jaw dropped and he frowned, trying to think of a way out, as he actually felt himself begin to blush. What the hell was the matter with him? What was it with this woman? She had a hide of steel. He tried to shake off the mental image that conjured up.

'That's really not necessary,' Zack spluttered a touch too forcefully, making a mental note never to help the kid again. He looked desperately around for Mike, who was watching the situation play out with great amusement and didn't appear tempted to step in. Zack knew Mike thought he needed a woman in his life, although he was sure even Mike didn't believe meddling Belle was the way forward for his friend. From what Mike had told him, she was a bit obsessive about the men in her life and didn't leave them alone, even after the relationship had ended. Her ex was a mate of Mike's and the man carried a constant pained expression.

Then Zack saw Mike signalling that he needed his attention for a moment and he thanked his lucky stars for a friend who understood how agonizing the unwanted attention of a lust-fuelled school mum could be, especially when his daughter went to the same place as her son. Imagine the gossip from that great big group of women she hung around with. They were like a pack of wolves, huddled together, giggling and hissing when he walked past. He wouldn't be surprised if Belle tried to pee on him to mark her territory.

Hastily excusing himself, and taking in a deep calming breath of the cool air, filled with the scent of the trees, Zack instantly began to relax. He walked in Mike's direction and heartily slapped him on the back in thanks as they both headed towards the staff office. 'Please make it stop,' he pleaded to Mike, who laughed good-naturedly, and appeared to be thinking only of how he could best wind his friend up.

'She's just asked me to book her onto personal tree climbing sessions with you next week,' Mike lied slickly, his eyes sparkling with mirth.

'What?' Zack stopped short and turned panicky eyes to Mike, before he saw his smirk. 'Very funny… not,' he said sourly. 'I've tried very politely to tell her I'm not interested, but she doesn't hear me. I can't be blunter than saying no thanks to her face.'

'She thinks you're playing hard to get,' said Mike. 'The guys here have a bet on how long you can hold out, before you get desperate for a shag and give in. How long is it since you've gone out with a woman?'

Zack tried to ignore the question and kicked idly at the soft earth of the forest floor, covering his work boots in mud. Mike walked ahead into the office, sat in the chair opposite Zack's and put his feet up on the desk, leaning back over his shoulder to look pointedly at Zack to let him know he wasn't leaving without an answer. Zack sighed loudly, stomped in, walked round the desk and plonked himself into his chair, forced to face the question.

'Come on. When was the last time you actually had any?'

'Any what?' asked Zack. Mike gave him a hard stare and crossed his arms over his broad chest, making his muscles bulge and his short-sleeved, khaki work shirt stretch tight, letting Zack know he meant business and was not about to move.

'Okay, okay,' said Zack, realising how strong they had both become with all the physical labour they now undertook, but wishing Mike would stop flexing his chest like a peacock. 'Maybe I should go on a date, but Belle would eat me alive.' He shivered involuntarily, feeling a bit sick.

'I could think of a whole host of women who would queue up to date you. I'm quoting my wife here,' he clarified, before Zack could make a wisecrack.

'Marlo talks about me?' Zack joked, flexing his own muscles.

'Ha ha,' said Mike sarcastically. 'Only because she thinks you're desperate and in need of a good woman.' Mike held up a hand before Zack could protest. 'She also said you would use not having babysitters as an excuse.' Zack had the good grace to look ashamed, as that was exactly what he had been about to say. 'Emmie would love to come over to our house to play, or for a sleepover. I know our boys are a bit younger, but you just have to take the plunge and let her out of your sight a bit more.'

Zack sighed and rubbed his temples. He needed a caffeine

hit. He had a headache coming and got up to use the trendy coffee maker he'd bought for the staff office. As far as he was concerned, if his staff were happy, then his customers were happy, so a few perks like an excellent coffee machine here as well as in the parents' waiting area were worth the investment, plus good coffee made him smile too.

'I'll think about it,' he said to Mike as the machine purred into life and began churning out fragrant coffee into the CloudClimb-branded Styrofoam cups.

Handing a cup to Mike and then reaching for his own, Zack took a heavenly sip of the warm delicious liquid and sighed in pleasure.

'What do you think about the new mum at the school? The hot brunette?' said Mike.

Zack thought about pretending not to know who Mike was talking about, but didn't have the energy. 'I've met her,' he said, picturing her slender curves and endless legs, surprising Mike as he barely spoke to anyone at the school. 'She's annoying,' he added for good measure.

'How the hell would you know that already?' asked Mike in exasperation. 'I've not seen you talk to anyone at the school, except Thea. How about Thea?' he asked suddenly, jumping up in excitement. 'She's pretty hot too.'

Zack thought about what Mike had said, and realised he was right. Thea was really pretty in a messy sort of way and he must admit he had checked her body out, with her womanly curves and gyrating bottom, but she had helped him with Emmie a couple of times and hadn't shown the slightest flicker of interest in him, for which he had decided he was actually quite grateful. She wasn't fawning all over him like some of the other mums and it made him relax in her company. He got the distinct impression that she wasn't looking for a man. Maybe she already had one stashed away somewhere? He hadn't heard her talk about Flo's father and he certainly didn't want to ask and have her tell him her life story. That would be too much, even for a great girl like Thea. He supposed he would help her if she needed him, but she didn't come across as the needy type. He wracked his brain and couldn't remember one instance since they had met when she had asked anything of him. She had offered help with Emmie, which was beyond kind, and he wouldn't trust his daughter to very many people in this world, but his gut told him she wasn't trying to get him onside to get into his pants or grab his estate. He fleetingly thought of Skye and the complicit smile they'd shared at school. Heat flared into his groin and blood rushed around his body, making him frown in annoyance.

'Thea?' questioned Mike again, with a sigh that seemed to signal impatience at his friend's lack of interest in the luscious mums that were always at the school. 'I give up,' he said, getting up and brushing down his uniform.

Zack sighed moodily and ran his hands through his thick black hair, before he remembered what this had done to Miles' hair and hastily smoothed it back, much to Mike's apparent amusement. 'I promise I will go on a date,' Zack acquiesced.

'A date?'

'Okay, a few dates then. If it will shut you up, it will be worth it. Actually …' he paused for effect, rapidly making a few mental calculations and smiling broadly, 'I was thinking of holding an event to launch the new-look business officially, with my integrated apps, so I might have some sort of marquee and music. Well, I was hoping you might know someone who could help me organise it?'

Mike reeled back onto his heels, seemingly shocked. 'A ball! Here? But that means you'll have to be social and talk to people? Someone …' he waggled his eyebrows suggestively and smacked his lips together, 'might get you drunk and pounce on those big pouty lips of yours.' Zack gasped in mock horror. 'Before we get ahead of ourselves, I'll believe the ball idea when I see you set up a planning meeting,' said Mike. 'There's a quiz night at the school in a few weeks. If you don't have a date by then, you owe me an extra week's holiday to enjoy some time off with my beautiful wife, who is complaining that I'm working every hour of daylight for my tyrant of a boss.'

Zack ignored him and pretended to look dreamily out of the

window at the trees. 'Ah, the gorgeous Marlo…'

Mike threw his empty coffee cup at Zack's head and he ducked good-naturedly, chuckling to himself – but also glad he had used the disposable cups for their coffee.

Chapter Thirteen

Thea smiled as she listened to the birds singing and smelt the fresh grass, which had just been cut by the school's caretaker, Mr Sawyer. She sent him a wave as he happily sped along the verges. He was a bit of a boy racer and she was sure there should be a speed limit for his lawnmower. He must have added a bigger engine to it, as he flew across the school field whenever he mowed it, almost leaving scorch marks. The headmistress was always too busy with the endless queues of parents and teachers who wanted to talk to her, and never quite managed to work out how Mr Sawyer completed his jobs so quickly.

Thea scrutinised an intricately-designed poster on the school notice board as she approached, and inspected the stunning landscape painting at its centre, which was breathtaking. It appeared that a local artist was having a private viewing of her work, but so many mums and dads were crowding around the poster she couldn't get near enough to see more. It looked like it would be a great success if so many people were clamouring to see the artwork. Thea stepped closer to see what all the fuss was about, and the main throng of people moved away to huddle round the circular bench located outside the school by the rain shelter. The bench was there for students to eat their packed lunches in sunny weather, but one or two parents used it if they were not standing in groups chatting with friends. Thea squinted and leaned in closer to the delicate writing at the bottom of the poster, which looked like it had been written by hand in intricate text and complemented the painting incredibly well. Thea gasped in shock, and did a double-take, as the surname of the artist was same as that of the mousy redhead, who always sat on her own. Thea looked up in astonishment as the woman blushed and parried questions from the usual 'mum scrum' that were, for the first time, huddled around her.

Watching Skye happily observing proceedings like a proud mum, Thea quickly walked over to join her. The way Skye was taking in everything that was happening, and looking very smug about it, made a weird kind of sense. Noticing Thea for the first time, Skye rapidly composed her features and turned to greet her friend. 'You did this, didn't you?' Thea accused. She didn't know how she knew Skye had a hand in it, but she just did.

Thea could tell that Skye briefly thought about lying, but decided to come clean.

'I have some contacts in PR and if Felicity wants to be part of that group so much, then she can decide for herself once she's in. If she realises they are all a bunch of airheads, then she can jump straight out again.'

'Felicity?'

Skye laughed at her friend's confused face. 'That's her first name... the redhead.'

'Is it? She's so quiet and always huddled into herself. She doesn't exactly give off the 'come and talk to me' vibe,' Thea indicated the buzzing group surrounding Felicity. 'I only know her as Sally's mum. They'll eat her alive.'

'Not now she's cool,' observed Skye. 'I reckon she'll last about a day before she's had enough of them. I introduced myself to her last week and nearly frightened the life out of her. She's actually quite nice and an incredibly talented artist, but boring as hell otherwise.'

'Skye!' gasped Thea, spluttering and covering her giggles with her hand. Skye had the decency to look abashed for about a second, before they both burst out laughing. When Thea had caught her breath, she stared Skye down with one of her piercing looks that Skye seemed to find it impossible to wriggle away from.

'What have I done now?' asked Skye.

'When are you going to tell me the real story?'

'I didn't make it up,' protested Skye, checking over the

heads of the mum scrum to see if 'Flick', as that was her new arty name, was surviving her ordeal. She actually looked really happy and her face was flushed and animated for once. 'Her name really is Felicity.'

'You know perfectly well what I mean,' said Thea seriously, standing with her hands on her hips to show she meant business.

'Oh, you mean about me?' asked Skye, innocently. 'What do you want to know?' she queried smoothly.

'Why did you move here?'

'My job brought me here,' parried Skye.

'You said you were an author, but I haven't seen any of your books online, plus you also said you were an Olympic squash and gymnastics champion,' Thea wasn't convinced at all by the tall tales. She wondered if Skye was a compulsive liar, who had been bored and got a bit carried away with her story this time. She probably hadn't thought Thea would actually listen, or care that much.

'Wow,' said Skye. 'You actually looked me up? If you wanted to read my work that badly, you could have just asked. My first book, on rock climbing, is with my new agent and she's trying to find me a publishing deal, which can take years and years,' she waved her hand around as if to exaggerate the point and distract Thea from staring at her so much. 'I don't have anything online or in stores yet, but thanks for making me feel like crap about it,' she said, seeming to lay it on thick. 'I came here to write another one, but I think the first one will die without trace and I might give up already.'

'Oh,' said Thea, looking a bit abashed. 'What about the last bit?' she continued. 'Is that how you know what to teach the kids? Did you win medals? Again, I couldn't find you online.'

Skye sighed theatrically. 'Do you do background checks on all of your new friends?' Thea had the good grace to look ashamed of herself. Skye was starting to look tense with all of the questions, but seemed to be steeling herself to answer. Maybe she had read one of those glossy magazines that you pick up at the supermarket, thought Thea. The kind of thing that said, to make girlfriends, you had to bare your soul and let

74

them into your life, or some sort of crap, or they would get bored with the lack of drama and gossip and go and find more interesting friends.

Chapter Fourteen

It had been a long time since Skye had let anyone into her life. Her old friends were from work and she had cut all ties with them when Reece died. They had tried so hard to be there for her, as Reece was their friend and colleague too. They had been like a tight-knit family and knew pretty much everything about each other, as this was the best way to stay safe. It had worked for a long time, until Leo had come along. Skye had missed their last rendezvous, to care for her child, and something had gone wrong. She didn't blame them... she didn't. It could have happened at any time. If anything, she blamed herself for not being there to protect Reece, but then perhaps Leo might have lost both parents and that would have been even more horrific than the hell they had been through. At least they had each other to hold on to. She might not be the best mother in the world, with her hair which hadn't been cut for years reaching halfway to her bum, plus her inability to provide her offspring with nutritionally balanced meals at the end of each day, but at least she was present. He had one parent to listen to him at night when he cried in his sleep with a raised temperature and one parent to watch his school play football at the weekend. Not that he played, as he had absolutely no interest in the sport, but they had got into the habit of watching Allie play; the girl had talent. Skye wouldn't let anyone harm a single follicle on her son's sweet head and woe betide those who tried. She couldn't let her son down the way she had his father.

She realised that Thea was patiently waiting for an answer to her question. 'You really wouldn't believe me if I told you.'

'I would,' said Thea solemnly and the mood suddenly felt gripped with tension, even with the high-pitched gaiety coming from the 'mum scrum.'

'I...' Skye began. Thea held up her hand to stop her.

'Let's take the kids to the park, somewhere out in the open,' she said meaningfully, making Skye start in surprise. 'We can talk there.'

Skye was awash with confusion. Thea had become very serious and bossy all of a sudden and she wasn't sure she liked this side of her friend. She did want to unburden some of her fears and finally be honest with someone, but she knew that could be dangerous and the last thing she wanted to do was to draw attention their way, or cause anyone to hurt Thea and her little family.

The people who had killed Reece were still out there. She had given up years of her life dragging Leo around the world trying to stay undetected, knowing that her former team had been targeted. They hadn't survived, only the back office remained intact and she wasn't taking any chances with Leo's life. He had happily adapted to each new place, but when he reached school age, she had realised she couldn't carry on this way. He needed some stability and she had to cure the wanderlust that clawed at her soul. Her son was more important than the overwhelming urge to run. If it wasn't for Leo, she would actively seek out the bastards who had killed Reece and make them pay for his senseless murder. They had killed him to stop her team from doing their job and the pain and loss tore at Skye's heart every minute of every day.

It ripped her apart daily without exception and she would kill herself with grief if she didn't let it go soon. Leo needed her and she knew this was what Reece would have wanted. She had to keep herself safe so that he wasn't alone in the world. Every time people started to pry into her life, invite her to parties and get to know her better, she packed up their belongings and scarpered to another location far away without a backward glance. She didn't need them and they didn't need her. Most of the people she loved got taken away from her, so there was no point opening herself up to more pain. It would finish her off.

Although Leo was pretty versatile and already spoke three

languages, she couldn't keep moving him around any more. Instead of opening up a new world for him, she often felt she had prevented him from making his own lasting friendships, because she was scared to let anyone in. Her previous employer had told her that she was safe and the people who killed Reece and her team wouldn't be searching for her, but she didn't trust anyone now. Reece's killer had meant to wipe out the entire active team, but she was still alive. They had been compromised somehow and the thought terrified her. They had walked straight into a trap and Reece had tried to save them. Skye originally contacted her bosses at work every few days, but they all knew it posed a risk each time she made the call and they tried to persuade her to come back to work every time she made contact. Whenever she finished the call she had a new burning desire to put further distance between them for the sake of her son. In the end, she had stopped reaching out to them, for her own sanity. It had been years since Skye had made contact and, in that time, she had begun to build a normal life for her and Leo.

Two years ago, she had been so lonely that she had opened a Facebook page with a few family photos, albeit under false details. She had been at rock bottom and had tried to make friends with people from Leo's old school. These days, people seemed to live their life through social media and it would have seemed strange if she wasn't on there. She had carefully selected a few pictures that didn't show their faces and stuck them there for the world to see. Regular people would just assume she was camera shy or was one of those parents that didn't let their kid's photos go on the school newsletter or on group chats. She would have to add further back history, but for now it would do. It hadn't worked anyway, as she had still avoided the groups of mums and dads and spent much of her time alone. In the end, they had got sick of asking her to places, being friendly, and being turned down, so they had started to keep their distance, assuming she was a miserable old cow.

Skye was surprised when the school bell rang, a piercing sound that made her jump and snapped her out of her maudlin reverie. Before she could calm her racing pulse, Felicity ran over and threw her arms round Skye in an exuberant hug, thanking her profusely at the same time for all she had done for her. Skye balked and backed away, mumbling that it was nothing, before the other mums had a chance to see them or hear what they were talking about.

Thea and Skye quickly drew the children aside and explained that they were going to the park to play, and for an ice cream each, which resulted in noisy whooping and high five hand slaps, making Miles scowl. He had just been told by his classroom assistant to ask his mum to see the head teacher. His mum had then turned, red-faced, and dragged him indoors by his ear for embarrassing her in front of such an important local artist.

As they reached the park, the children ran off to climb the colourful ladder that led up to a winding green slide, which looked like a slithering snake reaching for the ground. Other children spun round on the bright yellow roundabout and sang songs as their feet flew into the air and the swings rocked to and fro as young mums pushed their toddlers, while chatting happily about the day's events. Skye and Thea sank gratefully onto a wooden park bench, which was positioned far enough away to enjoy the lush greenery of the park without the ear-splitting noise of children having fun, yet close enough to watch them enjoying themselves. It gave the children a slight feeling of independence, while not realising that their parents were actually aware of their every move.

Skye got up and wandered over to the little coffee stall at the side of the play area and ordered two coffees, knowing they would be disgusting and taste like bath water, but wanting to put off her chat with Thea, who started settling Flo onto a soft blanket on the floor, in the shade beside the pram. Walking back slowly and placing the plastic cup down next to Thea on the blanket with an apologetic shrug of her shoulders, Skye grimaced as she tasted her coffee, then quickly spat the offending liquid onto the grass, which broke the tension and made Thea smile.

'Why did you buy the coffee when you know it's so awful?'

'I thought that, as they've had so many complaints, they might have changed the brand they use by now. Obviously not!'

Thea waved Skye to come and sit next to her and looked into her eyes as if deciding something important. 'Let me tell you about my past,' she said, surprising Skye, who slumped down next to her beside the blanket and started tickling Flo's feet, making her gurgle and her eyes sparkle with joy.

Skye, although quite happy to put off having to lie to Thea again, was curious to hear what Thea was going to say. She was getting a bit twitchy, while Thea appeared to have drifted off to an angry place in her mind by the way she was scowling. Skye berated herself for not continuing to present a professional front to everyone she met and preparing a proper back story for herself and Leo, but she had grown exhausted by all the running and she was emotionally drained from having no one to turn to. To be perfectly honest, she'd made the squash and gymnastics stuff up because she was bored out of her mind spending so much time alone. Maybe it was time to rejoin the world and get a proper job? Perhaps she could become a real author and write her own life story? It would certainly be a page-turner, although she doubted people would believe half of it. She would sound completely unhinged and they would probably cart her off to the place where they lock you in a room and spoon-feed you porridge.

Chapter Fifteen

Flo wriggled until she had managed to turn herself around on the mat by shuffling on her tummy and both women gasped in surprise. Thea grabbed her phone to take a photo of her brilliant child. She stroked Flo's soft baby hair and made her more comfortable, before she gave Skye a hard stare to tell her she was still on topic, and began. 'I'll go first and tell you about my past.'

'Okay,' sighed Skye, brushing a stray ant from her leg and making herself more comfortable on the grass.

Thea thought back over the last decade. She had been good at her job and had undertaken in-depth training for her new career. She had worked diligently and gone over and above what was required to prove herself worthy of her new role. She didn't talk about her life choices to anyone and certainly hadn't told her family, as it was top secret. They would find a way to undermine her decision and belittle her success in some way, without realising they could be in danger by association. If they ever caught a look at her bank account, they would drop dead in shock anyway. She didn't need to work for her sister; in fact, she never needed to work again, but she didn't want the insufferable woman to target her as competition. Even Flo already had a healthy trust fund, but it was easier to let her sister carry on believing that she was helping Thea out after she had made such a mess of her life again, getting knocked up and abandoned, penniless and destitute. The only actual way her sister was helping her, was by keeping her occupied using her as a ridiculously cheap child minder. If she wasn't looking after Allie, Thea knew she would be paying someone else to spy on her ex-lover and her old boss and the resulting chaos would be pure torture. Instead, she had packed up her meagre belongings, walked away from them both and added firewalls to her computer to stop her from cyberstalking them too. The problem was that Flo reminded her of her ex every single day.

'I used to work in an office,' she began, a wistful lilt to her voice. 'It was pretty run-of-the-mill, with rooms full of utilitarian desks, grey walls, and more grey shelves full of files of paperwork. It wasn't the most inspiring of places to spend ten hours a day. I was pretty good at my job, but I let them walk all over me.' Skye looked troubled and settled back onto her arms, waiting for Thea to continue. A couple of brown birds who were hopping nearby stopped what they were doing, and cocked their heads to one side as if they were eagerly waiting for the next instalment too, which made Thea smile. They quickly spread their wings and flew across the park towards a family who had just laid out a brightly coloured picnic blanket and were unloading an array of delicious-looking treats.

Glancing at the children, who had moved onto the swings, Thea took a deep breath. Maybe this was a bad idea, but she had trained so many teams herself now that she could draw on her own years of experience, and she felt that the connection she had with Skye went much deeper than a playground chat and a few fish finger dinners.

'One day, someone new arrived at the office; I certainly hadn't seen them there before and the tension in the room was palpable. I thought I was going to be sacked, but instead they offered me a job. I didn't understand what they were saying to me as they kept referring to my technical skills and saying they could utilise them. When I realised what I had jumped into, it scared the hell out of me, but I was too stubborn to run away and admit failure again.'

Skye's eyebrows shot up and she looked like she couldn't have been more surprised. Thea understood it would be hard to imagine someone like her in a dangerous job, as she appeared to be so scatty and disorganised.

'What was the job?' Skye asked, sitting up on her knees and

ineffectually brushing at the grass stains on her jeans. She took a small sip of the disgusting coffee and quickly looked round for a place to spit it out again, sighing in defeat before holding her nose and swallowing it. Thea smirked at her friend's antics. Skye really couldn't sit still for a moment. Maybe Thea was wrong about her? Surely someone this agitated couldn't be the person Thea thought she was?

'They asked me to come in and spend two years in technical training. It was like shoving me into a cake shop and locking the door. There was so much to learn and so many hidden depths to technology that I hadn't realised before. To be honest, it's scary how deep you can go, but I was mesmerised by the fact they were trusting me and I finally had some responsibility. I was only working for the benefit of my employer and I understood that, but I was on a power trip and couldn't get enough of the adrenaline it gave me to be told at last that I was good at something. They loaded me up with responsibility and I revelled in it. I used to arrange for people to become someone else, or even disappear from history completely, if I wanted them to.'

Skye jumped up in shock. 'What the hell?'

'Shhh,' said Thea hastily. Bloody hell! She had really misjudged this one. Maybe Skye was just a crazy woman and not what she thought at all.

'You're a handler?' asked Skye incredulously under her breath, suddenly looking from side to side and scoping the park very vigilantly. 'Are you here for me?' she demanded angrily, still trying to speak quietly and keep control of her temper. 'Who do you work for?'

'Of course I'm not here for you! Why the hell would I be? As far as I know you're an author who hasn't published anything and an ex-high-school gymnast.'

'What gave me away?' asked Skye, obviously kicking herself for becoming complacent for the first time in years.

'Nothing! It's just years of dealing with people like you. I recognise the harried look,' she tried to jest and dampen the deadly glow in Skye's eyes. 'I know your own tech team would have your details buried so deeply that no one could find them, but I think I could if I really wanted to. I just recognised your body language and I guess I was hoping I wasn't alone.'

Skye took this last comment in and thought about it for a moment. 'You say you could break my cover if you really wanted to? If you can, then so can others. I'm usually so careful, but meeting you, my standards have slipped,' she said accusingly like a spoilt child, anger flushing her skin red as she kept Leo in her line of sight at all times. 'And what's the likelihood of us being in one area at the same time?' she added, giving up the pretence that Thea didn't know what her real job was. 'Who do you work for?' she asked again.

Thea knew the drill. A knot of worry would be gnawing at Skye's stomach and she would feel queasy at the thought that maybe Thea was a threat. Was the way they had met and bonded a coincidence? Was Flo even her daughter, or Allie related to her at all? Skye knew how this worked. People who appeared to be part of a community with an ordinary job and family could be anyone. The mum or dad who worked away for weeks at a time could easily be on assignment. Thea knew how far her old boss would go to get a job done, and they had told her they would 'persuade' anyone who left to come back into the fold. They might push the boundaries, but pretending someone was a mum with a baby and a family was sick and unlikely. Skye would realise this as soon as she calmed down and began to think rationally again.

Thea saw the range of thoughts flitting across Skye's face, as her eyes darted from Flo to Allie. She looked like she was about to grab Leo and bolt. Thea reached for Skye's arm and restrained her gently, but she was easily shaken off. 'Skye,' reasoned Thea. 'I think we work for the same people. I'm surprised our paths haven't crossed before, if I'm honest, but there are hundreds of techy guys and girls like me. Your team must have had one.'

Skye's eyes narrowed and she scanned Thea's face, but obviously didn't see anything threatening there. 'Are you being genuine? What the hell is going on?

'You're hiding from someone, aren't you?' Thea asked

suddenly.

'Yeah, my boss!' said Skye angrily, kicking the base of a nearby tree, then probably wishing she hadn't as she yelped in pain. Thea wondered why Skye didn't feel ready yet to tell anyone about the danger she must have put herself in every single day. Thea raised her eyebrow at Skye's avoidance of her question.

'What the hell!' fumed Skye, stomping around in circles. Flo blinked her eyes wide and her lips wobbled at the tension she felt radiating from her mum. Skye slumped down next to Thea on the grass in defeat and put her hands over her eyes to shield them from the last few rays of the sun. 'I can handle seasoned interrogators, but I crumple at one raised eyebrow from you.'

'From what I can tell,' said Thea, ignoring her friend's theatrics and waiting patiently for Skye to stop sulking, 'you have the skills to determine fairly quickly who you can trust and you have training to back up your decisions. How the hell two of us ended up in this back of beyond with two children is what's worrying me.' Skye straightened up at this comment and looked into Thea's eyes to see if she was being played. 'I've never thought of what happens to people like us when they leave or retire. Do you think there are playgrounds all over the country full of dangerous assassins?'

Skye choked back a laugh and she begrudgingly sat up and stared at her friend. Thea's shoved her hand through her hair, which wasn't an easy feat with all those curls, and her forehead crinkled as she was deep in thought. Skye rolled her eyes, but Thea saw her. She knew Skye was trying to work out how such a messy and disorganised person as Thea could arrange the lives of so many other people? She used to be so efficient. Maybe she could use the excuse that having Flo had addled her brain?

'Are you working undercover?' asked Thea, as a horrible thought popped into her head. She suddenly reached forward and scooped Flo up into one arm, turning her back on Skye and grabbing the baby bag with her other hand, before swiftly getting up and placing her baby and her belongings into the pram with practised ease. She really was a klutz and wished she'd had this particular thought, that Skye might be dangerous, before she had blurted her whole life history out to a complete stranger. Something about Skye made you want to tell her your secrets, even though Thea had really only intended to say that she was a bit of a computer whizz, with a history of helping solve crime, and wait for Skye to spill her story. Thea could kick herself as she had blabbed like the needy creature she used to be, who couldn't survive without someone else validating her existence. She pushed her shoulders back and turned to face the astounded Skye, who had an expression like a slapped fish, as confused as hell.

'Are you?' countered Skye, who seemed to be trying to regroup, keep control of her anger and not frighten Flo, who was looking at them both with concern.

Thea thought about lying, but was too tired from lack of sleep and baby brain to be able to co-ordinate her ideas at that precise moment. Thank goodness she wasn't at work, or she might have sent people to the wrong locations, or put their lives in danger. Anger and tension flared into her bloodstream and she felt herself want to yell at Skye to move away from them, but she knew this could endanger everyone. Quickly dropping a kiss onto Flo's nose and unhooking the back of the pram so that Flo could lay flat and sleep, she signalled to the other children to come and collect some money for an ice cream, as the brightly coloured van had just pulled up at the side of the car park. She winced as the sound it played dropped out of key, drawing children from the far corners of the park, until the area was swarming with families. It looked like they were dancing around the van in anticipation as they tried to get a glance at the choices of ice cream in the window, even though they had all seen them a thousand times before.

Thea waited for Leo and Allie to join the queue before she continued. She had trusted Skye for a reason. She felt they were connected and she had never doubted her instinct when she was at work. It wasn't the time to do that now. She felt in her bones that Skye wouldn't hurt her, so she would have to find out what was really going on. Skye didn't look like she was about to be forthcoming on the real reason she was nervous, so Thea reverted back to her original plan, of drawing Skye's story out, by confiding to her a little of her own. Settling Flo, checking on Allie and then making the decision to sit down again, Thea waited for Skye to relax and do the same.

'Flo's dad was someone I worked with. I know, I know,' she held up a hand to stop Skye's surprised questions, so she shut her mouth and waited patiently. 'He cheated on me before I found out I was pregnant, so I decided my job wasn't an ideal place to stay and bring up his child, when I would want to beat him with a stick every day. Although, to be fair, he told me from the start that he never wanted children or any commitment from me.' Thea bit down on her lip as it wobbled a little and she turned away and ran her hands restlessly through her hair again, but they got stuck halfway in her curls, so she hastily pretended she was brushing a leaf away and placed her hands in her lap. 'Flo needed at least one parent who wasn't a knobhead to look after her, so I left.'

Skye seemed aghast. 'Didn't he come looking for you when he found out you were pregnant?' Thea had the decency to look a bit shamefaced and Skye asked, 'You did tell him?'

Thea ignored that question and started to collect the last of the detritus of Flo's toys. 'He couldn't come looking for me. Everything I put on my original job application was a lie.'

Chapter Sixteen

Skye couldn't believe what she'd just heard and threw her hands up in mock surrender. She must be really losing her mind, as she'd thought Thea was timid and scatty, but here she was telling her that she was a technical genius, who'd kept her baby from its father and who'd lied about everything, even before she was recruited to the agency. She was worse than Skye. Skye was supposed to be the best in her own field, but she had been out of the game for way too long, she could see that now. The thought frightened her, as she had always been confident that she could keep Leo safe on her own.

'I was so fed up with never getting a job and being compared to my sister on every level by my parents and family, so I snapped one day and made a new life up. My old company never even checked my pretend references,' Thea said, appearing surprised that no one had ever found her out.

'I lived in fear for years until the fateful day I was recruited. When I eventually left the agency, I presumed Flo's dad might look for me, but he didn't,' she said sadly. 'I knew how to cover my tracks, but he could have found me if he'd really tried. It seems either I'm not valuable enough to look for, or he doesn't need me right now, so he's left me alone. I know I look a bit of a mess, but I was one of their best code breakers and I can pretty much access any computer in minutes,' she said proudly, before seemingly realising that it made her look like a complete prat, as her bosses obviously didn't value her enough to try and get her back.

Maybe she wasn't as red-hot as she thought? sighed Skye. 'My background check?' she asked, not knowing what else to say for once and glancing over to see the kids walking back with melting ice creams and happy faces.

Thea nodded, looking a bit sheepish. 'I have a habit of

doing a basic background check on anyone I meet. It's a bit of an obsession. When I couldn't find more on you than the last couple of years, I knew it wasn't real. The only reason you would have a new identity would be for a career like ours, or if you were in witness protection, but the cover would have gone deeper for that.' She looked at Skye apologetically, but also with censure for not being more careful.

Skye could have used someone like Thea on her own team. Her handler, Marcus, spent so long moaning about all of the rules they kept breaking as a team and the risks they were taking, that it always took twice as long to achieve anything. Skye had a feeling that there was far more to the story about Flo's dad, but didn't push it for now, as she wasn't sure how she felt about him not knowing that he was a father. She was confident that Thea thought she was making the right decision, but what if she was wrong? Skye could easily do her own background check and find out about Thea, but if her cover ran as deep as she suspected, it would be an impossible task.

'It was my own fault for becoming complacent,' said Skye, apologetically. 'I was bored and made some silly stuff up this time. I'm usually pretty thorough and can do the basic wipe of my past history. I have someone I trust and he clears and resets the rest. This time I didn't even want him to know where I was. I wanted a fresh start away from my past, but then you popped up. I thought you would be a shining light for the new me, but instead you're entwined in the life I'm trying to leave.'

Thea looked hurt by this, but Skye was lashing out and had no one else to direct it towards. Skye's perfect ideal of a new life here was crumbling before her eyes and she needed Thea to persuade her that having a friend you trusted wasn't such a bad thing, but a bonus instead.

Skye helped Thea to collect the last of the bottles and toys and they unceremoniously shoved them under the pram, before following the children out of the park towards home. 'Don't think you're off the hook,' said Thea levelly, looking sideways at Skye who was scowling beside her.

Skye's step faltered a little and her shoulders slumped. 'Okay,' she sighed. 'What do you want to know?'

Chapter Seventeen

Zack had reluctantly let Emmie go to Miles' house after school for tea and was dreading having to go and collect her. He'd tried asking Mike's wife, Marlo, to pick Emmie up and drop her home, when she had popped in earlier to give Mike the phone he'd left on the kitchen counter before work. She had laughed in his face and told him to stop being such a baby and to man up. Bloody women! They were put on this earth to annoy the hell out of him. For some reason this had brought to mind a picture of his new tenant and the cheeky wink she had sent his way at the school. He didn't think she knew he was her landlord, but for some reason he wanted her to. Zack wanted her to know that he owned the bed she slept in at night and that he could walk in at any time he pleased. He knew he couldn't really, but she wouldn't know that. He wanted her to be aware of him, for some reason, as she had pretty much ignored him since the day in the field. His skin prickled when he was around her and he was sure that it was because, even on such a limited acquaintance, she got under his skin. She made his blood warm up and his mind immerse itself in lust. He tried his best to be angry with her and was sure he had riled her for how rude he was in front of Emmie, but that wink of understanding at the school had stayed with him and made him hot and bothered when he thought about it. He kept dreaming of those long legs in those skin-tight black jeans. He really needed to get a grip, or get laid!

The weather was starting to warm up and his tenant would have to peel off some of those layers soon and start wearing shorts or skirts. He began to salivate at the thought of her soft silken skin and what it would feel like in his hands. He sighed in frustration; he really needed to find a girlfriend. That woman was bloody annoying and probably just as manipulative as his ex and Belle. He shivered at the thought. He was much better off on his own.

Bending down to pick up a crumpled crisp packet discarded on the floor by the tree climbing area, Zack scanned the area for any other remnants of the day's activities. He had a small cleaning crew that did a sweep of the site every evening. He didn't want the local wildlife choking on the colourful plastic people carelessly left around. Zack had to adhere to strict health and safety guidelines now that he was running this business and it had been a baptism of fire on how quickly he could learn how to do it. He had been selling his app for a while now, so he knew how to run a business, but being swamped by kids and their parents or carers every day was not what he had down on his business plan. Both companies relied on the good faith of families, as they were the target audience for his apps and CloudClimb but, as a grumpy old goat, he preferred the distance he had from the customer with his app business, to the hands-on way he had to run the tree climbing centre. Now that he had actually come to terms with owning such a zany business, Zack found he wasn't as much of a recluse as he had previously thought, and was starting to unfurl his cold heart and enjoy seeing the look of delight on the children's faces when they finally climbed the big trees or even got to the lowest walkways, their faces shining in surprise at their achievement.

Zack was quite excited about how well his interactive app design idea was coming along. He was going to install cameras on the safety helmets and, for a small fee, parents and friends would be able to watch the tree climb from the safety of the refreshment hut, where several mini screens would be installed across one wall. He was also going to have screens set into some of the trees. They would be in waterproof surrounds, but would tell the tree explorers how high they were from the ground, what type of tree they were climbing, and what was the hardest or simplest route back to the ground via the course. He was even adding a couple of simple games for them to play at the press of a button while they waited on the crossing points for people to traverse between the trees. There would be extra strapping and tree links to be attached before the game would begin, so that everyone was safe and not distracted.

Some people took their time to cross the ropes, or got worried about the height, and this could mean a queue formed at the crossing posts. He felt the adrenaline hit his veins every time he thought of investing more money in this venture, but it was a good feeling and he had made the decision to move ahead and expand the business, so he might as well jump in and enjoy the experience. He just had to work out how to get the same pleasure out of his personal life and not spend practically every waking hour dreaming of computer designs and rope runs in the trees.

Zack felt annoyed by his own weakness, cowering away and hiding from a strong woman like Mirabelle. Trying to come up with a solution, he remembered something Marlo had said earlier in the week about the estate being a great place for a party, but what a shame the owner was a complete hermit. Marlo had laughed and Mike had snorted and turned away in mirth.

Narrowing his eyes in determination, Zack made up his mind. He knew that he had been manipulated by yet another woman when Marlo had set down the challenge, but he had been just too thick to realise it at the time. She was throwing down the gauntlet. He'd been goaded into responding. For a usually quick and alert male, he could be a bit slow sometimes. He'd had to take an old acquaintance to the school quiz night to shut Mike up, but now school gossip was rife about him again and Belle kept scowling at him.

He already had a few ideas for the ball he would hold in the grounds, though. He would use it as an opportunity to launch his new app design to the locals. They were his customer-base after all, and he wasn't about to let Marlo have it all her own way. If he had to socialise with them, then he would use it as a business marketing opportunity at the same time. Zack smiled widely and thought about how angry Marlo would be when she found out the ball he was proposing was going to double up as a work function. She would be cross for about a minute, then she would be nagging him about decorations and catering. He sighed and his equilibrium slipped a little. Maybe he would need some help, if he wanted to do this properly? He would need invitations that made people choose to attend in the first instance. He knew Skye was an author and wondered, if he tried his hardest and was nice to her for once, she might scribble down a few lines to entice people here. He was sure many would turn up for the free booze, but he wanted it to be strictly invitation only and he would have to ask a few local dignitaries. This meant a good invitation, so that they would want to come.

Zack thought back to the days when he had wooed Emmie's mum, Kay, with flowers and the most expensive perfumes and jewellery he could afford at the time. It had nearly broken his spirit trying to pay for them, but he had believed she was worth it. How wrong could a man be? He thought of Skye's sparkling eyes and silky dark hair and couldn't remember ever seeing her wearing jewellery. He didn't think she was the hearts and flowers kind of gal either. Maybe he could turn up at the cottage to inspect the property with a bottle of wine, and then ask for her help? That wouldn't work, as she would probably laugh at him and think he was a total creep. Seeing the mischief in her smile the other day at school, she would probably grab the wine first, then shut the door in his face. The thought didn't make him feel too good and Zack decided it was time he introduced himself properly and apologised for his previous behaviour.

Chapter Eighteen

Skye opened the door to the cottage and let Thea and the children precede her into the lounge. There were supposed to be four other children joining them again today for her new afterschool 'fitness club' and, for once, Skye was glad of the distraction. It meant she could put off Thea for a while longer. She didn't know how her life had come to this, teaching seven and eight-year-olds tactics on how to avoid Miles, while letting them think she was running some sort of afterschool club. What the hell had she been thinking?

She had decided it was time her son learned how to protect himself, and Allie was welcome too, but she didn't really like other children and, to make matters worse, the mums who brought their kids over for a play date tried to stick their nose into her business and would 'innocently' wander into the nooks and crannies of her home, their eager eyes darting everywhere, inspecting her credentials. She absently wondered what they thought of her little home, then smiled to herself as they wouldn't discover much about her personality from the furnishings, as someone else had bought every last thing in the house and she had relocated her few personal belongings upstairs.

The busybodies all seemed to sit and hover awhile, as if she would offer them coffee. Thea, who usually had to help herself to a drink, seemed to understand from the look of suffering on Skye's face she was not to offer one to anyone else, or get her own until they had vacated the building, in case they got any funny ideas about it being a coffee shop or a social occasion.

After the last mum had reluctantly left their child there and gone home (she was sure there were two more women than last week), Skye decided that if they wanted to snoop into her life so much, she would charge them for the pleasure. Surely after school clubs weren't cheap? She would have to get officially registered, which would be tedious, but she might start to enjoy herself and play with their minds. She could leave clues around the cottage about her life, for the school mums to work out, if they were so bloody interested. She smirked at the thought of them discovering her real job, they would run for the hills, but for now she could be a belly dancer, or an astronaut – although maybe the last one was a bit far-fetched.

Thea was standing by the entrance to the kitchen. The back door was open and the children were already practising their balancing skills on the slightly raised planks of wood that Skye had zig-zagged across the garden. She had spent hours building little supports for them, so that they were about two feet from the ground, and the children had their arms outstretched, concentrating on staying upright when moving from plank to plank. It was a simple but effective way to make them look where they were going, as they didn't want to fall, even though they could step down at any time. The planks were wide enough for their feet to fit on easily but, as the adjoining plank was always at an angle to the first and there was a gap between each end, all of the children were totally quiet and deep in concentration.

Leo had reported back to Skye that they had managed to dodge Miles quite well so far, as they were more aware of things being thrown at their heads, and they kept tabs on his whereabouts, so they could move somewhere else. The group of them made a game out of it and, apparently, more children now wanted to play with them, so Miles was becoming increasingly frustrated.

Skye knew this behaviour could escalate, but for now it was being neutralised while Miles tried to fathom out what was going on. Leo and Allie seemed much happier and that was enough for her.

She could sense that Thea's patience with her was wearing thin, by the way she was staring pointedly at her and tapping her nails on the grey granite kitchen counter. Skye sighed and walked over to pour herself a glass of lemonade. She graciously got out a second glass for Thea and took her time slicing some strawberries from the fridge, which was about as culinary as she got, to pop into the drinks with some ice.

Walking outside and placing the drinks on the little wooden table under the window, she lifted the plain green parasol to offer some shade from the last of the spring sunshine, which had unusually been blazing all day and was making Skye wish she was wearing a pair of shorts. As Skye turned and jogged over to the children, Thea took a long sip of the surprisingly delicious drink and watched as Skye hunched down and explained what she wanted them to do next, making them giggle and run off in all directions.

Finally, Skye returned and pulled out the chair opposite Thea, who still hadn't uttered a word. Skye gave in and lifted her hands in mock surrender, which made Thea raise half a smile.

Checking the children were busy with their next task and that they couldn't be overheard, Skye decided it was time she finally trusted someone and made a new friend. From what Thea had already told her, she was pretty certain that anything she said would be confidential and wouldn't make Thea grab the nearest phone and call the police.

'I was a field agent,' Skye began, speaking in a low voice and darting glances around out of habit. 'My job was generally to make first contact with our target and assess the feasibility of our operation. I worked as part of a team and it could get pretty hairy at times. My parents died when I was in my early twenties,' she paused in thought.

'They had me when they were quite old and didn't think being parents would ever happen for them, but when I surprised them by turning up, they never looked back.' Skye pictured her dad's gentle face and kind eyes and a ball of sadness unfurled in her stomach. 'It wasn't the case where my dad looked like a granddad bringing his granddaughter to school. Both were pretty crazy and grabbed hold of life. They gave me a zest for adventure and they were everything to me.' Skye's lip trembled and Thea reached across the table to squeeze her hand in sympathy. Skye gritted her teeth so as not to cry. She was pretty much hard as nails, but she hadn't spoken about her parents for so long and it felt good to remember them, even though it hurt today as much as it had then. She still missed them terribly.

'They died when my mum was seventy and my dad was seventy-five. They were on another adventure and the boat they were on capsized.' A fat salty tear slid down her cheek and she angrily brushed it away. She was too old to be crying over her parents. It was ancient history, she told herself again and again. Skye straightened her shoulders and refused to give in to the familiar sadness that threatened to engulf her. She had been extensively trained to suppress her emotions, outwardly anyway, but this sometimes meant she held them internally and she occasionally wondered if one day she would simply erupt and explode into an angry ball of hurt and frustration at the way her life had turned out.

'I didn't have any other family,' she continued sadly, 'not that my parents ever talked about, anyway. I used to wonder if they had pushed everyone away when they thought they couldn't have children and had come to terms with living their lives to the full on their own. When they finally relaxed, my mum got pregnant. You hear about that kind of thing all the time, don't you?' Thea nodded, but didn't comment in case Skye stopped talking.

'I was so lonely and angry when they died, I spent most of my waking hours in pubs, getting as drunk as I could before I passed out.' She raised her eyes to meet Thea's, waiting for the inevitable censure, but saw only kindness and understanding there. 'One evening, I got into a fight and this guy I'd never met piled in and saved me.' She pictured her first glimpse of Reece as he ploughed in, with bulging muscles under a tight denim shirt and soft blonde hair that looked like it had been kissed by the sun.

Her heart still flipped over at the thought of him and she picked up her drink and blocked her face with the glass as she took a sip, not really tasting the sparkling concoction, trying to avoid choking on the soft strawberries, defying herself not to cry again in front of Thea.

Everything had happened so quickly and, from what she could remember, she had been roaring drunk. The man who tried to make her go home with him had been pretty surprised when she had landed her first punch. He had been much bigger than her, though, and had regrouped from being winded pretty quickly, grabbing her arm painfully and pulling her towards the door. No one else in the pub had seen the altercation as it was noisy and packed with hardened drinkers, but Reece had seen her plight and stepped forward to block their route out of the building. She didn't even know him, but he had protected her and she had fallen madly in love with him in an instant.

Looking back now, she could see how needy and lonely she had become, but Reece's golden good looks and masculine charm would have worn her down eventually anyway.

'We fell in love,' she sighed miserably. 'He worked for the agency, LUCAN, but kept disappearing for work. I suppose I got jealous. I threatened to leave him. He couldn't confide in me about his real job, so he recruited me instead. He said he couldn't bear to be apart from me.' Thea looked sceptical about this declaration from what sounded like such a manly man. 'He decided this was the obvious solution,' continued Skye. 'It was such a shock to find out what he really did, but when I went into training, it was unbelievable as I was a natural. I think it might have irritated him for a while, but he soon got over it. The benefits of having me around all the time outweighed his ego,' Skye smiled sadly, trying to make light of an awful situation.

It was becoming clear that the story was going to go from bad to worse, by the way a steady stream of tears was trickling its way down the side of Skye's face. She kept swiping them away, but more followed. Thea reached into Flo's baby bag and handed her friend a tissue, which Skye took gratefully, mopping her face, leaving her with flushed cheeks and a slightly red nose. 'The training was pretty unbearable, but I got through it as I wanted to be near Reece. The team I joined became pretty indispensable for a time.'

Thea sat back and let out the breath she had been holding.

Skye assumed that she didn't want to say anything yet, as Skye was unburdening herself and, after all, isn't this what Thea had wanted; to find out more about this eccentric, crazy lady? She'd got more than she'd bargained for with Skye. The children started to look restless, though, so Thea jumped up and tried to pull down the hem of her creased skirt as it had got stuck under her. After a glimpse at Flo, who was playing with her toes in her pram, she gave the children a football that was in a basket by the back door and an ice lolly each from the freezer, probably hoping to distract and cool them down.

Thea then rushed back into the kitchen and looked to see if Skye had prepared any dinner but only found burgers and chips in the freezer. She hastily stuck them in the oven, on a low heat. Skye prayed it would give her a chance to finish her conversation with Thea and have dinner ready by the time the other mums arrived to collect their offspring. She was really hoping that they wouldn't hang around, as their own kids would need some dinner and the smell would prompt them to rush home.

'An unhealthy meal won't kill Allie this once, and I'll lie to my sister and tell her that Allie has eaten steak. It's the same meat after all,' decided Thea. Slipping back into her seat opposite Skye, who was in a bit of a daze, she gently nudged her arm to snap her out of it.

'I did enjoy the adrenaline of the job, but it was dangerous, as you probably already know. I was a bit of a maverick back then, although I still got scared,' Skye continued as if coming out of a trance. She looked up to see the children happily munching on ice lollies and kicking the football into the small goal she had purchased the previous week for Leo. She turned her wrist over and showed Thea the slivers of silver scars that criss-crossed her arms. They were so tiny, you could barely see the jagged lines, but there were quite a few of them. Thea cringed and looked horrified at the thought of something cutting her friend's delicate skin.

Skye smiled sadly at her scars; as if they brought back painful memories, not just of the physical pain, but of the mental trauma she had been through. 'I fell on a job once. I dropped through a window, just after I had found out I was pregnant. It cut my arms to shreds. Luckily, I had covering on every other part of my body, but my wrists got the worst of it. They were mainly superficial wounds, but they hurt like hell.' She rubbed the scars as if trying to erase the memory. 'I never made that mistake again.'

'I bet it wasn't your fault,' Thea leapt to her defence.

'It was. I got cocky and can't have checked my safety harness properly. The others in my team were ahead of me and I wanted to catch up and show them that I wasn't a liability. Funnily enough, I arrived first as I pretty much flew there. We lost the element of surprise and I got a proper bollocking from my boss, and then another from Reece when we got home for not doing the safety checks properly. He screamed at me that I couldn't take care of another human being, if I couldn't look after myself first.' She saw Thea flinch and sighed. 'I had never seen him so angry before. He didn't talk to me for a week after that.

'He eventually gave in, but made me promise to take time off to take care of the baby when it was born, until he came up with a better plan for how we would manage.'

Thea felt a big fat tear make its way down her own nose and she tried to sniff and wipe it away with a tissue she grabbed from an almost empty packet in the baby bag by her feet. 'I'm so sorry. I assumed that, like my own story, the man in your life was a self-centred cheat, but I've been wrong. He sounds a bit controlling, but still one of the good guys.'

'He was killed on a job when Leo was a baby. I crawled home to a tiny cottage my parents had bought on a whim one year. I hadn't ever got round to selling it as it was unregistered and probably illegally built. The architects had conned dad and made him pay in cash, so there was no trail to me. As soon as the builders had the money, they abandoned the place. My parents didn't seem to care as they thought it was a romantic setting. They planned to leave it for years so that the site became legally theirs and they could finish building their dream home. They died before this could happen. I carry the property deeds with me everywhere. Mum and dad would have been glad to know the house kept Leo and me safe. I stayed there licking my wounds. I must have known I would need the old place one day.

'I couldn't even have a funeral for Reece, as he didn't officially exist. There was an explosion when he was killed, removing all traces of him. My whole field team was gone and I was the only one who survived, as I wasn't there that day. I blamed myself for years. I still do in a way,' Skye mused sadly. 'If I had set the meeting up, maybe something wouldn't have gone wrong. Instead, I was sitting at home with a baby I had no idea how to look after, feeling responsible for killing his father.'

'One day I woke up, looked at my son and decided that I needed to start my life again before Leo's world crumbled to nothing, or someone worked out where we were. It was only a short while after Reece's death, but I knew that the people who killed my team were probably looking for me, too. I went in to work once after Reece had died, and they offered to hide me, but the only way our target could have found the team was for them to have had someone on the inside. The only people left were me and our handler, Marcus. It had to be him,' Skye said, with such hatred in her voice that Thea shivered. 'I couldn't risk him knowing where I was, so I disappeared. I'd cultivated a few tricks of my own over the years and had memorised everything in case I ever needed it. I had never been so thankful that I'm a quick study after Leo and I were alone. The agency wanted me to come in for a debriefing, but I told them I was too filled with grief, which was true, and they had no choice but to give me time to heal. I used that to run.'

Skye was emotionally exhausted and rubbed tired eyes, as her bones had become heavy and lethargic. 'I'm mentally drained now. It's been years and, although I'm good at hiding, if they wanted to find me, they would have done by now. I'm tired of running and Leo needs a home.' Thea got up and walked round the table, pulling a reluctant Skye into a warm hug. After a moment's hesitation at the unfamiliar contact, Skye sank into Thea's arms and let her friend comfort her. She hadn't realised how much she had missed having someone hold her until this moment, but there was no going back now. Her heart was slowly thawing and maybe she could finally re-enter the real world.

Chapter Nineteen

Thea slumped onto her couch in exhaustion. Flo had been really grizzly tonight and she'd felt a bit hot. It had taken ages to cool her off and bath time had been a struggle as they were both tired after a long day.

She thought back over the conversation she'd had with Skye and felt warmth spread in her stomach as she remembered the way her friend had trusted her with her life story. She felt proud that Skye had opened up to her. The story was so tragic, with both her parents and husband dying suddenly. She felt it in her bones that Skye was telling the truth but, as with many former agents, the lies were ingrained after years of being someone else and memories, many of which could be violent and disturbing, got distorted, lines became blurred and the real person inside could easily get lost.

Some of the people Thea worked with were positively glad to leave their old lives behind, but Skye was different. Thea could tell she still mourned the loss of her parents, and her husband must have been pretty special to have taken on a woman like her. From the love in her voice when she described him, Thea could tell he was the love of her life. Thea bit back the bile that rose in her throat as she thought about the man who had been the grand passion in her own life and sunk even further into the couch when she acknowledged, humiliatingly, that she had been used. A tear escaped from her eye and she angrily brushed it away. He'd had enough of her tears. She was stronger now and refused to cry over such a heartless man again.

She had thought she had found a love like Skye's, but she'd been so wrong. How she could have thought a man like Flo's dad would be interested in a fat dumpling like her, she would never know. She had grown in confidence over the years at LUCAN, but had been surprised when he pursued her. She had been so overwhelmed with lust that she hadn't questioned it. He was a professional liar and she should have known better.

She might hate her old boss for telling Thea she was sleeping with him too and was bored with sharing, but at least Thea had had the last word and left with her head held high. She had made ardent love with him one last time and then coldly told him she didn't want to see him again. She ignored his shocked expression and pleading tones and had literally disappeared. She knew how to erase any trace of her former life and, as he hadn't known her then, he couldn't start now. Not that he had looked for her anyway, as far as she could tell. Why would he? He didn't love her and she hadn't told him about Flo. What a chump! He'd said time and time again that he didn't want to bring children into this world after the atrocities he had seen. So, as far as Thea was concerned, she was protecting her child from a father who didn't want her and preventing her own heart from being broken into even more pieces than it was now. A wall of ice had encased her heart, until the moment she held her daughter for the first time, and it had come crashing down. The love she had for Flo was unparalleled by anything she had felt before. It was the one thing she thanked him for.

Thea derided herself that she could have probably given birth and barely noticed as she had so much blubber around her waist. She was going to stop eating cakes and start getting fitter, she decided tiredly, not having the energy to lift the glass of wine she had grabbed from the fridge in desperation before she sat down. She kept an emergency bottle in there, which was for times when she almost picked up the phone and told her ex about his daughter but, as she was breastfeeding, she hadn't even had the balls to take more than a sip each time. Thea pushed the glass away in disgust. She had finally begun to wean Flo onto solid food and formula, so she would soon be able to enjoy a glass without feeling like a bad mother. She'd been stuffing her face with cake to help with her desperation over her latest predicament, but if Skye could overcome what she had been through, then the least Thea could do was try harder.

She felt her eyelids begin to droop and she closed her eyes and sank deeper into the folds of the soft blue couch. If she could just rest for an hour or so, then she would have more energy to sort her life out, instead of existing from day to day in a haze of misery.

Thea started thinking back to the first day at work where she had walked into the discreet reception at LUCAN and a smile lifted her lips. It had been a fabulous time in her life back then and she had felt, perhaps for the first time ever, that she was competent and useful and could conquer the world. She had held her shoulders back and portrayed an air of confidence that she hadn't really felt. It was a new start for her and she had grabbed it with both hands.

Thea had been introduced to her team and told how the training would work. She had a room of her own onsite with everything she could need. It was like a small town and she couldn't believe she was part of such an important scheme. They had picked her for her ability to analyse problems and find a rapid solution and, over the coming months, she had honed her skills until she was the best she could be in her field. There was no more walked-all-over Thea, she was at the top of her game. Then her ex caught her eye and, although she was surprised he was interested in her, she grabbed him too. He had told her, much later, that he liked her calming influence and delectable backside! Thea's face had flamed with mortification but, in reality, she had been secretly flattered as nobody had spoken to her that way before. He said she reassured him and ignored his impulsive mood swings and crazy ideas about putting the world to rights. Thea listened without judgement and gave him the stability he needed to stop him from jumping into every dangerous situation he encountered. What Thea got from him, she now realised with clarity, was the amazing sex that had been missing in her life and, if she had to soothe him to get his beautiful body in her bed every night, then the deal was well worth her effort.

Thea had smiled constantly for the two years they were

together, and must have looked a bit smug right up until the day her boss, Lexi, had strolled in with her skinny jean-clad body and her sneering face, lips plastered with red lipstick, to taunt her. Thea had gasped in shock at the news although, if she was honest, she had always been waiting for this moment. It was as if she had expected that this happiness couldn't be real or last. Flo's dad was too wild and dangerous to be tamed by one woman and she had been a fool to believe she had finally been the one to do it.

Thea drifted off to sleep, remembering what it felt like to be desired by a man like that. He had made her feel like she was the only woman in the world for him. If only she had been.

Chapter Twenty

Skye and Thea had slipped easily into a routine over the last two weeks and Skye felt that they were connecting in a way she had steered well clear of in recent years. They were forming a strong friendship and had begun to rely on each other. Skye hadn't needed anyone for years and was nervous about being vulnerable again.

Skye walked Leo to school and felt physically drained. She had lain awake every night thinking about what Thea had said. How had they both turned up here? Was it some sort of test? Had they both been sent here on purpose? She recalled how she had found this place and chosen the estate cottages to live in, and her blood ran cold. She had used conventional methods, and not the internet, to find a new place to live. She had looked at newspapers and gone into the library of her old town and seen a poster about the estate and cottages and how they were being refurbished and would be ready for new tenants soon. She had also seen an article in a country magazine about an eccentric old man who owned the estate and cottages. It certainly hadn't been about Zack, as women would have flocked from far and wide if there had been a picture of his muscular frame and moody countenance, although the man in the photo did have Zack's dark eyes, she now recalled. He'd been about seventy and was dressed with the flair of the eccentric, with brightly coloured clothes and a cravat tied jauntily at his neck. He had been beaming into the camera and she had been drawn to him immediately. Skye had squirreled the magazine into her coat and taken it out to read in detail when she got home.

Skye's stomach flipped; could the article have been a plant? She used the library regularly, although she visited it at different times out of habit, so that anyone planning to grab her couldn't bank on her movements at any one time. Could they know her phone number and have seen the quick photo she had taken of the estate? She changed her number every time she moved, as she cut contact with everyone she left behind without a backward glance. She didn't keep their details, what would be the point? Skye generally became someone new every time she moved, but for the last two years she hadn't bothered to change things again. Leo was getting fed up with remembering each new name and history and she'd decided enough was enough. Only Reece knew the pet name her father had called her: Skye. He knew he could use it when they were alone and had loved their secret. He used to say she lifted him to the sky and the stars when they were together and the name was perfect for her.

Could LUCAN have used the photo to tempt her here? Hundreds of questions filled Skye's mind and her heart started hammering in her chest. Had Thea been planted here to remind her of her old job? Had they been placed together to make them realise that they could never really escape that world?

As they drew near the school, Skye bent down to kiss her son, who scowled with embarrassment and hurried off, stopping suddenly to send her an apologetic grin before seeing one of his friends and rushing up to greet them. Skye smiled at his sudden independence, then turned sadly away as she realised that he would be a grown-up before she knew it. He might want to travel and his plans would most likely not revolve around her. She would have to stop being so paranoid and make a life of her own someday soon and stop concentrating her efforts on her son.

Turning towards home, Skye kept her eyes on the ground. She wasn't in the mood to be polite to anyone today, not that this day was any different from any other, but she wanted to be alone to process what she had learned and assess their vulnerability.

As she turned the corner at the bottom of the road towards her cottage, the hairs on the back of her neck started to stand on end, and she instinctively looked around in time to see a man turn and cross the street in the opposite direction. She wouldn't normally make anything of this, but something about the way he turned at the exact moment he did, made her think he had been following her. She picked up speed and walked towards a different lane from her own, darting behind a low hedge as she passed, then slipping into a nearby field to place her back up against a tree and check carefully to see if he was following her. After an age of watching and waiting, she chastised herself for becoming so paranoid since she had met Thea. Why would someone be watching her after all this time? It was ridiculous!

Staying towards the edge of the field and then doubling back towards the road, Skye found a gap in the prickly green hedge and briskly jogged home, letting herself in with practised ease. Scoping the room and checking for any irregularities, she let out the breath she had been holding and sagged in relief when everything was as it should be. Out of habit, she ran up the stairs two at a time and flung open the wardrobe, sighing in relief that the suitcase she always had packed and ready with spare clothes and essentials was waiting patiently for her to grab at a moment's notice. Anything else they needed could be bought along the way. She would miss Thea, Flo and Allie, but Leo was her priority.

Throwing herself down onto the bed and putting her head in her hands, Skye felt like she wanted to weep. She had stayed strong for so long, but since she had come here, she had felt herself soften and some of the old Skye return. She had been called Sasha back then but, because her dad had said her eyes were as bright as the summer sky, the nickname had stuck. She wasn't sure why she'd chosen the name to use now but it had felt right, just as it had also been time to begin surveying a different area to start a new life.

Reaching into her jeans pocket for her phone, Skye wondered if Thea could get her a fancy one like hers, as she was pretty sure that Thea's phone was about as secure as you could get and was a better idea than Skye's burner model. She dialled Thea's number from memory. It was an old trick she had acquired, she never wrote anything down but memorised things, sometimes for years. She had put occasional numbers in her old phones, but mainly ones which she didn't use regularly, to throw anyone off her scent.

Thea answered after the third ring and sounded surprised to hear from her so soon, as they had spent all of the previous day together eating cake and enjoying the view of the muscly men that kept appearing at the door of the gym opposite the coffee shop they'd been in. But Thea had wondered aloud if Skye would panic about the bond they were forming and the secrets they had shared and said she wouldn't have been astonished if the next time she visited the cottage it was empty. Skye knew it was ingrained for agents to keep moving their base and to abstain from making real friends. It was safer for everyone that way.

'Thea,' said Skye urgently. 'Can you come round? Bring some ice cream and chocolate if you have any. It's either that or vodka and I know that you're not keen on alcohol at the moment. I'm feeling like running,' she said honestly.

Skye had put gravel on the little winding pathway up to the front door a week ago, and just ten minutes later it crunched underfoot, alerting her that Thea had arrived. Skye peered into the tiny glass spyhole she had discreetly drilled into the door and opened the door wide, just as Thea raised her arm to knock. Thea was dragging the pram along behind her, with a huge slab of chocolate cake balancing on Flo's legs, and the roses she had hastily grabbed from her garden on the way past were rammed in the basket underneath. Dragging the pram inside and knocking a few of the blooms off as she passed, Thea reached down and handed them to Skye with an apologetic smile at the state of them.

Skye took the offering with a wonky smile and walked the few strides into her kitchen, to see if the landlord had thought to add a vase to the cottage's inventory. Luckily, he had. It looked like it belonged to the original cottage as it was cut glass and didn't fit with the clean lines and minimal décor of the rooms inside. Skye held the vase under the kitchen tap, filled it and then placed the roses, almost reverently, into the water. Her eyes watered and she squeezed them tightly shut.

Thea came up beside her and touched her arm in concern, seeming surprised that bringing flowers had upset Skye so much. 'I assumed from the phone call that you were jittery from our daily conversations, or that you'd found out something more about Miles being a pain at school and decided you had had enough?' The tense line of Skye's shoulders and the tears in her eyes told another story. 'You're so strong, Skye. I thought you were joking around when you said you were thinking of running. A woman like you wouldn't be scared of what I told you about my past, surely?' Thea looked really troubled now and started pacing around the small room.

'Reece used to bring me roses,' said Skye, sniffing unflatteringly into her hand and wiping the tears with the back of her arm, leaving streaks of mascara running across her face. She placed the vase of scented blooms in the centre of her tiny dining table, underneath the window in the kitchen.

'I'm so sorry!' exclaimed Thea, seeming to kick herself for grabbing the fragrant offering impulsively as she left her garden.

'It's not your fault. It's not as if you're so desperate for a real friend that you picked up anything that might persuade me to stay.' said Skye morosely, not knowing how close to the truth that was. 'If I was nicer to people, someone else might have bought me flowers in the last seven years,' she tried to joke, but it fell a bit flat with the tension in the room. Thea stared at her sympathetically and gently pushed the vase of flowers further away across the table, although they couldn't go far as the surface was so small.

'Let's sit down and you can tell me what's happened.'

'I think someone's following me,' Skye said seriously, a steely tone coming into her voice. Thea looked really worried suddenly and Skye berated herself for being weak and burdening someone else. 'I should be handling this alone. Normally I would sort out the problem without a moment's hesitation, but this time my instinct was to call you.' The comment made Thea blush with pleasure as she looked at Skye.

111

'This, in itself, frightens the life out of me! I hate relying on anyone but myself, it just leads to pain for everyone involved,' said Skye.

'Why would someone be following you?'

'I don't know.'

Thea gave Skye one of her hard stares and Skye sighed in exasperation, pushing her chair back and moving to stand by the sink. Staring out at the back garden, she scanned every inch of the property. Thea sat patiently, hands in her lap, as though she was waiting to find out what they would do next. Skye realised Thea was usually the technical handler and organised the finer details, but that was after someone else made the decisions and told her what to do. No doubt she completed the task with expert skill and minimal fuss. But now it looked as though Thea was actually quite excited about the prospect of an adventure. She had probably been bored with babysitting and pretending to play dumb, however much she adored her daughter and niece, Skye realised.

'I may be overreacting,' said Skye carefully.

'But you don't think you are?' asked Thea, turning her chair to face Skye, who was now pacing the room. This wasn't the best idea as it was a tiny space and, as soon as she had taken three strides, she had to turn and come back again. Thea leant out an arm to stop her progress.

'We had several run-ins with the people who killed our team and I pleaded with our handler to move the task to another group at LUCAN as they were starting to notice us, but he wouldn't listen. The night of the explosion, two of their people died as Reece tried to fight his way out, apparently. It was horrific as our assignments were usually extracting important people or information from diplomatic situations and didn't involve people getting killed. I wasn't even there that night, but as part of a team which was assassinated, I'm determined they won't get me too. My son needs me.'

'When I was called in and was told what had happened, my world blew apart.' Skye drew a shaky breath and looked up to see tears in Thea's eyes. It was good to see that, after seeing so many people lie to, and kill, each other, Thea was still human and felt things deeply, probably especially since she'd had Flo.

Skye's own eyes were starting to feel a bit red and sore. 'They said the target had gone to ground and they would have to give me a new identity for my own protection. For my team to have been hit, someone must have known they were coming. I told Reece I had a bad feeling about it, but he shut me out and told me I had to protect our baby. They must have had someone on the inside and I couldn't take any chances, so I went to my parents' cottage and pretended to wait, while I found a way to get us to the safe house Reece and I had built in case we ever found ourselves in trouble. I was so full of grief and anger that someone had betrayed Reece, and might try and hurt Leo and me too, that I used my own contacts to get us out. Then I found I was scared there, too, after a while and I ran again.'

Thea turned towards her and it was clear that her earlier adrenaline rush had turned to fury at the thought that anyone would dare anyone try to hurt Skye and Leo. Skye knew the other woman felt an unexpected connection to her, full of sadness and anger for the way they'd killed her field team and now they wanted to kill her too.

But Skye's stomach plummeted. This was a quiet suburban area and Thea's whole family lived here, as well as Skye and Leo. If there was an assassin out there, she knew he wouldn't hit civilians, but if anyone close to the target got in his way, he wouldn't think twice about taking them out too. It would have to be done with minimal fuss as they wouldn't want hysterical locals running amok, nevertheless, they would get the job done.

Chapter Twenty-One

Skye watched the tumult of emotions flit across Thea's face and felt sick that she had ever brought her to her house. She should have known better and would understand if Thea ran for the hills or exposed her secrets to the other school mums and dads, as she and Leo were a very real danger to their offspring.

'I'm sorry for asking you round, Thea. It might not be safe for you to be here. You should go.' Skye began collecting Flo's baby bag and placed it over the pram's handles.

Skye didn't know Thea well enough yet, but she could sense she was obstinate and telling her to go snapped her out of her very real concerns for her friend and made her focus on what to do.

'You said you're not safe. What's changed since last week when you were looking relaxed and settling in? Why are you suddenly sure they are looking for you after all this time?' asked Thea.

'I think I've seen the same man watching me twice now, but he's clever and I never get a proper look at him. It's what alerted me to him in the first place. It's an occupational hazard to scan every face I pass and I notice people's body language.' Skye saw Thea's body go stiff with alarm and she could see the pulse racing in her neck. She hated scaring her, but this could be a very real threat. 'The signals he was giving out were quite off. It's exhausting to be constantly alert, which is why I'm probably scowling half of the time,' she joked, trying to lighten the mood and not terrify poor Thea. Skye could see that her friend was visibly shaken and realised that she probably didn't get to see any dangerous activity from her fortified office at LUCAN. Skye was scared, but she was ready to take action. Thea had gone red and looked like she might vomit at any moment.

'Have you got a plan?' asked Thea, visibly trying to calm herself down and not be a baby in front of Skye, who had dealt with things like this every day when she worked at LUCAN.

'Track him down and dismember him?' said Skye, in mock seriousness. Thea appeared slightly shocked and Skye laughed finally as Thea slumped further into her chair and smiled too. 'I'm only joking. I have had to fight people, but I haven't actually killed anyone. That's not to say I haven't knocked out a big beefy guy or two,' she winked with a conspiratorial smile.

'Do you really think you're in danger, or are you just feeling a bit spooked?' asked Thea, straightening her back as if garnering strength from Skye's no-nonsense approach. Skye had been visibly shaken when Thea had arrived, but her training had kicked in now and she was striding around the very small kitchen again and reaching for a box that Thea looked horrified to see contained a very sharp set of throwing knives.

'I'm not sure,' replied Skye honestly, absently picking up the knives to check they were razor sharp, then putting them back in their box and tiredly rubbing her eyes. It was at times like this that she wished Reece was around to share the burden of protecting their son. 'He didn't seem threatening and I've just glimpsed him from a distance. Have you noticed anyone following you?'

Thea rubbed her muscles and Skye could see she was tense. 'Mentally scan the last few days to see if you've seen anyone new around town.'

'I don't have your training Skye, so I could probably walk straight past someone and not think anything of it at all. You're trained to decode body language and the nuances of a person's behaviour whereas, unless I was aware of a threat, I wouldn't know how to stay undetected.' Skye knew she was right. Thea was trained to hack computers and create new identities for people. How the hell was she supposed to know if she was being followed? They could walk straight up to her and she would offer them a wave of welcome and a jaunty 'Hello.' Skye sighed in frustration.

'I really have no idea,' Thea said honestly, watching Skye place the box of knives back up high above the kitchen cabinet.

'We've spent a lot of time together, so I think I would have spotted anyone following you,' said Skye absently. 'I'm sure I'm overreacting. They told me the threat had been neutralised, but I didn't know who to trust.'

'So why did you run?' Thea asked. 'I really want to know the answer to try and work out who you are. If you thought it was safe, why run?' she asked again when Skye didn't immediately answer.

Skye raised her face to the heavens as if asking for forgiveness and took a deep breath to steady her nerves. 'I was angry at Reece for not being more careful and mad as hell at LUCAN for not protecting my team. I know they said I was safe, but they also said that about the original operation the team was on.'

'I heard about your team,' said Thea very quietly, as if she didn't want Skye to hear her. Thea began wringing her hands in her lap and Skye noted the movement and frowned again at the sign that Thea was deeply uncomfortable about something and it was more than just a possible stalker.

'What?' said Skye, thunderstruck. 'How?'

'We'd all heard about you lot. You were the elite team that always got results with nominal disruption. We didn't know exactly who you were, but there were rumours about you. We also heard about the explosion,' she said as gently as she could. 'Everyone was in shock. If it could happen to you guys, what hope was there for the rest of us? We were told that the whole field team died,' she said apologetically.

Thea looked like she had something else to say, but was hesitant about divulging too much and Skye gave her a hard stare and told her to get on with it. She didn't mean to be harsh, but this day was getting worse by the minute!

'I do think you're safe,' Thea conceded. Skye noticed she was trying to avoid looking straight into her eyes, as if she knew she'd see censure there for letting Skye suffer if there was no cause.

'Why?' Skye demanded to know.

'Because they caught your handler, Marcus, trying to run. He'd made a deal to eliminate your team. Everyone was rocked by the revelation that we had a mole at LUCAN. Security was changed and all protocols tightened up. I was based in Norwich, but was called over to your area in London.' Thea hesitated before continuing, still looking at the floor. 'Everyone in the agency started questioning everyone else's motives for a time. It was horrible to have that fear every day,' she looked up apologetically at Skye when she saw her flinch.

Skye was furious. She'd been carrying that burden for years and the strain was starting to show. She gulped down the bile that was forming in her throat, her mouth dry from being so tense.

'Everything settled back down after a while and it was work as usual,' Thea said hesitantly, waiting for Skye to explode in anger.

'Business as usual,' said Skye bitterly. She let out the breath she had been holding but squared her shoulders. 'You don't think there's danger? Why the hell didn't you tell me that straight away when I said how worried I was?' she raged.

'No, I don't think there's any vulnerability, if that's what's causing you to worry.' Thea was wringing her hands in her lap again. She must have realised by the spark of anger in Skye's eyes that she wanted to slap her for being such a wimp. How could she not have told Skye about Marcus straight away? 'I didn't tell you as I thought it would cause you even more pain. You trusted him and he let you down. I'm so sorry, Skye.'

'I knew it had to be someone on the inside,' seethed Skye. 'I want to kill Marcus. He assassinated my whole active team.' She put her head into her hands and tried to stop the pounding in her brain. 'He murdered Leo's dad.'

Thea looked like she was about to burst into tears herself, but rushed forward to take Skye into her arms as she wept. 'Skye,' she pleaded. 'LUCAN took care of it.'

117

'What if they didn't?' said Skye, angrily brushing the tears from her eyes for being so pathetic and weak and not wanting to listen to reason. She never usually cried and having one friend wasn't about to make her soft all of a sudden. She shook off the fragility she had shown and stared at Thea.

'They did,' said Thea miserably, visibly quaking with nerves at being faced with the real Skye. 'He had a terminal illness and wanted money for his family. He was already getting paid a fortune, but he was using heavy drugs to ease his pain. Someone found out and blackmailed him. He didn't know they wanted you dead, just out of action.'

'I still want to kill him!' raged Skye, without a moment's hesitation. She was fleetingly sad for his suffering, but the grief and misery he had caused so many others was beyond comprehension.

'He's dead, Skye,' said Thea as Skye slumped down into the chair opposite her and grabbed some painkillers from the drawer near her seat, throwing them into her mouth dry and gulping them down with difficulty. 'He explained to the agency that he told the target you were dead. He was horrified that they'd killed everyone and full of terrible remorse. He thought they would just beat the men up a bit and frighten you all into leaving them alone.'

Skye lifted her head and gave Thea a watery glare. 'How do you know all this?'

'I was brought in to clear away any history of you all. For your safety,' she hurried on at Skye's look of sadness that there would be no record of Leo's father now.

'I had to interview Marcus while he was berating his own weakness and raging at the lies they had spun him. I'm so sorry,' cried Thea, shaking. 'I felt sorry for him at the time as he was so pathetic and ill, but he was also deranged and babbling a lot from the drugs he'd filled his body with.'

Skye got up and moved over to the sofa in the little lounge for comfort and wracked her brain to see if she could pinpoint the start of Marcus' betrayal. Had he seemed different before the explosion? Had he been unwell and had she been too wrapped up in her pregnancy to notice? She had thought they were friends and she now questioned her own judgement. He might have been a hard taskmaster and an annoying perfectionist, but she had trusted him with her life, time and time again.

'His illness progressed really quickly and there was no cure.'

'He was an easy mark,' sighed Skye in exhaustion.

'He told me he had started slipping up and the target found him drunk in a bar and offered him drugs. They let him talk and drew him in with offers of pain relief. Once he took their drugs he was hooked.' Thea got up and followed Skye into the lounge before continuing. 'They made him pay huge sums that he couldn't afford. They offered him a deal. By then he owed them so much, he couldn't refuse.'

'He could have, though,' said Skye angrily. Skye thought back to the time her harness had slipped and her wrists had got cut. She had almost died then. Had Marcus tampered with her harness? She didn't believe for one moment he would have wanted them to live. Then they would be around to find him and discover his secrets. Maybe he had tried to start with one of the team, then moved the bar and decided to make it seem like they had been ambushed and clear them all out in one go? She remembered his piercing brown eyes and the way he looked right through you sometimes. He was quite mercenary, but she had mistakenly thought this would help him cover every planning detail of the job. It turned out he wasn't as thorough as he thought, as she had lived and he hadn't. Thinking this way made her stomach rise up and threatened to make her vomit. Thea reached across and gently helped Skye to her feet, a look of sympathy on her face.

'He couldn't have told the target about you, as no one knew you weren't there that night. Reece must have been covering your back, as he was the one who told you to stay away, and the team notes hadn't changed. Marcus thought you died too. I had to clear everyone's history, including yours. You didn't need to create your own cover as you don't officially exist now either.'

'There are always ways of finding people, Thea. You know

that. I have probably left a trail somewhere.'

'There is a way,' she conceded, 'but no one is looking for you. You're dead.'

'The man in the street?'

'Probably just a man in the street,' hedged Thea. 'Maybe you noticed him because you haven't properly looked at a man in years? It's about time you stopped running and made a home, for Leo, if not yourself. It doesn't have to be here, but I have a feeling you feel at home?' Thea called over her shoulder as she went to make them some tea, glancing up at the cupboard where the knives were stored as she passed.

Skye knew that Thea's easy stride hid the fact that she had a heavy heart. She liked Skye and really wanted her to stick around. She'd told Skye she'd assumed she would be a nightmare at first as she was secretive and grumpy, but said she was also sweet, funny, kind and fiercely loyal, which had made Skye blush. No one had said anything nice about her for so long.

Thea flicked the switch on the kettle, visibly exhausted from the day's emotional turmoil, and opened the soft grey cupboard doors to find some mugs. Skye cringed as Thea must have noticed that Skye was a bit obsessive, as the colourful mugs were all lined up with handles pointing outwards to pick up easily.

'Ever efficient,' Thea smiled. 'Tea, the British answer to many distressing situations; it can soothe a broken heart and wash away troubled thought.' Keeping the tea strong by adding just a dash of milk, she put in a spoonful of sugar, from the metal tin on the kitchen top, for good measure. 'We could do with a sugar rush,' she sighed, rolling her shoulders as if she was trying to ease some pain. Then she brightened up.

'I've just remembered the huge slab of chocolate cake I shoved onto the pram,' she held two mugs in one hand and grabbed that as she passed too. Skye sagged. She needed her blood sugar levels to return to normal after the shock of finding out about Marcus and his treachery, plus the realisation that she had put herself and Leo through hell by running for so many years, without reason. At least she might start to feel safe now. Thea could help her with that, she resolved.

'I have the uneasy suspicion that you won't let anyone get close to you, you'll use your old life as an excuse to move on soon, just in case you began to care about anyone again.' Thea gritted her teeth as she was up for a fight. She looked into Skye's tired eyes. 'I'm determined to change the outcome this time.'

Chapter Twenty-Two

Zack was beginning to regret telling Marlo about his plans for holding a summer ball in the grounds of his house. She had squealed in delight when he had told her the previous week, clapping her hands in glee and jumping up and down until he had to ask her to stop because she was frightening the wildlife. It was just a party, for goodness' sake! You would have thought he had just offered her a tour round her favourite rock star's boudoir, while the said rock star was stark bollock naked in bed, by the way she was acting.

Marlo had babbled excitedly about canapés and champagne as Zack walked away, having already listened to her for ten minutes, making his ears bleed from the 'ka-ching' of the cash register that rung in his head every time she had a new idea. Zack had been thinking of putting up a big tent in the meadow between his house and Skye's cottage, but Marlo, annoyingly quite insightfully, had pointed out it should be situated next to the climbing centre, where people could admire his new business and learn about his plans for integrating his app idea. She had said the locals would get drunk and fall in the pond which sat behind the main terrace if the tent was placed there. The pond faced towards the meadow, so that your eye was drawn into the garden, and he didn't want strangers creeping round and peering in windows. He shivered at the thought.

The pond was only small by estate standards and was fenced in, because of the dogs more than Emmie. After he had spent a week of evenings getting covered in gunge, shovelling years of sludge out of it until it had looked as new as a hundred-year-old pond ever could, the dogs had decided it was their personal bath. It was in surprisingly good shape once it was empty and filled with fresh water, but the dogs had jumped in at every opportunity and petrified the poor fish that Emmie had carefully chosen one weekend. Zack had had to rush out to buy identical ones after finding a couple of them floating, lifeless, on the pond's surface one morning, while the dogs sat panting happily after another early morning dip.

The fence was more for his peace of mind than anything. Emmie could wander into the garden whenever she liked and it stopped him from having to follow the dogs around with an old towel, cleaning every surface they passed as they coated it in designer paw prints.

Marlo had popped by that morning and actually brought a colourful little pad with her. It was full of lists and Zack had gulped at the seemingly endless jobs that she thought he could fit into his already full days. Mike had laughed and told him that he was in for it now. Apparently, Marlo loved lists and left them stuck all over the house to remind Mike of the many tasks he forgot to complete each day.

Mike told Zack he had devised a game with his sons to see how many they each began the morning with. The highest score was six so far, but the habit was getting worse. Marlo's current choice was little square neon notes. She loved them because they were already sticky and she could slap them everywhere, including the back of the bathroom door, to remind them to put the toilet seat down. As if they would ever forget, living with a neat freak like Marlo. If she hadn't been so sexy, Mike would have put his foot down and stopped the silliness years ago, but it made her happy to put the colourful little square notes everywhere and they pretended to take notice before shoving them into the nearest bin, just in time for another colour to appear hours later.

Mike winked at Zack, seeming to enjoy the pained expression on his friend's face. It looked like it was comforting to see someone else on the receiving end of the lists for a change.

'Right!' Marlo had said, making herself comfortable and blatantly ignoring the fact that this was her husband's place of business, she was talking to his boss and it was the start of a working day. Zack was sure she thought they swanned around all day drinking beer and chatting to the trees. In fact, their day began at eight when they checked the site before the rest of the staff arrived. They went over the whole rope course and wrote safety notes in a journal, which would be monitored each week to assure everything was in full working order at all times. By 9am the whole site was ready for their first visitors of the day.

Mike had been sceptical when Zack had first proposed working together. The site had been more of a playground than a business, but Zack knew he now gave him credit for seeing its potential and taking the time to learn everything he could about the business he had inherited, only investing where his advisors told him to.

Zack had admitted to Mike, over a beer after a long day at work, that the estate had been dumped on him by his incorrigible granddad, who Mike said sounded like a real hoot. The place had been half-finished, then left to rot, and was eating money. Zack had confided that he was completely clueless about this type of business and hadn't wanted to take on such a huge house in the first place, but Emmie had needed a place to grow up and he was at such a low ebb, his granddad had caught him unawares by inviting Emmie and Zack round, then buggering off and leaving them here with a note to say it was theirs. Mike had joked that he sounded like the kind of relative he wouldn't mind having.

As the evening had progressed, and Zack dropped his guard a little, he started telling Mike about how the place needed so much work, but that there were a few surprising antiques inside, disregarded by his granddad, which he could sell. He had taken Mike on a tour, while Emmie slept, and Mike had been astounded by the state of the interior. Zack had admitted that, at first, he had wanted to grab Emmie and run, as it was an ongoing story with his granddad; buy a new and exciting toy, run it into the ground, then expect your family to bail you out. The house, although stunning, was a money pit. Selling would just about mean breaking even, so it wasn't all bad, but Zack was the one left sorting out the mess… again.

Zack had decided to shoulder the responsibility after Emmie started crying and refused to leave the dogs that had been abandoned with the house, and they'd been here ever since. Zack had hired two up-and-coming, hotshot adventure centre designers who had come in and verbally ripped the place to shreds, describing it as a monstrosity, whilst also admitting that it had potential. Zack listened carefully to their advice, then jumped in and paid them to train him, then his first four staff, for several months. He knew from his family history that some investors disregarded market research and advice from professionals in their field, thinking they knew better, but he wasn't about to do that. The first year and a half here had been spent gutting the tree climbing business and rebuilding it. Zack would have loved to grow more trees and forget about the place, but Emmie had seen it and fallen in love with the idea of being able to see the stars from the trees. He still hadn't worked out how to say no to her yet, even though it had probably cost him hundreds of thousands not to do so. CloudClimb was Emmie's name for the trees, as she had said she felt as if she could reach the clouds, when she climbed the ropes with her dad one evening, and the name had stuck. It seemed to astound Mike such a small child could dictate to a big, strong-minded, stubborn man like Zack, but Emmie just had to wobble her bottom lip and he was swooping her up to console her. Zack could see he was spoiling her, but he had his reasons.

Zack had spent months finding out from the local community and businesses what they were looking for. Admittedly, he had paid someone to do this as well but, for a guy with as much cash as he had now, it made sense to use it intelligently. Zack knew that Mike thought he was secretly glad to have been landed with the estate. His app development business was very solitary and, under duresss, he had had to make friends here. Luckily, with a place like this, he could run both businesses as they were so different. One funded the other and, by the way things were looking with CloudClimb, he was emerging as a savvy businessman and his first two ventures were turning out to be pure gold.

Mike said he'd assumed that someone who could afford a place like this would be a complete snob, but he'd acknowledged that Zack was the exact opposite. Zack had explained in down-to-earth fashion about his ex-wife and how he had been left holding the baby. On top of which his eccentric granddad bought places, then left them to go to ruin when he discovered a nubile wench to run off with. Mike had said he hadn't realised that life could be so exciting.

After doing his research, Zack had zeroed in on the local corporates, as he really didn't want the place crawling with kids. Mike seemed to find his friend's aversion to other people's children amusing. But as soon as the grapevine had come into play and they had heard about the new lord of the manor, mothers had flocked to the tree centre, dragging their children behind them and spreading the word about this wonderful new play centre for adults and children alike. The gossip caught fire, which Mike had said was because they glimpsed Zack's smouldering good looks and bulging muscles. He'd punched Zack's arm lightly and laughed that even Marlo had mock-swooned when they had first met.

'So,' said Marlo, demanding Zack's attention and ignoring her husband, who was sniggering behind her back as she wiggled her bottom in Zack's chair to get comfortable. 'First on the list is hiring a marquee,' she said seriously, providing a printed list of preferred suppliers and their contact details. 'I think we should stick to local, as they might advertise that they are going to be here and that could have a positive effect on your business.'

Zack raised his eyebrows at Marlo's professional tone and Mike just shrugged and rolled his eyes heavenward. Zack thought of the corporate clients due to arrive at midday, for team building in the trees, and shuddered at the thought of more customers. He had gone all-out to set the business up, as the house had been haemorrhaging money, but he already had his hands full with the clients he had and wasn't sure they could cope with too many more of them. Marlo was just getting started, though, so he bit his lip and looked daggers at Mike, whose idea it had been to involve his wife in the party idea.

Mike had confided the day before that he'd been worrying that Marlo was bored now that Tim and Rory, their sons, were at school full time. She had been writing more lists than usual, which was making him nervous. She needed to have something else to occupy her before she drove them all mad. Zack could sympathize, but didn't really want to get involved.

'Then,' Marlo continued, 'I've found a company to provide a cocktail bar and sexy waiters.' Zack opened his mouth to speak, but Mike was waving frantically behind her back, so he shut his mouth again and listened quietly. He would get Mike for this torture.

'Well?' Marlo said pointedly, looking behind her to see what her husband was up to, before shooting him a dark stare and continuing to list even more obstacles that Zack would have to climb over to hold the stupid party.

Mike smiled sweetly and eased himself out of his chair before rapidly exiting the room. Zack looked over helplessly at him, which Mike apparently found quite funny, as he whistled as he walked towards the refreshment building to make himself a coffee before the rest of the staff arrived sharp at 9am.

Zack despaired. Mike had said that Marlo was taking all this so seriously that she had asked Thea to collect the boys at 8am that morning, on her way to school, which had confused Thea as she usually left for the fifteen-minute walk at 8.30am. When Thea had dutifully arrived at 8am, not knowing what she was going to do with the children for the extra half an hour before school, Marlo had literally shoved them out of the door so that she could catch Zack for a meeting before the other staff arrived. Poor Thea, who had been looking constantly harassed these last few days, had practically sprinted there to get the boys before circling back the other way to collect Allie. She didn't complain but offered a weak smile to Mike as she left, making him fleetingly wonder if everything was all right in her world, before realising that his wife was raring to go, even though he was already late for work.

Marlo had insisted on coming with Mike, which had meant they'd both arrived late. Zack just tapped his watch in jest when he'd seen them and walked into his office, not really expecting Marlo to march in behind him.

Half an hour later, a bemused Zack had joined Mike by the coffee machine. Zack had agreed that, because Marlo had insisted on joining them first thing, he would complete today's safety checks an hour earlier by himself, which meant they now had a short interval of peace before the other staff arrived.

'She's still here?'

'She's taken over my office and computer!'

'Better get used to that, mate,' said Mike, slapping him on the back good-naturedly and handing him a cup of coffee in a clean mug with the CloudClimb logo emblazoned on the side.

Zack inhaled the heady scent of the coffee beans before slumping into one of the chairs and scratching his head. He wasn't exactly sure what had just happened, but it seemed that he had agreed to everything, and offered to let Marlo use his office, without saying a word. Now Mike held up a hand to stop him as well. 'Just give in mate. It's so much easier.'

'But…'

'No buts. She'll do an awesome job. She used to rep for an events business before we had the boys. I wouldn't completely throw you under the bus. She knows what she's talking about, but you'll discover lists everywhere until after the ball. Just agree to do what she says and ignore the little colourful squares stuck all over your office. Not only will your life be easier, but the ball will be a great success.'

Zack eyed him sceptically, snorted in disgust, then got up without a word and went to find out which of his team members had arrived, for the working day to begin.

Chapter Twenty-Three

Skye nodded to Thea, who pulled out her usual chair at the table in Skye's back garden, and smiled when she heard the children's squeals of delight as they conquered yet another challenge. Skye knew she was more relaxed after the long chat with Thea the previous week. She still scoped the area, but was more chilled and actually smiled occasionally, rather than scowling at everyone. She knew she was a hard taskmaster, but made the work a lot of fun.

Skye walked over and slumped into the seat opposite Thea, while checking to see if the children were practising the latest move she had taught them. This involved keeping one foot firmly on the floor, lifting the other leg up at a right angle and holding a beach ball in front of them to improve posture and balance. There was lots of giggling as they fell over, then got up and tried again. Occasionally, Skye threw a soft ball their way and they had to dodge it, while staying upright but, mostly, she left them to it for a while.

'You realise that other parents know this isn't a 'fitness club', don't you?' asked Thea, a small smile playing on her lips.

'What!' gasped Skye in surprise, almost tripling the strength of her softball throw by mistake and knocking Leo into a heap on the floor. She watched Allie jump over and help him up. She hadn't really given it much thought and assumed the children lied to their parents and said they were coming round to play. She really did need to swot up on her mothering skills. Of course, kids told their parents pretty much anything at this age. It was later that they started craving freedom and wanted privacy from the grown-ups. Little ones blabbed. How could she have forgotten that? Skye vaguely remembered joking that this was a gymnastics club at the start, but hadn't really cared enough to think about it other than fleetingly. If parents didn't want their children to come round any more, they could bugger off somewhere else. It was of no concern to her, as she didn't want them here in the first place. She did concede, on knowing them a little better, that they were actually great kids, but still... They all had so much fun here and they were polite, although they had looked at her like she was a bit mad for the first few weeks, until they got used to her unusual methods of teaching and play.

'They think you're training them in self-defence... which they love by the way, as they all detest Miles.' Thea looked at Skye's shocked face and carried on regardless, knowing Skye would start to rant and refuse to let them come round any more. 'Amy's mum asked if you train adults? She said they could avoid his mum too! Word is spreading, not about Miles, they keep that quiet, as they all know that Miles' mum would kill you if she ever found out.' Skye raised an eyebrow and Thea laughed out loud, a real belly laugh that made the children stop and stare for a moment before grinning at Skye's nod of the head and running to the back of the garden for a game of football.

Trying to keep a straight face and failing miserably, Thea continued. 'They keep asking me if they can book their kids into your club. You're so popular,' she winked, making Skye smile too. 'Although you're too scary to approach personally as you constantly scowl at anyone who invades your personal space.' She giggled, leading Skye to kick her in the shin.

'Ouch!' said Thea, rubbing her sore leg, but looking relaxed and seemingly enjoying herself immensely for the first time in days. Skye knew she'd been so tired recently as Flo was teething.

'I don't scowl!' protested Skye huffily. 'Okay... I do,' she conceded, picking up the can of drink Thea had thoughtfully provided for her after she had realised that all Skye ever had was an old bottle of lemonade, or wine. The tangy orange fizz hit Skye's tongue, perking her up as the sugar reached her bloodstream.

'What do you think?' Thea asked, waggling her eyebrows suggestively.

'About what?' asked Skye.

'You know what,' chastised Thea gently. 'None of them had the courage to come up to you for a friendly chat. Maybe you could soften up a bit. Smile occasionally?'

Skye grimaced, but she did sigh and wiggle her toes. She hadn't bothered to put shoes on in the garden as the weather had begun to warm up. 'I'm totally approachable,' she harrumphed moodily, slouching into her seat.

'Hmm,' said Thea thoughtfully. 'You don't let them stay for five minutes when they collect their kids; you run a mile when anyone approaches you at school, other than Felicity. You act as if they've all got rabies!'

'Oh…'

'You shuffle them out of the door so quickly that they don't know if they've actually been inside. Miles has started picking on several other kids since ours keep out of his way. Billy's mum says Miles is a menace and she wished she wasn't so scared of Belle, or she would have put a stop to it ages ago. Loads of parents have complained to the headmistress, but she's so busy fending off complaints about Miles from the teachers, that the mums don't get a look in. I don't know why she doesn't just boot him out. I'm all for equality, but the boy's a menace.'

'She's his godmother,' said Skye.

'What?' spluttered Thea, almost spitting out the fizzy orange she had just started to swallow.

Skye felt really smug at Thea's surprised look.

'That's why she ended up at the school in the first place. She's Belle's oldest friend. They used to practically live together, their houses were so close. If she booted him out, it would cause an almighty fracture in the family.'

'What the hell?' said Thea, throwing her arms up and banging them down again on the table, wincing as they made contact with the smooth surface.

'You really are a wuss these days,' scolded Skye. 'I looked her up, I'm surprised you didn't, Thea,' she tutted with good humour, her spirits much restored now that Thea was annoyed too. 'I thought there had to be a good reason that Miles has never been suspended, for the amount of pencils he steals, at least. He could open his own shop with the rulers he's acquired, too. Who needs forty bendy rulers, for goodness' sake?'

Thea looked slightly miffed that she hadn't thought to look up the headmistress, Mrs Moswell. It wasn't as if Skye had much more than the internet to do a search with either. It must irke Thea that she was losing her edge with baby brain, sniggered Skye.

'I knew it,' said Thea, in exasperation.

'No, you didn't,' joked Skye, nudging Thea's leg good-naturedly and getting a swift jab in return. 'Ouch,' she complained, rubbing her shin.

Thea stuck her tongue out at her friend and Skye guessed that the childish gesture made her feel marginally better. 'No wonder she lets Miles get away with murder. The teachers despair of him, but they can't discipline him as Mrs Moswell always says it wasn't his fault. Talk about nepotism! She'll have to do something soon, or there will be a riot. I heard that two of the teachers have threatened to leave if he's not disciplined soon. They've given up telling him off in class as his mum storms in after school and gives them an earful. They just ask him to sit outside the classroom and work on his own, which he loves as he gets to muck about there too.'

'Maybe he finds the work too hard?' suggested Skye. 'Some kids are naughty to disguise the fact.'

Thea looked thoughtful for a moment, then shook her head, sending her curls dancing in every direction. 'No... he's just a little monster. Allie says he's really clever, but he's bored. His mum's always busy and I think he likes the attention. At least when she's sticking up for him her focus is on him, not her. The teachers at the school are great, they would have noticed if he was struggling. I think he's simply spoilt rotten. He gets everything he asks for to shut him up, so he thinks it's his right to take what he likes from others, as he's never disciplined. His mum just laughs it off, if the staff mention it.'

Skye shrugged. 'Miles seems to be leaving our kids alone now, so we'll have to be content with that. I didn't come here to solve everyone else's problems when I have enough of my own.'

'You're probably right,' sighed Thea, picking up her drink and sighing at the cooling sensation in her parched throat. 'We should count our blessings and lighten up.'

Skye gave Thea a sharp look to see if that was another dig at her, but she had picked Flo out of her pram, sitting next to her by the kitchen wall, and was now making cooing noises into her daughter's face. Skye got up from the table and started to round the children up for their next task, before the horde of nosey parents arrived to give her another headache.

Chapter Twenty-Four

Skye jumped in surprise when someone sat down heavily next to her, in her regular spot on the low wall that ran behind the bike shed. No one else usually sat there, as it was prone to damp and moss and there were some perfectly good benches to rest your posterior on, just by the school gates. Skye had sussed out pretty early on that she wouldn't be drawn into any gossip from here, plus she had a great view of everyone who walked through the school gates. She must have been too distracted, working on ways to smile at these women, rather than grimace, and hadn't expected anyone to join her here. Skye looked up in annoyance, before remembering what Thea had said about looking less frosty. She had been trying to decide how to be nicer to people, but she hadn't had much practice over the years and she didn't really know where to start. She wasn't sure if she really wanted to know about their toddler's bowel movements or the colour of underwear they were wearing to excite the latest bloke they were shagging. Plastering a polite smile onto her face, she was astounded to find Zack sitting next to her, smiling at her strangely.

'You look like you were about to break my legs,' he joked, not knowing the thought had actually crossed her mind when she had first met him. When she didn't reply, Zack sighed and ploughed on. 'I wanted to apologise for being an arse in front of Emmie.' When Skye put her head to one side, measuring him up, and didn't gush that it was okay like he'd obviously expected, he continued, slightly wrong-footed. 'I've been trying, and failing miserably, to discipline my daughter, but she starts to sniffle and I give her what she wants every time.' Skye nodded as she already knew this fact, which was probably rather annoying to him, but she didn't care.

'I was at the end of my tether that day,' he explained, 'and I took my irritation out on you. I'm sorry.'

'Apology accepted,' said Skye simply, not making a fuss.

'Oh... great,' he said, smiling into her sparkling eyes with obvious relief. Skye thought she had been relatively easy on him, so she wasn't sure why he was sweating slightly. It was all a bit embarrassing, but he was twitching like an adolescent who hadn't been able to stop thinking about her and this was the only idea he had come up with to approach her without looking like a total creep. He probably hated apologising for anything, and had an ex who complained all the time that he had done something wrong and he would bow down to her to keep the peace, even if it wasn't his fault. He looked the type. Skye wished she didn't psychoanalyse everyone she met. He looked like he wasn't used to someone accepting an apology with good grace either.

'You okay?' he asked as she looked around to see if the other parents were staring at them. No one was watching, they were all busily catching up on the day's gossip and not paying them any attention. They couldn't really see them from this angle, in any case, as the bike shed was in the way.

Skye thought for a moment before answering and decided that actually, yes, she was okay. Her chat with Thea had allayed most of her fears and she had finally been able to make some peace with Reece's death. It was time to move on. She sent Zack a dazzling smile, which seemed to surprise him so much he almost fell off of the wall in shock.

'I'm fine, thanks.'

'Great... I was wondering if I could ask you for some help?'

'Sure,' she replied, interested to see how this might pan out. Being so near to Zack was making the hairs on Skye's skin stand up on end, and she was sure she looked like a school kid herself, wanting to talk to the cool guy.

'I'm having a party to launch a new product I've designed,' said Zack.

Skye's eyes went wide in surprise, as though this was the last thing she expected him to say. For years, she had had to compute every possible outcome of every situation, but she was completely out of practice and hadn't done any homework on Zack. Maybe she should look him up? He really was gorgeous in a rugged, manly sort of way, and her thoughts were getting muddled as his leg kept brushing hers. It was taking all of her concentration not to jump off the wall and hide in the bushes, it had been so long since she had been so near a man. If Zack noticed that Skye was distracted, he didn't show it. She knew she would have to practice her charm skills if she wanted to dip her unpainted toes back into the dating pool.

'I live in the estate house now,' he said. When she didn't look impressed or fall at his feet, he clenched his teeth as if he was trying to keep his ego in check. 'I also run a tree climbing business, CloudClimb, on the estate. I don't know if you've heard of it?'

'Thea has mentioned it,' Skye conceded, trying not to look at his lips as he spoke. 'My son, Leo, has asked me to take him one day.'

'Would you have time with the self-defence classes you run?' Zack joked, eyes sparkling.

Skye smiled and blushed a little. 'You've heard about that too? I just found out today that the kids had squealed on me. I'm waiting for Belle to try and lamp me one.'

Zack laughed, a deep baritone sound, and Skye's mouth went dry.

'I think she only picks on weak men like me who don't look like they can cope on their own,' he said and, seeing her grin, continued. 'I'm pretty sure she hasn't heard yet, but you might want to think about moving out of the area when she does.' Zack seemed determined to make some sort of truce with her and although she was responsive to him, she decided to make him work a little at winning her over.

She was so out of practice at trying to get men's attention that she had no clue of her success rating, or if they even noticed her, so Zack could be her trial run. 'I had heard she has a penchant for sexy estate owners,' she parried, winking at him. 'You might want to move out first.'

Zack's eyebrows shot up and he smiled into her eyes. He now knew she found him sexy and was confident about telling him so. She wondered if he had never met anyone as straightforward as her before. She was annoyed with him, but forgave him without any drama and she thought he looked good, so she told him so. It was probably a refreshing change from all of the games Thea mentioned that Emmie's mum played and the subterfuge that Belle created.

'Maybe we should hide in the woods together?' he said, grinning at the way she blushed and looked away, stuttering that he had called her bluff. Maybe she wasn't so confident after all, she sighed.

Skye had forgotten how to flirt with handsome men, although it had been part of her everyday life when she was working. She had thought nothing of charming information out of them. She had been sleek and groomed then and hadn't doubted the effect she had. Now, she was a messy shadow of her former self, but she could feel the first flicker of attraction and she actually allowed it to unfurl instead of shutting it down. It had been years since anyone had excited her, and she'd barely noticed anyone's interest in her, beyond assessing how much of a threat they could be to her family.

'The party?' she queried, trying to change the subject and get rid of the very vivid image of them both naked in the woods.

'Hmm?'

Skye raised a questioning eyebrow at his memory loss and wondered if he had drifted into a similar fantasy, which made her legs turn to jelly.

Skye had touched Zack's leg to get his attention and he stood up rapidly as if his trousers were suddenly uncomfortable. She was surprised at his knee-jerk reaction to her touch. 'Yes, the party. My main business is building apps, but since my granddad ran off with the local barmaid and left me with an estate full of debts, I've been trying to save the place, as Emmie loves it here.'

Skye looked at him curiously, as he seemed to be blushing himself now and was babbling like a schoolboy. The thought that her touch had made him react like this made her want to run her hands down his chest and tease him some more.

'Is your granddad the eccentric man in a cravat?' she asked jovially.

'That's him. I thought you only moved here recently. Have you met him?'

'I saw a poster and article about the estate in my old library. There were photos of your granddad in front of the house. His smile captivated me and I loved his taste in cravats, so I called the phone number on the advert and rented a cottage in the grounds. Your cottage, I guess?' she asked, feeling strange that she had been sleeping in his bed all this time. The thought made her kind of giddy.

'What a coincidence. That must have been a fairly old article. It took me a while to update the cottages. You would have been living in a hovel if you'd got there when Gramps was here. They were disgusting!' exclaimed Zack, wrinkling his nose up at what Skye assumed was the memory of the smell when he had first set foot in one of the cottages.

'I love my granddad, even though he's a complete nightmare and a liability; the old goat is my family and he always manages to make Emmie laugh, even when he's being incorrigible.'

'I'm sure it wasn't you I spoke to when I rang the estate. The man sounded much older and really posh,' said Skye.

'Gramps had an estate manager, it must have been him. I would be surprised, though, as he never actually did much. I think they met in the pub and decided that, as he could cut grass, he could manage the estate so that Gramps didn't have to. I think he paid him in beer. He retired recently, when I came. From what I saw he spent his days asleep in the barn with the dogs at his feet. He did handle the bookings for the cottages, though. I was just too snowed under to care at that point. Sorry.'

'Your Gramps sounds like quite a character.'

Zack sighed heavily and Skye remembered his granddad's smiling face from the magazine article, then imagined his apologetic face when he abandoned another mess of his own making. 'He buys random places, has mad ideas for making them into something that will make him millions, he spends millions... then loses interest and flits away, leaving my dad, and now me, to sort out the mess. If we left all of the places he's bought alone, they would fall to pieces and cost us another fortune to look after. These great big buildings are wonderful, but they eat money for breakfast, lunch and dinner. Gramps usually meets a new wench in each place, then gets distracted by another one and disappears with her, surfacing months later in a new location with a completely different woman.'

'Family trait?' Skye teased, enjoying finding out that there was more to Zack than tight pecs and a cute bum.

'Hardly!' he laughed out loud. 'Emmie's mum left me holding the baby, as we were broke, and ran off with a millionaire with halitosis. I haven't had a lot of time to date since then, what with bringing up a child I had no clue how to raise, and attempting to build a fledgling business every night while she was asleep. I think I was sleepwalking for the first few years of her life.'

'Sounds familiar,' Skye smiled, empathising with the struggle of bringing up a child alone, and how isolating it could be. 'Although I didn't come across a millionaire with halitosis, thank goodness. You can't exactly be broke to run an estate like yours,' she said candidly, then put her hand to her mouth in surprise at her own rudeness, but Zack laughed heartily. She liked the sound of his voice and squirmed a bit with embarrassment.

'Say what you mean, Skye,' he said with mock sarcasm.

'I always do,' she blushed, liking the way he said her name.

'My granddad spends all his money and I refused to take any anyway, which frustrated the hell out of my ex, Kay. When she left me I was on the verge of a breakthrough with my app design, but she just walked away and said she'd heard it all before.' Zack looked at his feet and kicked a random stone into a nearby hedge at the memory. Skye was sad that it still made him so angry, even after all these years.

'How could she walk out on us like that? I pretty much

begged her to stay,' he admitted as the school bell pealed.

They looked around like guilty lovers, stepping away from each other and anxiously noticing a few stares coming from a group of mums who had just detoured round the bike sheds to avoid the sudden rush of children into the school playground.

Noticing Felicity sitting on her own a bit nearer to the school, dabbing the tears from her eyes, Skye said a reluctant goodbye to Zack, touching his arm softly as she left and enjoying the warmth that seeped through her palm. She felt a weird sense of responsibility for the timid woman, now that she had thrust her into the lion's den, and her gut feeling was telling her it could only get worse.

Just before she went over to Felicity, Skye turned back to Zack as an afterthought and spoke quietly. 'Why don't you and Emmie pop over to the cottage at six tonight and we can chat about the party then?'

Zack looked surprised at the offer, but when he nodded his head in assent, Skye gave him a quick grin, then went to see what disaster had struck the resident artist now. She was too distracted by Flick's distress to think about whether it had been a good idea to invite Zack and Emmie round but, from the way the little girl had peeked over the wall with such longing, and the speed at which she ran to her dad every night while doing her best to avoid Miles, who was often clinging onto her school bag until he got a glowering glare from Zack and scuttled off to his mum, it was the right thing to do. Not that Skye had been watching him, of course! Maybe a new, gentle friend like Leo would be good for Emmie, too?

Skye lightly touched Flick's shoulder as she hiccupped and tried to brush her hair out of her face and blow her snotty nose before Skye saw what a mess she was. 'They're awful!' she ground out fiercely.

'Who are?' asked Skye, already knowing the answer, but Felicity was mid-rant and wasn't about to stop now the emotional roller coaster she had been on for the last couple of weeks had come to an abrupt halt.

'They suck you in and bleed the life out of you,' she sobbed vehemently, seeming not to care now who was looking at her, although most of the parents had grabbed their children and were out of there with a swift, polite smile before you could wave goodbye. 'They all want me to paint for them, for free, for the 'publicity' it will get for my work. I would have to paint non-stop for the next five years if I were to take on all of those commissions, and I wouldn't earn a penny,' Felicity gulped in some air and appeared a little steadier once she had calmed her nerves.

Skye sat next to her and was uncharacteristically patting her arm, noticing the contact made Flick flush with pleasure. 'I have no idea why you deemed me important enough to notice, but I will be eternally grateful that you've uncovered my hidden talent,' blushed Flick. 'I dreamed of being a proper exhibited artist, with people strolling around admiring my work and then pulling out handfuls of cash for it. I wanted posh assistants scurrying around with glossy brochures, sticking red dots all over the walls to tell other hungry buyers the paintings were already sold and they were too late. Well, that was exactly what happened. The exhibition you arranged for me was amazing,' Felicity gushed through her tears, 'but I already have two major commissions from that interview you set up with the local paper. I won't have time to paint them if I keep doing freebies for my so-called friends.'

'Tell them no,' Skye said simply, not understanding the dilemma, as she had never cared much about what others thought of her before she came here. She did wonder what it would feel like if Thea suddenly made demands on her, but although Thea was mightily bossy and had a death stare that could make grown men weep, Skye couldn't imagine her being selfish or inconsiderate. The thought did make Skye a bit nervous. Would she become needy, like Flick was with the other school mums? The idea of relying on someone horrified her. She was beginning to lean on Thea for emotional support, and enjoyed her company. Skye had even invited her round on a day that wasn't a club day, and that had never happened before, and had bought a packet of biscuits that Thea might like... Skye's hands began to tremble in shock, so she steadied herself on Flick's arm and stamped on her own toe to snap herself out of it. Felicity looked a bit taken aback as Skye's suddenly jumped up and began hopping from foot to foot – that had not been a good idea. The weather was warming up and she had forgotten she'd finally thrown her boots into the little cupboard under the stairs and was wearing flat sandals. Felicity was looking at her pityingly now, as if suggesting saying no to Belle and her crew made Skye a bit thick.

'I could break their legs for you?' said Skye, returning to her usual banter. Flick started sniggering gently, obviously assuming her friend was joking, and quite enjoying the mental picture conjured up of Belle hobbling along, red hair flying in the wind while Skye tried to catch up with her.

'I'm currently hiding behind the bike sheds so that they don't break my legs when they find out I'm too busy to do their paintings. Belle wants me to paint her in the nude as a present for a gentleman friend.' She screwed up her face in disgust, just as Skye did the same thing and made a gagging sound.

'I think I've just been a bit sick in my mouth,' said Skye as they saw each other's scrunched-up faces and burst out laughing.

'I saw you talking to Zack,' said Felicity casually. 'Lucky lady,' she blushed at her own brazen comment.

'You like him?' asked Skye in surprise. She had been ignoring men for so long it hadn't occurred to her that others still saw them as something beautiful. She wondered fleetingly if anyone ever looked at her that way? Although she doubted it, with her grouchy demeanour and distinctive wardrobe of black and more black.

'Not really,' admitted Felicity, 'although he is pretty as a picture,' she giggled at her own joke, making Skye smile as Felicity's gentle personality began to shine through. 'I've got my own beau, although I wouldn't tell anyone here. They would tear him apart for wearing a bowtie and wonky glasses. He's an art critic I met recently, and he's gorgeous,' she exclaimed, blushing again at her own passionate outburst. 'I would never talk to anyone else like this, but your quiet, no-

nonsense manner makes me want to tell you everything. How do you do that?

Skye lent down, grasped Flick's hands and squeezed them gently, ignoring the question. 'Hold onto that feeling that you have something of your own, and you will get stronger from it. You don't need these school mums in your life, now. You're free to choose your own friends. Why don't you make new ones that you actually enjoy being around?' Flick looked stunned, as if she hadn't thought of that before. Skye gave her a swift hug as she saw Leo walk out of the school building and look around for her. Allie was close at his heels, as usual, and Skye stepped into the sunlight and raised her arm in greeting as she moved towards them.

Chapter Twenty-Five

Walking home, Skye mulled over the idea of adding more children to her new self-defence classes. She really, really wanted to feel good about becoming more open and helping others, but she hated people. She loved being around the kids, but the chit-chat with parents confused the hell out of her and left her cold. She could converse with anyone on practically any subject, and was well versed in politics, but personal small talk had her running for the hills. She hated talking about her real self, as most of her life was made up. She knew that being here meant a lot to Leo, so she had had to curb the expansive lying that was part of her former job. Now that she couldn't lie so much, she found she actually enjoyed making stuff up. Most people labelled themselves by their status, job or talents. What could she say about herself? Multi-skilled ninja school mum? The thought still gave her a frisson of adrenaline and she pictured their faces if they ever uncovered the truth. It was a sobering thought. Leo would lose all of his friends, except Allie, as her aunt was just as bad!

The other thought was that she liked having other children near her for an hour or two, once or twice a week, but by the end of each session she had just about reached her tolerance level for being around others these days. She was accustomed to hiding away, and had lost the social skills she used to have in abundance. She needed to work on her 'being nice' skills. How hard can it be? she thought morosely.

Skye pondered the way Zack had approached her, and admired his courage. Making a move in her direction couldn't have been easy. She wondered what he wanted to talk to her about? It was actually good timing that he was popping over; because he was her landlord, she would need his permission to use anything from the field behind the cottage. She'd had the idea to expand the space the kids worked in, as the number of children was still creeping up. Where the hell did they all come from? She was sure Thea must be lifting them over the back wall while she was indoors. There were definitely two more children than last week. She had decided it was time to really challenge them and, for that, she would require more space. She knew Thea was organised and would have lists with the kids' names and addresses and contact numbers hidden somewhere in case of emergencies. She bet Thea had even showed them some DBS checks and explained that, although Skye was too busy to chat, she was perfectly safe to be around their children, which was why more kept arriving each week. Well, they couldn't be more checked out by the government than Thea and Skye, she giggled to herself. Thea was responsible enough for the both of them anyway.

There was an upside to having the kids in her house. Skye hadn't had the heart to charge them an entrance fee yet, as it wasn't an official club and, as far as the parents knew, she wasn't professionally qualified, unless Thea had blabbed about that too. The children just seemed happier and enjoyed coming to her home to be bossed about and have some exercise. The upside was that the mums had taken to bringing round all kinds of food, which, when you put everything into perspective, was pretty good news. They arrived with anything from dainty iced cakes to full-on chicken casseroles, after one or two had managed to take a quick peek at her empty fridge when grabbing their child a glass of squash. She didn't know whether to slap Thea for letting on she was a dismal cook, or hug her friend for helping her to receive a ready supply of fresh dinners and desserts at least twice a week.

Leo and Allie certainly didn't complain about her usual food, and they knew better than to rub in how delicious the new meals were. She wasn't so stupid or stubborn that she couldn't recognise a gift when she saw one, and determined quickly that she could now spend even less time in the kitchen and more in the garden with the kids. She realised that she had come to rely on Thea and the madcap group of children more than she could have imagined.

Skye had decided only the previous night that she would approach Zack to ask him to lease out the field behind the cottage. He might be stubborn and not let her build the climbing apparatus she wanted to, but he had a whole tree climbing business, for goodness' sake, so he couldn't really complain about a few low climbing walls and an assault course.

Luckily, it seemed that he needed her for something, so she hoped she would be able to cajole him with a bit of bartering. She picked up her pace as she noticed the kids had started walking up the pebble-strewn pathway to the cottage while she was daydreaming. She realised that this was the first time she hadn't been scanning the streets for threats, too. Perhaps they might settle here and she could build on this new life?

Skye thought of Zack's strong physique and wondered if he would help her set up her new business, for that was what she had just decided it would be. She would need some muscles to help her build it. She would give up the pretence that she was anything else, saying she had decided on a career change and would set up a self-defence business from home and, to be fair, she was actually qualified even though she hadn't shared that information with anyone but Thea. It had been part of her initial training at LUCAN. There would be no more lying from this day forward, as the new and improved Skye-Safe classes started today. She had a feeling that the children, and maybe even adults at a later date, would love the excitement of challenging themselves on her assault courses.

Maybe she should approach this differently if she wanted to sell the idea to Zack; butter him up a bit and beguile him with her feminine charms? She grew a bit hot at the thought of seducing him, but didn't back down from a challenge, and thought it was about time she woke up her sleepy libido. If she was going to jump back into the dating game, she may as well aim for the top and enjoy herself.

It wouldn't cost much to put the course she had planned for the field together, not that she was short of cash, but with her expertise and his bulging biceps, they could come up with something special if she didn't get too distracted by his snug jeans and firm hands. If she was so out of practice at getting her own way and he said no, she would just have to cut back on the number of kids that arrived each week.

The doorbell rang at six o'clock sharp, but Skye had been so busy trying to get the parents to leave, while shoving their latest offerings into her fridge and oven for dinner, that she had almost forgotten that Zack and Emmie were coming round and hadn't had time to get changed or, at the very least, brush her hair. Leo excitedly ran to the door to see who it was, then stopped in stunned silence when he saw it was Emmie and her dad. Emmie was looking at her feet and seemed embarrassed at being dragged here, even though she must have been to the cottage loads of times with her dad before Skye and Leo moved in. Skye wondered if Emmie felt annoyed that she'd had to be invited by Leo's mum to come round, and not Leo, and could have kicked herself for being so tactless once again. She hadn't considered how Emmie might feel, or Leo, come to that.

Had Emmie heard whispers about a mysterious club that Skye ran, or seen a glimpse of it when she had spied on them over the wall? Skye felt sorry for her as she looked mutinous, as if she was damned if she was going to beg anyone to include her. After her chat with Zack at the school, Skye could imagine that Emmie might have been mortified when her dad had told her they were coming here tonight. Maybe she'd even ranted she didn't want to come but, for once, he had apparently stood firm and told her she was accompanying him regardless, as here they were on her doorstep. Zack had mentioned to Skye that he was useless at disciplining his daughter, so Skye was impressed they'd made it. Skye could see that Emmie was curious about Leo and his mum, by the way she was peeking under her hair into the house when she thought no one was watching her. Skye winked at Emmie who, she guessed, had finally decided to let her dad have his own way if he was going to be grumpy about it, although she wasn't about to make it easy for him judging by the scowl she sent him. Skye smiled, glad it wasn't her problem.

She rushed forward and ushered them inside, giving Leo a breezy smile and a swift push in the back to propel him forward, as he seemed to be rooted to the spot. He was usually quite sociable; with his start in life he'd needed to adapt to so many new places, but he was blushing furiously, so Skye tried to cover his embarrassment by making him move away from the door.

Seeing Zack walking into her home, and filling the space with his masculine energy, wrong-footed Skye and she began to feel her cheeks grow hot as if she was going to start blushing too. She had to stop acting like a pre-pubescent teenager and persuade him to let her use the field at the back of the cottage, without making a complete idiot of herself.

The food was fragrant and bubbling temptingly in the oven as they reached the kitchen, which didn't take long in such a small house. Skye ignored her grumbling tummy, she had forgotten to eat lunch again, and led them outside to the garden, before stopping short and realising what it must look like. The beautiful kitchen garden that bordered the lawn was still there, but in the centre was a latticework of tree trunks and climbing apparatus which might not look so good to the owner of such a quaint and perfectly-formed cottage.

She hoped he saw the positives in the situation. She was helping the local community, surely? Thea was Zack's friend and Thea's niece was getting free tuition and scrummy food from the other mums and Skye was being kept out of trouble. What more could they ask for? Thea always gave in and helped Skye to drag the trees over the wall and into the garden, then sat sipping tea while Flo gurgled on her playmat and Skye got out her electric saw and began carving the little trees up. Both Thea and Skye were getting fitter and Thea had told her she could actually see her toes again as her tummy was shrinking and her boobs weren't quite so gargantuan and bursting with milk any more. She thought fleetingly that maybe it wasn't best to share that last point with Zack, so she straightened her face and turned to him with a brilliant smile. Ushering him towards a chair outside as a distraction technique, she resisted the urge to cup a hand around his impressive derrière. She held herself in check and prayed that Thea had been shopping and stocked her fridge with drinks and, if she was really lucky, a good bottle of wine.

Zack sat down but looked stunned, and as though he was about to ask her what the hell she had done to his lovely garden, so she cut him off. 'Drink?'

Quickly moving away before Zack had time to respond, Skye grabbed some cans of lemonade and a jug of orange squash, sending a silent thank you to Thea for always bringing sustenance with her and filling the cupboards with tasty food these days. Skye returned and her stomach did a somersault at the sight of Zack, sitting in her garden. She had to find a way to stop him telling her to get rid of the training equipment.

Chapter Twenty-Six

Zack's mouth hung open in shock. The last time he had been here, he had spent hours digging up the turf and planting stupid flowers to entice a tenant. Now, you could barely see the lawn, or surrounding flowerbeds, as a low-level structure of wooden planks covered the whole lawn! He had heard rumours that she was running a self-defence class here and it hadn't really bothered him that she hadn't approached him for permission. Skye was new here and he saw it as an excuse to contact her if he needed to. It had worked like a dream and she had invited him round, but now he was regretting letting his libido control his business and was kicking himself for assuming she was a bit of a flake. From his own experience of setting up CloudClimb, this looked like it had been designed by a professional. Zack hated it on his lawn, but was intrigued at what she had achieved in such a short space of time. Ideas were starting to whizz around his brain at finding out who designed it, and how they could incorporate a similar design into the centre. He had been thinking of trying to find easier climbs for smaller children as, although he didn't encourage them, they turned up at the centre anyway. He might as well make money out of it and not have them hanging around annoyingly while their older siblings went on tree climbs.

Looking beyond the assault course, Zack could see the end of the garden was untouched, other than two football goals. He didn't know whether to laugh or cry at the thought of how perfect the garden had looked before, and how many hours he'd spent digging the soil to make it presentable.

'Leo, why don't you and Emmie go and explore the garden? You can explain to her what everything is,' said Skye, looking at Zack for his consent and, after a short nod of his head, the children ran to explore. Emmie had been so wide-eyed with excitement when she had seen the course that Zack didn't have the heart to say no or embarrass her by wringing Skye's neck, which was what he felt like doing. He tried to rein in his rising fury and bunched his hands into fists to control himself.

Skye innocently looked up at him as if she had completely forgotten that she had built her training course and basically commandeered the garden without asking permission for the changes she had made. From his professional point of view, it looked like she had begun with a few fallen tree trunks that she had found on a stroll through the woods behind the cottage. He admitted to himself that he had been kind of hoping to bump into Skye; preferably half-naked, in a bikini or the vest top and shorts she always seemed to wear, as the weather was warming up. A few months ago, he would probably have run a mile if he saw her dragging a small tree through the woods. He wondered if she'd called Thea and blackmailed her into helping her steal the tree-trunks, as they looked pretty heavy and those two were inseparable these days. Perhaps her excuse was that it was for the kids, she wasn't charging them to come to her home, as far as he knew, and the lord of the manor would never find out. He tried to control his temper and remember that he had been so enthusiastic about his new ideas for CloudClimb after years of procrastination and isolation, that maybe Skye hadn't dreamed that anyone might not love what she'd done here either.

'I probably should have mentioned this to you before,' said Skye, 'but I hadn't really thought about it.' She gulped at Zack's stern look and questioning stare, and tried again. 'I can see how this might look a little odd…' she joked.

'A little?' asked Zack, checking to see where Emmie was and finding her grinning, as Leo held her hand and helped her to walk along one of the mid-height beams. 'What is this?'

'It's an assault course,' Skye said simply, as if he must be really thick. She sat down opposite him and took a cooling sip of her drink. Maybe she needed to calm her racing nerves, he thought, as she must know how bad this looked and be worried about his response.

'An assault course, in a cottage garden?' Zack clarified, keeping a firm check on his anger, but wanting either to put her over his knee to spank her, or kiss her until they both forgot she had pretty much destroyed all of his hard work. Both thoughts made it uncomfortable for him to sit opposite her and he stood up abruptly to go and look at the course, putting some distance between them, before he slung her over his shoulder and carried her into the woods. The woman was reckless and annoying, but he couldn't get her out of his mind.

Skye jumped up and followed him, which made Zack even angrier. Didn't she know enough to leave him alone before he did something silly, like pin her to a tree and run his hands along her taut thighs, embarrassing them both?

'Uh… yep. It's an assault course in a cottage garden,' Skye said, reaching out to touch his arm to regain his attention.

Zack looked at her hand on his arm for a moment before responding. 'Why?'

'It's for the self-defence training you mentioned earlier,' she said casually, then she seemed to realise she hadn't removed her hand from his arm, before whisking it away, flushing and trying to change the subject. 'The course does take over the lawn, but it is perfectly formed and built to function in a fairly small space of grass, compared to the full version I really want to build.'

'Why is it here, though?' he asked patiently, as if she was a bit dim.

'Well… about that,' she hesitated. 'I was hoping to ask you if I could relocate into the field behind the garden,' she pointed vaguely in that direction, as if hoping he would give his assent, then move on to the reason he had approached her about at the school, as they seemed to have moved off topic. He watched her surprisingly powerful arms wave in the direction of the wall, but he was distracted by how soft her skin looked and the amazing smell that was wafting through the open kitchen door and window. Skye must be a sublime cook if she could create meals that smelt like that. His stomach rumbled in protest and he wished he had managed to eat more than a couple of slices of toast that day.

'Would you like some dinner?' Skye asked, openly pouncing on a way to ease the tension surrounding them. He had noticed a magazine that had been left open on the sofa as he'd walked past earlier. He'd glanced at the headline, which basically read, the way to woo a man was to stuff him full of tasty food. He grinned and wondered if Skye was trying to win him over? His timing couldn't have been better as today the fragrance coming from the kitchen smelt like a chicken casserole and he'd spotted a Victoria sponge cake sitting on the counter. What man could refuse that?

'Um…' his stomach growled again and they both smiled.

'I think your stomach is trying to tell us something?'

'Well, it does smell delicious, and it might distract me from the huge pile of logs you seem to have constructed in my garden,' he scolded, trying to lighten the atmosphere a little. 'Plus, I do need to ask you a favour and I may have a way to make us both happy about your destroying the garden, without my having to resort to my earlier thoughts about slinging you over my shoulder and spanking you,' he winked, making Skye flush red all over and her jaw drop open at his blatant flirting. She would be able to see he was still angry with her, but he was now using that energy to his advantage and had quickly worked out how he could benefit from it. He hoped she was impressed by the speed at which he had turned the problem around, and might be intrigued at the way he'd gone about it. Instead of stamping his feet and shouting, he was bartering with her and trying to be sexy and mysterious at the same time. It was a natural skill, he grinned to himself. He was an astute businessman who didn't waste an opportunity to utilise anything as an asset, and was annoyed that she thought she could use him in some way by forgetting to ask for his consent. He assumed she was like Kay, and would expect him to be floored by her beauty (she would have to work on her grooming regime) and astounded by her business acumen (she would also have to start to treat this game like a profession, if she wanted people like him to take her seriously).

Skye looked a bit put out that Zack was concentrating on whatever it was he needed from her and thought a few sexy innuendoes would sway her, but mainly she appeared cross with herself for falling for it. He recognised that she wanted to take control of this situation, not be controlled by him, but this was his land and he was going to enjoy the process of making her see things his way.

Chapter Twenty-Seven

The children looked a bit wary about eating dinner together when Skye called them over to ask them, as a way of avoiding looking into Zack's teasing eyes. They appeared sceptical about their parents sitting around a dinner table together, and Zack understood this probably seemed like an intimate act and Leo might not have had to share his mum's attention with another man before. Zack hoped not. He could see that Leo wasn't sure he liked the idea of them being there, by his wobbly bottom lip. He'd enjoyed playing outside with Emmie, and had politely smiled and shown her how to use the assault course, but she was one of Miles' close friends and it was conceivable that Leo was regretting being so nice to her now that they had to sit across the dinner table from each other. Zack wished Miles would go and find other friends and leave Emmie to play with kids like Leo, who seemed really polite.

The aromatic casserole melted in Zack's mouth and he quickly forked in some more. It really was delicious. He'd forgotten to leave anything out for dinner tonight as he'd been so distracted by the thought of seeing Skye again. Emmie was glaring at him mutinously, but she was eating her dinner and being fairly polite to Skye and Leo. Skye was chatting about inconsequential topics while the children were with them and he found the soft lilt of her voice relaxing and surprisingly sexy. She always walked around in skinny jeans and black T-shirts, with those horrendous biker boots, and looked like she'd forgotten to brush her hair half the time, but the way she moved so fluidly and always seemed to be alert and vibrant (when she wasn't scowling at someone) made him want to get to know her better. The sleek and well-oiled mums at the school held no interest for him although, he had to admit, he'd never really given them a chance.

Skye scooped up their now-empty plates and dumped them into the sink to clean later. She grabbed some ice lollies from the freezer and asked Leo to take Emmie to eat them in the garden. Leo looked like he was loath to leave this man alone with his mother, but was too polite to object in front of another adult. He had a determined look on his face that suggested he would certainly have to talk this through with his mum later though.

'So, what do you want from me?' Skye asked boldly, seating herself opposite Zack again and resting her elbows on the small wooden table that could just about squeeze four people round it if you folded it out.

'You really want to know?' he asked cheekily. Skye was more relaxed around him now, but the sexual tension was still there and he gave her a steamy look that made it clear that he fancied her and wasn't just trying to throw her off centre with his flirty comments. He couldn't believe how forward he was being after avoiding women for so long.

'I do,' she said, giving him her best beguiling smile but not blushing this time.

Zack laughed heartily at this and felt his pulse quicken again. She was such a mix of confidence and bashfulness, that he didn't know if she was playing with him or not. 'What I really want is you sitting on my lap,' he said cheerfully, almost making her fall off her chair in shock.

He was highly amused at her reaction and he wondered if she would run away or call his bluff. He'd never been so brazen with a woman before, but wanted to stake his claim on her before anyone else did. She was so adorable and crazy that she drove him nuts, he wasn't about to let her get away from him now that he had her attention. She certainly wasn't the most beautiful woman he had ever seen, with her distinct lack of grooming and dire wardrobe, but there was a quiet strength about her that drew him to her, plus she had gorgeous long legs and silky-smooth skin.

Skye's face flamed, but she took on the challenge and straightened her back. 'It's a shame the children are in the

156

garden, or I might just have done that,' she purred, making his eyes go wide. He knew she was teasing him, but before she had time to check his response, Zack moved round the table in two strides, checked to see that the kids were still in the garden, pulled her to her feet and pushed her up against the wall in the living room. Zack's mouth swooped down before Skye could protest and, as his lips touched hers, his senses exploded and, instead of grabbing his arm behind his back and throwing him to the floor for approaching her, which he was worried someone who ran a self-defence class might do, she wrapped her arms around his neck and wove her fingers into his hair to deepen the kiss. Hearing a noise from outside they sprang guiltily apart, both with glazed eyes and panting heavily. They looked at each other and then bent over laughing at their own behaviour.

'Wow!' said Skye, touching her hand to her swollen lips. 'Maybe we shouldn't have done that?'

Zack tried to compose himself, but the memory of her lips touching his had literally blown his mind. 'I want to do it again,' he said gruffly, reaching for her, but she danced out of his reach as she saw Leo nearing the back door.

'What else did you need me for?' Skye asked, catching her breath and disappointingly not swooning as the children walked into the kitchen and looked their way.

'Huh?' he asked groggily, not understanding the swift mood change before spotting the children. 'Oh, that? I was going to ask you to help me write the invites for a ball I'm thinking of holding, but that was when I thought you were quietly sitting here alone writing a book. I thought you said you were an author?' he raised an eyebrow in question.

'The book business is a bit slow,' Skye countered, as Leo filched a huge slice of Victoria sponge for himself and Emmie, dragging her back into the garden. 'It takes ages to write a book and I got a bit distracted with the success of the 'self-defence' classes: your description, not mine. I call them playtime for kids, or Skye-Safe.' She stuck her chin into the air defiantly as if challenging him to question her.

Zack really wanted to push her against the wall again and

bite into her delicate skin until she groaned his name, but the kids arriving had forced him to step away and see things more clearly. Skye was so independent and didn't look like she needed a man in her life, although she had all but burst into flames when he'd kissed her. She did what she liked and to hell with anyone else. Did he really want another headstrong female in his life? Zack's raging hormones gave him the answer and he made a rapid decision about an idea he'd been mulling over during dinner.

Zack brushed past Skye, hearing her gasp softly as he touched her briefly, before continuing on to stand in the kitchen doorway and take a better look at the assault course. 'I want you to relocate this to the base of the CloudClimb centre,' he said steadily, not giving her time to argue. 'You shouldn't have put this up here without permission and it conflicts with my business.' Skye opened her mouth to protest, but Zack put up a warning hand to silence her, clenching his fist again and dropping it to his side to stop himself from reaching out to pull her to him.

'You'll have room to expand the site there and it will complement what I offer. I've been looking at ways to keep the smaller children occupied while their siblings climb trees. They're starting to drive me mad.'

Skye smirked at this, then evidently remembered she'd told him that she didn't like small children either and cringed. Zack was steamrolling her and was completely satisfied that she would obey his every command. 'I quite like the idea of moving the course away from my back garden and the snooping parents I told you about over dinner,' she said thoughtfully. 'The drawback being I would have to learn to cook for myself, which would be a nightmare as the mums pay me in food,' she giggled at his shocked face as he glanced at the remainder of the delicious Victoria sponge, then laughed too.

Zack considered her options. It would mean fewer children in her home, but maybe more contact with school parents. She would have to smile at them and exchange pleasantries while they waited for their children and she had told him she was quite solitary and preferred working alone. She needed to make a choice but would be able to see, by the look of determination on Zack's face, he wouldn't be swayed lightly and would possibly make her dismantle the course she already had. She sighed theatrically, as if this was a hard decision and she was doing him a massive favour to help his business.

'Okay,' she said, 'I agree in principle to your idea, but I have a few terms of my own.' Skye's eyes were sparkling and she began restlessly moving around the room before he reached out to stop her and scooped her into him with a sigh of pleasure.

Skye undeniably enjoyed the feeling of being in his arms as she moulded into him, before pushing away and standing next to him and staring into his eyes. 'This would mean big changes in my life, and maybe finding a permanent home in the village, but I feel that it's the right resolution.' She was plainly used to making decisions very quickly and didn't flinch at this change of plans. 'I would want to design the course myself and check the ground was suitable. You would have to do the promotion with your business and I would have use of your refreshment facilities, which I hear are sublime by the way,' throwing in a compliment and a dazzling smile at the end to distract him from her demands.

Zack started to feel his confidence drain away slightly. He had thought Skye would simply refuse, or shout and scream at him for ruining her plans. He had assumed he'd have to spend weeks talking this idea through and find ways to make her succumb to his plans for her and her business. Instead, she had turned it to her advantage and he felt like he would be the underdog in the deal. 'Designing and implementing a full assault course might cost tens of thousands,' he said grumpily under his breath.

'It won't,' Skye said simply, giving Zack the impression that she knew what she was talking about. She had impeccable hearing too. He could see from the back garden that whoever designed the beams had a lot of experience.

'Will you use the same designer as you did for this one?' he asked, indicating the back garden.

'It was me,' Skye grinned, making Zack splutter slightly. She happily slapped him on the back, a little too hard, to help him regain his composure, then let her hand slide down his body for a cheeky feel of his bottom. The bold action made Zack jump in surprise and grab Skye's hand, before trailing soft kisses on her frantically racing pulse, making her squirm in delight.

'How?' he began to ask, lifting his head to look into her eyes, then deciding he really didn't want to know. As long as she accepted all of his rules, then they could work it out later. Preferably when they were in bed and after he had checked over every one of her delightful credentials. Lust aside, he knew a good idea when he saw one, and this could add great value to his business. Considering he had been avoiding women for years, suddenly he wanted to chain this one to him as swiftly as possible and in any way he could think of.

'It will be expensive,' Zack continued, thinking he would have to be generous if he wanted to partner a deal, in both senses of the word. He would make sure he had the greatest share capital in her business in return for investment, but the scent of her perfume was clouding his mind and all he was really bothered about was how he could get inside those skinny jeans. Ideas were whizzing around his brain and excitement at how this could solve some problems at work, and earn him some more of her company, was setting in.

'I have money,' Skye said.

'It will cost a lot. Having the tree centre fully designed by professionals cost me a fortune.'

Skye gave Zack a pitying look. 'I am a professional. I set this course up safely, with minimal fuss, with just Thea's help. I can upscale it with a few talented men or women, as long as Thea is employed too. It's one of my stipulations for our contract,' she said with a wink, making him wish he'd kept his mouth shut and let her have her garden full of logs. 'Plus, I have plenty of money to set up a mainstream business,' she said, surprising him again. 'I won't need investment except for the land and location, which now you have mentioned it, will benefit us both if we're becoming partners.' Skye gave Zack a cheeky grin and stepped closer to him. He backed away and into the garden, knowing he had been out-manoeuvred, but finding it particularly hot just the same. He grinned at her wolfishly and let his gaze slide up and down her body and Skye flushed at the memory of the taste of his lips.

'It's going to be fun,' he grinned back, pinching her bottom before calling for Emmie that it was time to go home.

Chapter Twenty-Eight

Zack put one foot inside his office and was about to do a rapid retreat, when Marlo caught sight of him from her seat... his seat, Zack fumed silently.

'Oh hi, Zack.' Marlo waved him to come and sit opposite her, not seeing the irony of what she was doing. When he didn't take a seat straight away, she stared him down until he gave in and swung himself into the chair opposite her. He didn't want to do as he was told, but grumpily admitted that it was almost as comfortable as his own chair; the one Marlo was happily sitting in.

'I have got the contracts here for you to look at for the marquee hire. I've also signed up the caterers and that DJ and the sexy singer you liked.' She gave him a meaningful look but, with all of the preparations for the ball and the way Skye had taken him at his word and begun to set the foundations for their new business venture, Zack hadn't had time to catch his breath. He had completely forgotten his passing comment about how hot the singer was when they had originally watched some footage of events to decide on the entertainment for the ball. The singer was a contact of Marlo's and he got the feeling she was in matchmaking mode.

'Great,' was all he could think of to say. He wanted to get to his computer and look at the finances before Skye arrived and started organising her ground team, as they were setting the foundations for the new assault course today. It had only been four weeks since they had talked it over. She had turned up the very next morning, after the school run, and he had wanted to drag her upstairs to his bedroom, but she had been all business, as if nothing had ever happened between them. Women confused the hell out of him. He'd been trying to get her alone for the last few weeks, and had only managed to shut them into the refreshment building once for a heated embrace before they heard someone approach and she'd run away again. Ever since then she'd made sure others were around them. He was so frustrated.

Marlo raised her eyes to heaven in apparent exasperation. He knew she had put hours and hours of work into this. The least Zack could do was pretend to be interested. He spotted Skye jogging past as she directed some guys to the new climbing area.

'Skye!' Marlo shouted after her and she stopped and looked around to see who'd called her. Zack winced and rubbed his sore ears.

Skye clearly realised Marlo was in Zack's office and was calling out her name again, as that woman had some lungs and you could probably hear her from the village. Skye changed direction and bounded into the office. Zack grinned at the sight of her endless energy. He would take any opportunity to see her, even if it meant Marlo was there. Skye looked from one to the other in evident confusion as to why Marlo was sitting in Zack's chair and Zack shrugged good-naturedly, while jumping up to offer her his chair. He cringed as Marlo noted this with interest, and winked his way as she waited for Skye to get comfortable. The girl was such a fidget; she didn't stop moving.

'Zack and I need your help, Skye,' she said, undeniably thinking that two women might have a better chance of convincing Zack that he did want to spend another couple of thousand pounds on the ball, when he didn't.

'Oh? What can I do to help you?' Skye turned and smiled sweetly at Zack, who grinned back wolfishly. Skye had told Zack that she had spoken to Marlo a few times in the last week and she seemed like a complete whizz at events management. She'd said Zack was lucky to have found someone like her, and she was planning to talk to him later in the week about putting her on the marketing payroll. Zack thought that sounded like a terrible idea. Marlo was so bossy!

'I was just about to explain to Zack that we really need the

163

ball to look, and feel, luxurious. I've booked some of the things we need, but I was thinking a cocktail bar with bartenders who twirl. I know it's an added expense, but it will be a talking point.'

'What's wrong with a few beers and bottles of wine on a table?' asked Zack in exasperation, trying hard not to look down Skye's top from his vantage point behind her.

Skye and Marlo exchanged conspiratorial glances. 'Skye?' asked Marlo. 'What do you think? Will a few beers on a table send the right message to your customers?'

'Hang on a minute!' said Zack, snapping his attention back to the impromptu meeting. 'The ball is to launch my new app and introduce the tree climbing business to the local community. What's it got to do with Skye?' he said, looking at her apologetically.

Marlo smiled as if he was a bit thick but she was indulging him anyway. 'I thought you said that Skye was your new business partner?' she said innocently.

'Well, she is … just not for the whole business. She's a partner in the new build.'

'Exactly,' said Marlo. 'The timing couldn't be better. You are launching at the same time, so why not incorporate both in the launch to save money later?'

'Well… yes, but…' stuttered Zack.

'It makes sense,' put in Skye. 'I'm not a partner in CloudClimb, but Skye-Safe will be ready to open for a promotional day by the time you hold the ball. We would save money on marketing in the long run. You did agree to add in promotion for the new joint venture in our agreement.' She offered him such a guileless smile that he couldn't help but stare. These women were railroading him.

'I know Skye has lots of strong young men around her today, what with the support beams going in for the assault course,' said Marlo sweetly, as anger and jealousy flittered across Zack's face before he realised she was winding him up, 'but I think it would be a good idea if the two of you went to check out these bar suppliers. They're holding an event tonight and said I could pop along to see if they would be a good fit for us. Unfortunately…' she sighed dramatically, 'I can't go this evening as I've got to finalise plans for the ball. Maybe you two could go for an hour? You can drop the kids with Mike and me, or Thea. They can watch a movie.'

Zack wanted to say no to Marlo so badly, but they both knew he wouldn't. He would have to be a bit more subtle when he looked at Skye, and not stare at her with rampant lust, as it was obviously plain as the nose on his face if Marlo had worked it out so quickly. He looked to Skye to see what she thought. She just shrugged her shoulders. That was helpful! Skye had been avoiding getting to know him better, he was sure. Now they would be alone together for a short time, he could find out why. 'Sounds good to me,' he said.

Chapter Twenty-Nine

Mirabelle tapped her foot on the concrete of the school playground in irritation. She had heard through the school grapevine that Zack would be hosting a ball in the grounds of his estate. She was fuming that he hadn't told her personally so that she could be the one to break the news to everyone. She knew how much Zack appreciated having her around and that he had a special connection with Miles, as he was always buying him crisps and getting him into his tree climbing gear before the rest of the children. She hadn't seen as much of him lately as he was constantly busy with Leo's mum and her interfering ways.

Belle had heard whispers that the kids who seemed to congregate at Skye's house now were doing some sort of self-defence classes, but why would kids need to do that? Miles had seemed pretty grumpy about it when he found out, but he amused himself with other kids in the class anyway and didn't have much to do with that group now. She hoped they weren't being nasty to Miles, or she would have to grab a parent or two and bash their heads together until they saw the light. Miles had complained that Emmie was spending more time with Leo, which was annoying as she had high hopes for Miles and Emmie being best friends. It would mean she saw more of Zack and she could find her rightful place as lady of the manor.

She grimaced when she saw Skye breeze through the gates with a harassed-looking Thea in tow. Thea was looking more and more haggard of late. Belle wondered if she was having some sort of mental breakdown. She had actually had the audacity to snap at Belle yesterday when she had tried to enquire if Zack had a date for the ball. Thea had told her to ask

Zack herself and waltzed off to the end of the playground without a backward glance. What was up with everyone at the moment? She watched Skye slink off to her usual place behind the shed by the wall, and gritted her teeth when she saw Zack head that way too, as soon as he walked through the gates.

Belle had seen the new assault course when they had last been at the tree centre and, although she was irritated that Skye was spending more time with Zack than she was, she dismissed Skye as a potential threat as she was a bit plain, and dressed so boringly in black. Plus, it seemed she worked for Zack now. The girl needed a serious makeover and her hair could do with a treatment or two to iron out the kinks.

Glancing down and smoothing over a non-existent crease in her own pristine jeans and tight blouse, Belle sighed in frustration. When was Zack going to man up and ask her out? She'd made it plain enough that she was interested in him, so she couldn't fathom why he hadn't made his move yet. He must be incredibly shy. Maybe he would ask her out at the ball? She would just have to work out a way to get him to move faster and ask her to accompany him. It would be a real coup for her to arrive with him on her arm. The school divas would be so jealous and it would stop them from snapping at her heels for a place at the top of the pecking order. They should all step back and give her the respect she demanded.

Maybe she needed to start with Skye and squash that little blossoming friendship? Or perhaps the smarter way would be to get her onside? Skye didn't conform with the usual mums at the school, who either tried to befriend the queen bee, or deferred to her and kept aside. She sat by herself, didn't really try to talk to anyone other than Thea, then went home again. The woman was not only poorly dressed, but extremely dull and a mystery. Belle scrunched up her forehead in thought, then realised this would give her worry lines and quickly rearranged her features into the usual impassive façade.

Chapter Thirty

Skye quickly retreated to her space behind the school gates and hoped for some peace and quiet. She wanted to find Thea, but she was nowhere to be seen. She had been a bit standoffish with Skye lately, and not her usual sunny self, which made Skye worry that she had upset her in some way. Things had changed because they were still running the club from her garden at the moment, but Skye was spending more and more time between her house and the estate. Thea seemed suddenly to have an issue, and be uncomfortable with Zack and was a bit growly when he was near Skye, which was weird.

Maybe she fancied Zack after all and was feeling jealous? Skye had thought Thea would want her to move on and finally meet someone she liked. The more she was around Zack, the more she wanted to make excuses to be alone with him. These new feelings had scared her a little and, at first, she'd avoided him, but it was impossible now they were setting up the assault course and he had taken to cornering her and brushing up against her at every opportunity. The man was incorrigible! After so long alone, Skye was gradually working herself up into a fervour of desire and being around him, and not giving in to him, was torture.

She tried to make herself comfortable on the wall, but she was still craning her neck to find Thea. Where was she? Skye had noticed a man in the field behind her cottage earlier today. She had seen him from her bedroom window and was sure he was looking at the house. She had run to the side of the window and stolen a quick glance around the frame, but by then he had gone. It made her wonder if she had imagined him, but she was sure she hadn't. She had carefully scouted the area and locked the house securely before she left for the school, and even looped back on her route to make sure she wasn't being followed, but there was no one.

Thea had assured her that Marcus was dead and that she was safe. What if she was wrong? What if the guys who hired him were refocusing their efforts and had found Skye? Her insides went cold and she felt terrified for the first time in ages. Sweat broke out on her top lip and she started to shake. She knew she could deal with a threat, but if they had found out about Leo, then she would be vulnerable. Why else would someone be watching the house? She vaguely thought that maybe Zack's ex had decided she wanted him back and set a detective onto her to find out if she was suitable to be near her daughter, but Kay hadn't been around for years as far as she knew, and Skye would easily be able to tell the difference between an assassin and a private investigator.

Maybe the man in the field just worked for Zack? She tried to calm her pulse and think clearly before panic set in. Zack must have sensed she was thinking about him, as he walked around the gate and came and sat next to her. When he saw she was white as a sheet he moved closer and took her hand in his. It was freezing cold, even though the sun was shining today. She watched him dart a glance around to see if they could be seen by anyone, then must have decided he didn't really care if they did. He had told her he was fed up with worrying about playground gossip but he suddenly looked really concerned about Skye. She glanced down at their hands but didn't pull away, so he began to smooth his hands over hers to get some warmth into them.

'Skye?' he asked gently.

Turning to face him, she pulled her hands out of his grasp and put them on her lap. 'Do you have anyone working in the fields behind my house?'

Zack seemed surprised by the question, but could clearly see she was deadly serious and he frowned. 'There's no reason for my staff to go into the fields. Did you see someone there?'

'Yes,' she said simply, as if this explained her concern.

He sighed with noticeable relief that this was all it was. 'I often come across ramblers who have strayed off the path and wandered over to look at the house. Did someone give you a fright?' He smiled in reassurance.

Skye hated showing she was vulnerable and actually human, and not the self-sufficient superwoman she made herself out to be. Zack wrapped an arm around her shoulders and pulled her into his side for comfort, smiling at the way she moulded into him. 'Hikers sometimes cut across the fields if they see the house and want to come and investigate further,' he soothed, smoothing down the hair at her neck and nuzzling it slightly. 'There are signs to say that it's private property, but they do get knocked down by the wind and falling branches, or sometimes they just get ignored. I'm really sorry if someone gave you a fright. I should have mentioned it.'

Her body sagged into his and she let out the breath she had been holding. Hikers! Of course. Why didn't she think of that? She felt really foolish now, but was slightly mollified by the warmth spreading through her body at the touch of Zack's lips on her neck. She looked up and went cold again as Belle poked her head round the gate, looking like she'd just swallowed a lemon, before stomping off in indignation.

'Belle's just seen us!' Skye said, jumping up in despair.

Zack chuckled, indisputably glad to see Skye's pale face infused with colour. 'Is that so terrible?'

'What about the kids? The gossip?'

'The kids have a fair idea already and Emmie told me she thinks you're kinda cool,' Skye looked up in surprise and she couldn't drag her eyes away from his as the school bell rang out. 'Do you care about the gossip?' Zack asked, seriously.

'I care about Leo,' she said with a grimace, worrying already if someone had told her son. She could see Zack trying not to look hurt as he brushed her comment aside gently.

'I understand, but I hope you're starting to care about me, too, and maybe we should mention to the kids that we're dating?' he asked, looking hopeful. Skye's eyebrows shot up in shock and then she saw the funny side and bent over laughing. 'What's so funny?' he asked in a hurt voice.

'Dating?' she giggled, making him smile and swat her bottom as she turned around, making her chuckle more. 'How

170

old are we?'

'Okay, we'll tell them we're having hot passionate sex,' he parried, making her gulp and start to sweat at the thought of his naked body. Zack was doubtless enjoying teasing her, as she seemed to have got over her earlier concern, so he risked a quick peck on her lips as he stood up, before they heard the children thunder out of the school classrooms.

Skye stared at him and licked her lips, as he'd made her want to grab him and ravage him in the bushes, which would be totally inappropriate considering their surroundings. He'd managed to get her to agree to the date Marlo had set up for them and he'd whispered in her ear that he was determined it would end up with her in his arms or, at the very least, with an agreement to more 'dates'.

'I will try and talk to Leo tonight,' she promised, liking the way Zack was taking charge and not letting her back away from him. 'Knowing him, he's sussed it out anyway.'

Chapter Thirty-One

Thea had avoided Skye today as she saw her with Zack at the school and didn't want to interrupt. Half of her was pleased that Skye was finally moving on, but the other half was concerned for her own mental state. Thea knew she had been distant lately and she admitted to herself that she was jealous of the way Skye had seamlessly met Zack, a gorgeous multi-millionaire who wasn't a complete lothario. To be fair, she knew from Skye's history that she hadn't met a man in years, but why now, when Thea was there to fill the gap Reece had left? They didn't need men to mess up their lives. Thea had hoped they would support each other and forget about anyone else, as men only signified trouble as far as Thea was concerned.

She thought of Flo's dad and how surprised he would be to find out he was a father. It served him right to be in the dark after the way he'd treated her. She had thought he was the perfect man; charming, edgy and great in bed. It turned out he was a lying, cheating bastard, who was sleeping with half her team, including their boss. He'd made it clear he hated children, but he had made Thea feel like she was the only woman in the world and really important to him for the two years they had been seeing each other. How could she have got it so wrong? She had loved him and he'd disregarded her feelings and done whatever he wanted to anyway. More and more lately she had been questioning her decision to run, though. Maybe he would have accepted Flo and they could have worked things out? She hadn't given him a chance to explain or to lose the other woman and, every day, the burden of keeping the secret from him weighed down on her. She knew she looked a mess and was distracted. Even Allie had asked her if she was okay. She would have to snap out of it and make a decision. She either told him straight out, or kept the secret forever.

She was close to Skye now, and she hadn't ever expected that to happen either. When they met, Skye had been suspicious and prickly. Thea had assumed she would be self-centred and hard-hearted, if she was honest, but she was the complete opposite. Skye had a brittle edge, but Thea had decided that this stemmed from years of neglecting her own needs.

Thea was trying to be excited about Skye's new business venture and couldn't believe how quickly she had made the decision to set it up and then jumped in and made it all work. The rumours Thea had heard about Skye's team, before she knew her, were of cold and ruthless men and women who didn't leave a detail to chance, until their final job. They were an enigma whose reputation went before them. From what Thea now knew of Skye, she saw efficiency, razor sharp intelligence and humility, which she hadn't expected at all.

Thea had wanted Skye to like the village, and for the kids to be friends, but now it was looking as though they were setting up a permanent home, Thea was beginning to think it might not be a good idea. She wanted to bring up Flo here, and supposing someone did look for Skye one day, or LUCAN decided they wanted her back? There must be at least one person who knew she was alive and well somewhere, even though Thea had been thorough when she'd deleted her history. The thought didn't sit easily with Thea and she was beginning to regret telling Skye so much about herself. She should have just got to know her from a distance, like she did with everyone else, and then she wouldn't be feeling so bad about the fact that she was angry at Skye's success. Why couldn't she find a great guy to look at her the way Zack drooled over Skye; the way most men seemed to drool over her? What was so great about wearing hardly any make-up and boring black clothes all the time, anyway? Thea needed to shake herself out of this funk, stop worrying about things she couldn't control, and start being a better friend. Grabbing a

173

mouthful of wine from the glass that always seemed to be at her side these days, she got up and decided it was time she got a haircut and began to sort out her own life.

Chapter Thirty-Two

It had been surprisingly quick to set things in motion for the new assault course, as Skye had already drawn up plans of her ideal layout for the field behind her cottage. Deciding to work as a team towards building a new climbing course meant Skye and Zack spent more and more time together. Last night they had gone to the wine bar Marlo suggested, to meet with the cocktail waiters and waitresses Zack had decided to hire for the ball.

There had been full glasses of crisp red wine and they had tasted morsels of mouth-watering food, while they relaxed, listened to the music, and laughed about they way some of the customers were clinging onto each other and dancing after one too many cocktails. One woman had shimmied over to Zack and tried to drag him away, even though he had been sitting opposite Skye and gazing into her eyes all night. The woman had been so persistent that Skye had told him to make the woman happy with one dance, but instead he'd smiled seductively, pulled her into a quiet corner and slid his hands around her hips. He moved her body with his as the beat got slower and his lips dipped to her shoulder blade and left searing heat there, making her forget that anyone else was around. She'd wound her arms around his neck and pressed her body into his to let him know her intentions. As Leo had stayed over at Thea's cottage, they had spent the evening laughing and flirting until the early hours. He'd tortured them both by waiting until the last song had finished and had then led her out of the bar with a smouldering look.

At the end of the night, Zack had driven her to his home and led her up the stairs to his room without a word. As soon as she saw the huge bed she had balked slightly but, before she had time to think, he'd backed her up against a wall and his lips plundered hers. She'd gasped in excitement as every nerve in her body came to life as his hands roamed over her hips and then moved around to cup her backside and pull her towards him to let her know the effect she had on him. Skye had felt like she was on fire and she'd responded with such passion that it took his breath away. There was no going back for her now and Zack had worshipped every inch of her body until she was completely intoxicated by his caresses and they moved together in rhapsody. She moaned as he trailed kisses down her neck and bent lower to taste the swollen buds of her breasts and then moved lower still to send her over the edge of ecstasy.

The next morning, Skye had woken dreamily in dishevelled sheets next to a smiling man, who actually looked a bit smug, but she found she didn't care as she felt rapturous. She had forgotten how nice it was to wake up in someone's arms, to snuggle into their warmth and feel the intoxication of their first night together. Zack had jumped out of bed naked, which astonished her but she certainly appreciated the view. Then he made her breakfast, insisting that she wasn't allowed to rush away at the break of dawn, as Emmie was at Mike and Marlo's house until later that morning. Skye had begun to feel a bit weird about the domestic scene, though and, after an hour or so, had slipped from the bed and made her excuses to go and freshen up while Leo was at school.

As soon as Skye arrived home she had been torn between euphoria and restless bewilderment, and had headed back to talk to Zack about what they had just done. It changed everything for her, but she wasn't ready to be vulnerable to another man again.

Chapter Thirty-Three

Mike was working in the CloudClimb office when Skye appeared. He told her that Zack had just left for a meeting with suppliers and wouldn't be back until school pick up time. As Skye headed for the door, Mike shrugged and left her to it. He had discovered over the last few weeks it was best to leave her pretty much to her own devices. She would ask for his opinion with the site, but usually already had an idea of the answer. She wasn't girly and giggly like some of the other women who hung around Zack, and she didn't really seem to notice he was there much, which must drive him nuts, Mike smirked. Zack was used to women swooning at his feet, but this one was different. Mike could see the appeal, though. She had a lithe, athletic body and long dark hair. She dressed with minimal fuss, which seemed to suit her personality, and Mike was enjoying gradually getting to know her. Marlo was desperate to find out more about her, but she was a bit of a closed book on that front.

Mike looked at the computer screen in front of him and sighed at the list of jobs he would have to do that day. The climbing course was shut for the day as it was Wednesday and Zack liked a day to have some peace and quiet for his app design business. It didn't mean Mike had a day off, though, as there was always a ton of bookings to go through for the following week and, for some reason, he had been voted as the member of staff who should look after their Facebook and Twitter feeds, even though he hadn't a clue what he was doing and it often took a whole day to update everything. He could just stick a photo of Zack on there each week and customers would flock from miles around. Mike grinned at the thought and decided it was time he got his own back on Zack for

177

lumbering him with this job when he knew he hated it. He was sure Zack did it because he knew it would wind Mike up. Zack said it was time he moved into the right decade with technology and educated himself on other ways to support the business. Mike secretly thought Zack wished he was more 'techy' so that they could discuss his app business more, but Mike had no idea how any of it worked and had spent months training each Wednesday, and still arrived each week without a clue where to start.

Scrolling through the computer and finding a few old promotional photos that Zack had refused to let the PR team use, Mike smiled to himself and hit send, to post one to their social media pages. He was sure Zack would see the funny side of it, but Mike did actually think it would bring in more business and Zack might just have to put up with it. Marlo would be proud of him for his inspired idea, too.

He felt a bit bad, after his initial burst of happiness, at the joke he'd just played on Zack, then decided that maybe it wasn't his best idea and he scrolled around the computer trying to find out how to delete the picture. After twenty frustrating minutes, he gave up and angrily slammed the computer shut. He remembered that Skye was around somewhere and decided that she might know how to take the photo down without Zack ever finding out.

After walking around the CloudClimb grounds, and not seeing Skye, he was about to leave but a slight noise alerted him to someone in the trees. His pulse began to race and he started to run towards the highest point of the course. He grabbed the phone out of his pocket to dial for help if someone had gone onto the course without the proper safety checks, and then stopped, dumbfounded, as he saw Skye leap from one tree trunk to another with such grace it took his breath away. What the hell? He stood stock-still in shock as she bounded round the course, before he came to his senses and called for her attention. He didn't want to scream and scare the hell out of her, in case she wasn't wearing the correct safety harness. Zack would kill him.

Skye looked surprised to see him, but didn't break her stride and his heart felt like it was in his mouth as, although he could now see that she was wearing a safety harness, she was deftly clipping and unclipping it between the stations so quickly that it was as if it wasn't even there.

'Skye,' he called. 'What the hell are you doing up there? Get down!'

Skye simply nodded her head at the command and clipped herself onto the high-wire zip line, while Mike looked in awe as she flew down the line in seconds and was standing at his feet grinning with the adrenaline of leaping around in the sky.

'What the hell?' said Mike, angrily. 'You could have been hurt.'

Skye looked abashed for about a second, then grinned so widely that he couldn't help but grin back. 'You've done this before, haven't you?' he asked, still cross, but she looked so happy it was hard to stay mad.

'I used to climb all the time with my dad,' she said simply, her eyes clouding for a fraction of a second before she covered it and smiled brightly again. 'I apologise if I scared you. It's how I know so much about the assault course. I climbed for years and years. We had to do all sorts of technical training for the mountains and I was quick to learn. I went back years later and did an advanced climbing course. I was thinking about being an instructor, but my parents died and that led me on another career path.'

'I'm so sorry. I didn't know,' Mike said, pulling her into a hug and feeling her body go rigid, so he quickly let her go. 'Zack didn't tell me,' he apologised, feeling a bit silly for trying to comfort her. 'Otherwise, I would have left you up there soaring though the trees.' He tried to joke to lighten the mood.

'It's my fault,' Skye said, putting an arm awkwardly around his shoulders then letting go and walking amiably by his side. Mike understood from her actions that she was trying hard not to keep putting distance between herself and everybody else, as she definitely wasn't a 'hugger'. Not everyone enjoyed human contact, and he tried not to second-guess her reasoning and let it go. 'I haven't told Zack yet.' When Mike started in surprise but didn't say anything, she carried on. 'I've been coming here every Wednesday for months.'

'What?' gasped Mike.

'No one expects me to be here and it makes me feel so free to climb the trees. I guess I owe you lots of entrance fees,' she said solemnly.

Mike doubled over in laughter and Skye put her hands on his back to control his mirth. 'You'll have to take that one up with Zack,' he gasped through his tears of laughter.

'Take what up with Zack?' asked Zack, walking towards them and sending a glare of ice to them both at the sight of Skye's hands on Mike's back. Mike knew he would be thinking of Kay and that this couldn't be happening to him again. He would be trying to figure out what the hell they were doing, sharing a personal joke?

Mike stood up and looked Zack straight in the eye to quash any stupid ideas. Zack had the good grace to look a bit ashamed of his assumption. Mike winked at Skye and said, 'I was just telling Skye how I uploaded a gorgeous photo of you to our Twitter feed, then thought I'd better delete it. After finding out I had no clue how to do that, I asked Skye if she thought you'd mind. She said your profile is too cute to hide and we should leave it there.' He checked to see if Skye was with him on this and she nodded vigorously, while Zack howled in rage and started running towards the office faster than he had ever moved before. Skye snorted with mirth and she grabbed Mike's arm as they both ran after Zack to see what would happen next.

Chapter Thirty-Four

Belle sipped the last dregs of her fragrant café latte and crossed her jean-clad legs. She seethed quietly as the quivering school mum in front of her found enough courage to tell her that the new woman in the playground, Skye, had been running some sort of 'defence against Miles' club, to keep the children away from her son. If it was true, then heads were going to roll! How dare she exclude Miles from his friends and alienate the rest of the class from him? He barely had anyone to play with these days and now it seemed that this had all been planned from the start by the interloper. Belle crunched her knuckles and felt fury rise in her chest.

She was already feeling sick at the sight of Skye and Zack kissing in the school playground, which was disgusting! She had marched into the headmistress's office yesterday and demanded that she do something about it. As usual, Penny was so insipid that she had tried to smooth things over by saying there were no children present, as they were all in school and no one else had complained. Penny had only got the job as they were family friends; if she stopped being useful, then Belle would find a replacement who was.

Her heart was hammering in her chest and she stood up and prepared to leave the coffee shop, straightening out her jacket and looking stonily at the woman in front of her who was blushing and cringing in her seat. Belle patted her arm perfunctorily as, after all, she might be a complete bore, but she knew which side of the fence to come down on. She was loyal, unlike Penny, and deserved something for telling her what had been going on at the school when it seemed no one else had the balls.

'Thanks for letting me know, Naomi,' Belle said tightly,

trying to force a smile while mentally scrolling through the faces of every school mum and dad to see who the traitors were. She could instantly peg a few, but would soon work out who to tackle first. Grabbing her bag, she stalked to the door, turning briefly just in time to see Naomi sigh in relief that the encounter was over and grab her phone to spread the word. Ignoring the sense of self-doubt for a moment, Belle made a decision and headed for CloudClimb. After all, that seemed to be the most likely place to find a snake in the grass, amongst all those trees.

Belle saw that Marlo was just about to head out of the office hopefully to try to find Skye, but stopped short and ducked back inside when she spotted Belle marching through the front gates. Belle knew that woman was gutless. She saw Marlo frantically wave her arms around from her hiding place just in Belle's line of vision, as they had both just seen Skye walking towards them from the other direction.

Skye frowned when she saw Marlo's weird mating dance, then evidently realised what she was doing when Marlo pointed at Belle before moving further back into the building. Skye shrugged and walked towards Belle, which made Marlo rush forward again with excitement to watch the inevitable explosion. Belle was ready for a fight. She'd discovered that most parents at school now knew about Skye's self-defence classes and were sad that they would soon be stopping. They were very excited that she was opening a new assault course with training sessions, though, which sounded much like the ones she had run from home. The school grapevine even said that Skye had discussed with Zack the possibility of running adult classes in the evening as a future business add-on, fumed Belle, who had needed to call in a few favours to find this information that should have been readily available from her friends. She would certainly be 'talking' to them later.

Marlo had gossiped to her friends that she was enjoying watching their fledgling romance grow, and that Mike took every opportunity to wind his friend up about it whenever he could, too, as Zack couldn't seem to stop touching Skye at every opportunity. The man was acting like he'd never had sex before, which was disgusting. Seeing Skye approach Belle at a leisurely pace while Belle strode ever nearer, Marlo darted a glance round for a first aid kit and Belle sent her an evil glare.

'Nice to see you here, Belle,' said Skye in a friendly voice. 'I had been expecting you to talk to me while we were at school,' and appeared surprised it had actually taken the grapevine so long to get the news about the kids to her, which made Belle flinch with embarrassment. She noted Marlo was peeking around the edge of the office door, but hadn't come to join them. Some wingman she was.

'Really?' hissed Belle, looking about to see if anyone was around to witness Skye's downfall and peering down her nose at Skye's toned legs, which were encased in a pair of tiny black jean shorts that looked like they had been severed at the legs by a pair of scissors, from the amount of loose strands that hung down her tanned limbs. The girl really needed to learn how to dress. Disappointingly, there didn't seem to be anyone else here other than Marlo, who was still peering out from the building next to them, but hadn't walked over; the coward. She was a friend of Belle's and she would have expected her to have told her about this. Okay, maybe they weren't close, but still… 'I've just been informed that you've been running an unauthorised after school club and, as chair of the PA, it's something we take quite seriously.'

'Is it?' asked Skye in some confusion. 'What's serious about some kids coming round and playing after school?'

Belle didn't like Skye's flippant response, or the way she was standing straight, slightly in Belle's personal space now she thought of it, and annoying the hell out of her with her smug face. 'I heard it's a self-defence club and you started it to keep the children away from Miles?' she raged, stepping backwards and feeling suddenly uncomfortable. This wasn't going quite how she planned it. Skye didn't look in the slightest bit flummoxed or intimidated as she had expected, nor had she looked embarrassed at being found out. What the hell?

Skye stood a bit straighter and looked Belle directly in the eye. 'Why would they want to avoid Miles?' she asked innocently. 'Of course, it's not an official self-defence class, although it did give me inspiration for this place,' she continued, without giving Belle a moment to say more, and tilted her head towards the new climbing area she had constructed. Belle followed her line of vision to the low-level climbing apparatus by the CloudClimb centre.

Belle somehow felt that Skye was playing with her, but couldn't put her finger on quite how. It made her start to stutter before she snapped herself out of it, taking a step towards Skye. Skye planted her feet and stayed put, which meant Belle had to sort of sidestep her and then pretend to walk over and inspect the assault course, feeling like an idiot. 'Why would someone tell me your 'club' was to isolate my son?' she demanded to know, her face turning puce. Skye patted Belle's arm, a bit patronisingly, but it stopped Belle's face turning even more purple, as she felt she might combust at any moment.

'Look,' said Skye, 'when my son Leo joined the school he didn't know anyone. I started inviting various friends round to play. As you can see from this construction, my field of expertise is in climbing and fitness training. I was having a career break when I arrived and had no intention of doing anything like this. I was actually going to try and write a climbing book and throw in some romance about a couple who got lost in the mountains. What a stupid idea! I thought maybe a writer's life would be creative and relaxing, but when I tried to write a book and sent it to an agent, she told me it was dismal.' Belle stared in shock at this sudden sharing of confidences and felt a warm glow that Skye had told her something she was sure none of the other mums knew about her. The gossip would be pure gold. Skye waved her arm around to encompass the low-level climbing course, which seemed to be her pride and joy. 'I had to think again, and when the children seemed to enjoy playing in the garden so much, I approached Zack about expanding his business. Luckily, he was already looking for a way to keep the smaller children occupied while the older children were on the CloudClimb course. The idea grew from playground chat. You guys gave me the idea.'

Belle glowed with the praise that she had actually helped this poor failure of a writer to find another dream.

'I had a small climbing frame I'd built in my garden and the kids asked me to help them learn how to balance. It became a weekly play session, not an after school club.'

'Why wasn't Miles invited round, then?' asked Belle, not really knowing where this conversation was heading. She had really wanted to slap Skye's stupid face earlier and now she was very confused about how she felt.

'It's not like he and Leo are best friends, is it?' asked Skye candidly, making Belle frown.

'You have loads of kids there, apparently,' said Belle, trying her best not to sound petulant. Skye would have to start thinking of Leo's school life and not keep putting herself first, the selfish woman. Surely she must be aware that Miles was a sought-after friend in school and upsetting him was not an option. Belle didn't like the thought that Miles was now feeling segregated from other children because of this woman and her son.

'Only as many as can fit in a cottage garden.' Skye didn't expand on how huge the garden was. 'Miles would have been welcome but, unfortunately, when more children asked to come round, I had to say no,' she sighed as if this was such a chore and she was speaking to a four-year-old, then caught herself and sent an apologetic smile to Belle, which she grudgingly accepted. 'I guess that, thinking about it now, there might be other mums who are upset with me. Do you think the whole class wanted to join in?' asked Skye innocently.

'Oh no!' exclaimed Belle, realising she may have overreacted and not wanting to see Skye upset over such a silly misunderstanding. 'I'm sure most of them aren't like my Miles, who loves it here at CloudClimb. They probably hate sport and wouldn't want to come to such a pokey space anyway.' Skye grinned at Belle, who had no clue how insulting she was being.

'Obviously, we now have much more space with a low-

185

level assault course for small children to climb on, but the older children can use it for self-defence training. It really was the school gossip that gave me the idea,' said Skye, as Belle flinched at the inferred 'we' of Skye and Zack as a team. 'Sometimes gossip can work in your favour,' she smiled, as if hoping her comment would hit the mark.

Belle flushed red again and cleared her throat. She didn't know who to believe, but it seemed maybe bloody Naomi and her cronies had got it wrong this time. Why would anyone want to keep away from Miles anyhow? He was the most popular boy in school. Maybe if Skye was going to be a permanent fixture round here, she would let her into her inner circle? Especially if she was with Zack. The girl would be loaded and in need of direction. Belle would have to forget Zack, it seemed, and give Gerald a call at last, to accept his offer of that weekend in Provence.

Belle cleared her throat and turned to see if Marlo was watching; she was. 'Well, I'm glad we got that sorted out, Skye,' she said patronisingly, as if Skye had bowed down and apologised to her. 'It seems we had crossed wires, but I'm glad we can be friends now,' she continued, patting Skye's arm. Skye looked down at the gesture before darting a glance at Marlo and raising her eyes heavenward.

'I understand from Zack that he's having a ball here soon? That sounds like great fun!' Belle chirped, suddenly playful as if confiding in a close friend. Skye sighed and let Belle score one point.

'I think I saw your name on one of the invitations on Marlo's desk. Would you like me to grab it for you before you go?'

'That would be lovely,' exclaimed Belle, as if the thought couldn't have been further from her mind, but she was secretly rubbing her hands with glee. At least one good thing had come out of today's fiasco.

'Stay here and I'll grab it for you before I walk you out,' Skye darted off before Belle could answer and she felt slightly awkward at standing in the middle of the trees all by herself. Skye ran to the office and Belle gasped at how fast she moved when motivated. That girl could run.

'What happened?' Marlo demanded to know as Skye arrived and she checked her for bruises.

'Don't ask me now, just hurry up and write her name on an invitation to the ball.'

'What?' cried Marlo. 'I had put her on the list, but Zack scrubbed it off.'

'Stick it back on again, then, and write her name in your best fancy writing as if it's been there for ages,' Skye urged, not even the slightest bit out of breath from the run she had just done. 'She's waiting outside. I hope that the golden ticket and gentle push for the door will make her get lost and leave us alone. I've reached my limit for being nice and I know Zack will flip out at me inviting her to the party. But, everything else aside, she is the local queen bee and it makes sound business sense for her to be invited. Zack will still sulk though.' Seeing Marlo standing open-mouthed, she grabbed her arm and ushered her to the desk, where a pile of pristine invitations sat waiting for the names to be written on. Skye picked up a pen and placed it in Marlo's hand, and she sat down and began to write as fast as she could. 'I don't want her wandering anywhere else before I can get rid of her.'

'You bribed Belle with a ball ticket?' gasped Marlo. 'That's such a great idea. I'll have to think of a few things she'd like, to shut her up if she ever gets a bit narky with me, too.'

'Of course I bribed her,' giggled Skye, taking the ticket and rushing back out of the room. 'She's really shallow!' she added with a wink as she flew out of the door and started guiding 'Mirror Ball' Belle back towards the entrance.

Chapter Thirty-Five

Thea started clearing up the mess she had made with breakfast and hadn't had time to deal with. She walked passed the pretty mirror she had in her kitchen, which Allie had decorated with shells, and admired her new haircut. She had finally decided that morning to get her hair chopped off, and it was now a manageable crown of curls rather than her usual unruly mess. She had to admit that she was looking more like her old self lately. She'd stopped gorging on wine and cake and her clothes felt much looser. In fact, she could probably do with a return visit to that boutique with the snotty shop assistant where she had first met Skye, to buy a dress for Zack's ball. She might even need a smaller size. Now Flo wasn't breastfeeding, her breasts had shrunk back to their admittedly still fairly humongous, but not quite so offensive, state.

Thea finally felt that she was getting hold of her life again, and not slipping into the pool of depression that had been clawing at her over the previous few weeks. Maybe she'd had some sort of minor breakdown, or postnatal depression, since Flo was born? It wasn't like she could ask a hard nut like Skye about feelings, or approach her spiky sister for advice. She would simply bite her head off, or laugh in her face for being so pathetic.

Thea also admitted that she had been jealous of Skye and Zack's blossoming romance. She'd watched them holding hands when they thought no one was looking and seen the way Zack managed to brush past Skye at every opportunity, whether it be a soft hand on the arm, or a swift feel of her backside.

They were so natural around the kids too. They made sure Allie was included, but Emmie and Leo seemed to have fallen into a pattern of spending hours playing in the estate garden with the two lolloping dogs, while the adults worked together. The natural progression of Skye being at CloudClimb all the time was accepted by everyone and it had made Thea a bit bitter at how easily she fitted in. Even 'Mirror Ball' Belle was suddenly gushing about how wonderful Skye was, much to Skye's disgust.

Seeing how Zack looked out for the kids, even though he wasn't Allie's or Leo's dad, made her question her decision to keep Flo's dad in the dark about his child again, too. It had been making her sick with worry over the last few weeks and she had finally decided that it was time to call him and let him know where she was. Maybe she could forgive him for Flo's sake and they could start again? Her stomach crunched at the thought of seeing him and she badly wanted to reach for a glass of wine, but she held herself in check and put the remaining dishes back into the cupboards. She smiled at the clutter of mugs and cups in her kitchen, compared to the borderline obsessive sparseness of Skye's, then her smile slipped as she remembered how drunk she had been the previous week.

She cringed in embarrassment and was glad she hadn't caved in and confided in Skye. Before Thea had come here, she had gone into her old work files and left a trail for Flo's dad to find, if he chose to look for her. She knew it was cowardly, but at least that way he wouldn't be able to say she hadn't given him a route to his child. She wasn't completely heartless. He was a smart man and he would see the clues if he looked for them.

Thea gulped in some air as her face flamed in embarrassment. Why would he be looking for her anyway? He had scores of women and probably hadn't noticed she wasn't there. Why would she want a bastard like that as a role model for her daughter, when he hadn't come knocking on her door so far? She felt her face flame and berated herself for being weak and trying to contact him. She was glad he hadn't answered when she'd drunkenly called him last week. He wouldn't recognise her new number anyway.

She should have been strong, as Skye had been for years, and survived devoid of a man. If it hadn't been for the guilt she felt about Flo growing up without knowing her dad, Thea would have probably tried to forget about him. She knew, deep down, that she was finding it hard to cope without him and she was so weak she would probably have found an excuse to contact him at some point. Not just for Flo, but because her body craved him like a drug and she needed a fix desperately. She was so ashamed of herself, it had been making her ill, but she'd had enough of the self-pity now and was trying to pick herself back up off the floor for her daughter's sake.

Straightening her back and flicking her hair off her face, she decided it was time she started sorting her own life out and not comparing herself to Skye all the time. Skye was an emotional desert and maybe she wasn't the best person to emulate. Lifting the pram and turning it to face the front door, she scooped up Flo, from where she was happily playing on her baby mat with some toys, and decided she would buy herself a complete new wardrobe and settle on what kind of woman the new Thea wanted to be. If Flo's dad did turn up at her front door, then she would look slick and amazing and he would beg for her forgiveness and never let her go.

Turning as she locked the cottage door, she thought she saw a movement by the side of the estate gates, but as she squinted to get a better view, she saw one of the CloudClimb staff arrive, strolling down the lane, and frowned. She could have sworn there was someone else there, but the road was clear. Waving back to the young man that Skye had just recruited to help them with Skye-Safe, she pushed her bag under the pram and briskly walked towards the high street.

Deciding she was being paranoid after her earlier thoughts, as Flo's dad had obviously either not found the messages or chosen to ignore them, Thea pressed a button on her phone to activate the voice control and told it to call Skye, while she parked the buggy outside the boutique. Ignoring the delicious cake smells that were wafting down the street from the café, Thea eyed a beautiful purple dress in the window and waited for Skye to answer. It was about time they both threw out their drab wardrobes and let some vibrant colour into their lives, although by the rosy flush of Skye's face these days, she was probably getting enough sex to power a town and might not have time for clothes shopping with her friend. They were both young, rich and sexy women and Thea decided they should stand on a bench in the village and shout to the rest of the world about it. No more hiding in shadows. It was time to start living.

Both she and Skye had been so busy setting up Skye-Safe that they had forgotten to buy a dress for the ball and it was only a few days away. She would get Skye down here and then into the hair salon if it killed her. They'd been drifting apart a bit lately and a bit of girly shopping was the remedy to most things in life. At least it would be a start and, once again, they could reinvent themselves, but maybe this time without hiding the real person inside.

Chapter Thirty-Six

The children were all running around Zack's house as if they had eaten a plateful of coloured sugar for dinner, instead of the spaghetti Bolognese Skye had prepared. They had all recognised, pretty quickly, that it was the only edible dish she could safely cook. It had been decided that Thea and Flo would come round and they would all get ready for the ball together. Zack had hired a team of child-minders, who were actually a group of bored local grandparents who had decided to set up a childcare business at big events. It worked like a dream, as everyone knew them and they often had a brilliant time dancing with the children too. Zack had been introduced to them by Mike and they had been an instant hit with the kids.

Zack walked past the open door and did a double take when he saw the two women standing there smiling at each other. Wow! Neither of them was the type of woman to primp and groom themselves every minute, but hell, when they did his heart nearly stopped at the sight of them. He didn't let them know he was there, but drank in the sight of them, enjoying how happy they seemed.

Thea twirled round in front of Skye in her purple dress and Skye clapped her hands in pleasure. Thea looked amazing! Her dress flowed around her ankles and dipped seductively at her breasts. Skye had told him that she was pleased to see the old Thea gradually returning lately. Skye had been so tied up with the Skye-Safe launch, and the rush to get everything ready, that she'd been preoccupied. As Thea was helping out too, it had been a nightmare to get together and chat. Every time Skye had approached the topic, Thea had shut her down and said she was fussing. It made Skye uncomfortable to discuss personal topics as she wasn't a girly girl, but for Thea, she had tried. She should have tried harder, though, she'd said. Skye had a knack of getting people to share their innermost secrets, as Zack seemed to be sharing more of his feelings these days, but something about Thea's behaviour had been really bothering Skye and she had backed off from finding out the truth in case Thea slipped back into the doldrums. Skye was finally building a life for herself here and she, selfishly, didn't want Thea to ruin it. So much for being a good friend, she'd sighed, but Zack had told her she was an amazing friend and she'd hugged him so hard he'd thought she might pop a rib!

From the door he watched Skye impulsively reach over and hug Thea tightly, making her giggle and blush. Thea hugged her friend back fiercely and then held her away to take in Skye's dramatic midnight blue dress with tiny stars dotted all over it. It was so fluid, it clung to her svelte frame. It was as if you were staring at a moonlit night; she looked breath-taking. 'Zack will drop down dead in shock when he see's you,' she giggled and he almost had, as he'd never seen either woman look so beautiful.

Everything they had worked for was coming together. Skye-Safe was set up and ready to show to the public. Zack had finally managed to incorporate his app designs into the main tree climbing area and walking trails in the woods. Marlo and Thea seemed to have been welcomed as part of the main team and were expected to look glamorous, but be on duty to wine and dine their new clients tonight. It had been exhausting but exhilarating over the last few months.

He had developed such strong feelings for Skye recently, but she was still a bit nervy around him, especially if he tried for an open display of affection. It frustrated the hell out of him, but he was trying with all his might to take things slowly and not to scare her off. It was so difficult, when every time he saw her he wanted to back her into the nearest room and touch every inch of her skin. Seeing her standing there looking like a vision of the night, he gulped in some air, as Thea turned and noticed him. She went over, kissed him on the cheek, winked at Skye and left them together.

'Stunning!' was all he could say, taking her hands and

starting to kiss her neck and trail his fingers down her naked back, making her pulse race. She kissed him on the lips and then placed her hands on his solid chest before they got carried away again.

'You like the dress?' she asked flirtatiously, moving away to put a little distance between them. He knew the children were around and she still had mixed feelings about open declarations of affection in front of Leo.

'I love the dress.' Zack didn't let her have the space she craved and pulled her back into his arms, passionately kissing away her lipstick until she was breathless and pliant in his arms. 'I love the woman inside the dress more,' he whispered into her ear, so that no one else would be able to hear, and felt her stiffen in his arms for a fraction of a second before she realised what she was doing and noticeably forced herself to soften again. It was too late, though, and he had felt her resistance.

Zack needed Skye to want this relationship as much as he did. He couldn't lay himself out to be crucified again in the way Emmie's mum had done. It had taken him so long to unfurl and become human again. Letting a woman know he cared about her, let alone how intoxicated he was with Skye, was almost intolerable to him, but he felt compelled to try. The feeling he had when he was with her, and he managed to coax a genuine smile or helped her relax and enjoy life a little after the trauma of losing her son's father, was worth every minute of self-doubt he had about opening himself up to the pain of rejection again. He couldn't get enough of her. The problem was, the more she backed away, the more panicky he became. He knew it was a bad idea to push her so soon, but he hadn't been able to control himself and, from the alarm he had seen in her eyes a moment ago, he might have gone too far.

They had spent so much time together lately and she was coming round to the idea of Leo and Emmie being happy with the idea. He had drawn her into his house with many excuses to try and make her comfortable here. He didn't want her in the stupid cottage; he wanted her in his bed! If he had to evict her to get her there, he would play dirty and tell her he had a long-term tenant who wanted the cottage and she would have to move into the estate. Then he remembered that she had her own money and realised that was a bad idea, as she would just buy a house further away from the estate. She was maddeningly independent and she infuriated him. He didn't even know when he had fallen in love with her, but he thought it had probably been the first day he had seen her, holding Emmie's hand across the field, when he had been so angry he'd behaved like a complete jerk. He was lucky she had spoken to him at all after that, he thought.

'Come on,' Zack said, trying to stop his stomach from turning over with the sick feeling he now had. 'We need to get to the marquee and greet our guests or we'll never hear the end of it from Marlo. I think she'd shoot us both.'

Before he could leave, Skye reached up and gave him the sweetest kiss, which silently told him she had heard him and they would talk about it later. He tried to rein himself in and not kiss her back but he couldn't do it, so she held his hand and they walked towards the sparkling entrance to the party which was adorned with fairy lights that lit up the pitch-black sky.

Lights hung from several branches of each tree of CloudClimb, and tiny glowing white stars had been hung from the Skye-Safe assault course. Candles in lanterns lit the pathways and the app screens glowed in the trees with pictures of the marquee's interior.

Tables adorned with silver plates and goblets were arranged around a dance floor, and beautiful displays of branches and leaves sprang from the centre of every table. The ceiling had been blacked out and stars twinkled in the night.

To one side of the dance floor was a huge screen where guests could see, for the first time, how the games, interactive walking trails and tree apps would work. There was a buzz of excitement in the air from the staff who were all dressed in their finest clothes, with discreet CloudClimb badges on their lapels, ready to direct people to gaze in wonder at the spectacle before them. Marlo really had worked her magic and the setting was a complete triumph.

More staff were stationed by the estate entrance to guide guests along the candlelit pathway, winding amongst the trees, where they could see the interactive screens, then into the marquee, where a delicious cocktail awaited them and an evening of decadence and mystery would unfold.

It was the conclusion of months of planning and Zack couldn't afford to be distracted, but he was aware of every move Skye made across the room, and he felt himself become more and more tense with every man she smiled at and greeted, while they took in how sensational she looked in that dress and salivated all over her. He could feel his fists bunching up and his shoulders pushing back, before Mike came over and slapped him quite hard on the back when he saw how feral he was looking, staring at Skye and the group of school parents who were currently surrounding her.

Snapping his attention back to his friend and trying to loosen the grip he had on his beer before he snapped the glass in two, Zack grimaced at his own stupidity. 'Uh-oh,' joked Mike good-naturedly. 'Man, you have it so bad it hurts.'

Zack turned away from Skye and looked sulkily at the floor. 'This is your big launch night,' said Mike in a no-nonsense tone. 'We've all worked so hard to get us here and my wife, in particular, has slogged her guts out to make it perfect. You have a beautiful woman of your own who clearly adores you. Don't screw it up.'

Zack sighed and decided to chill out, looking his friend straight in the eye. 'You're right. I'm being an idiot. Marlo has excelled herself, as I have told her a million times already. You and the staff have been great and, you're right, Skye looks like a million dollars.' He glanced across the room at her and smiled as she laughed at something one of the school mums said. She still held her body in check and didn't throw her head back and immerse herself in it but maybe, with time, she would become more comfortable with them all and let them see the real woman he saw.

'Glad we finally agree on something,' joked Mike, grabbing his arm and steering him over to join Skye and start mingling with his guests.

Chapter Thirty-Seven

Later in the evening, after speeches that made everyone laugh, and dancing, Zack was feeling more relaxed, as Skye had pretty much stayed by his side all night and, when she didn't, he realised it was ridiculous to smother her to get her attention. The evening was still in full swing and so many people had congratulated them on their interactive app idea and the new assault course. He was extremely proud of what they had achieved in such a short space of time and it felt strange to remember a time before Skye had barrelled in and taken his world by storm. Zack felt more alive since he met her than he had in years before that. He could understand that soppy grin Mike had when he looked at Marlo now and even why he would drop anything if she said she needed him. It had been such a brilliant evening. The children had all gone inside the house to watch a movie with the childcare they had booked, then a bit later, they would all go to sleep in one of the rooms they had set up for a giant sleepover. Mike and Marlo, as well as he and Skye, and even Thea and Flo, were all staying tonight. It was like a giant slumber party and a great way for them all to have been able to join in without stress.

Most of the talking to potential customers had been done by his staff, as he hated that part of the job, but he had reluctantly given a speech and it had been well received, judging by the number of people who had patted him on the back afterwards. He was finally enjoying himself and he had had a few glasses of wine, and a beer or two, and wanted to drag Skye onto the dance floor as a slow number had just come on and he was desperate to mould her body, in that dress, to his.

He walked over and whispered into her ear, not caring if he was interrupting her conversation with Felicity, the arty school

197

mum that everyone was raving about. The woman giggled tipsily and moved away as he pulled Skye into his arms and they swayed gently to the music.

'Are you having a good evening?' he asked seductively, nibbling on her ear and making her press her body into his. He gasped as the warmth of her skin came into contact with his, as she slid her hand down his back and under the hem of his tuxedo jacket. She brushed her fingers along the waistband of his trousers, just beneath his shirt, and touched the sensitive expanse of skin at the top of his toned bottom. He nipped her earlobe to tell her to stop and she laughed and slid her hand to the safety of his waist, over his clothes and not anywhere it could cause major damage to his already stretched control.

Although Skye's dress was floor length and the colour of the night sky, the top layer was almost translucent in certain lights and, every so often, her movements gave a glimpse of endless leg and slight cleavage from the side slits and scooped neckline underneath. It had been torturing Zack all night.

'I'm having an amazing time,' she smiled into his neck, plainly enjoying the playfulness after his words earlier. He understood that it had probably been on her mind and, although he knew she had begun to feel love for him too, his open declaration, so soon, evidently reminded her of Reece and had her backing away the moment he said how he felt. He could have kicked himself for not having more finesse. Surely she realised she must have hurt him by not responding in kind? She must know how he felt about her by now? Did he really need her to say the words back, he wondered? Undeniably, he did.

'Your app design has totally blown their minds tonight,' she said proudly, recapturing his attention. 'You will have so much business we won't have time to see each other,' she teased, snuggling in to the warmth of his arms around her.

Zack frowned at her tone and felt a slight undercurrent to her words. He knew she was proud of him. She had told him over and over, which made him want to succeed more, but the thought of loads more people around, and not being able to see her so much, made the blood freeze in his veins. What happened if he was too busy to spend time with her? Would she get bored and run off with someone else, like Kay had? He tightened his hold on her and drew her to the side of the room where they could sit down with some privacy.

She was still smiling, but it faded as she noticed his serious expression. 'What is it?' she asked with a frown, placing her hands in her lap and waiting, not moving a muscle. 'I knew this feeling of happiness was too good to last,' she said quietly, breaking his heart in two.

'I want a commitment from you, Skye,' he said gently, taking her hands in his and trailing his fingers over hers. 'I don't want confusion from the school mums, from our children, or from us. I love you and I want us to be together publicly.'

He looked into her eyes and implored her to want the same thing. 'I don't understand,' she said, her bottom lip quivering slightly. He could see she was trying not to upset him, but she looked panicked, as if she was about to pack up and run. 'We are together a lot of the time and most people must know about it by now, unless they're a bit thick or have been visiting Mars for the last couple of months.'

'I want you and Leo living here,' he gestured towards his home, 'with Emmie and me. I hate you going to a different house each night, and I'll evict you if I have to,' he tried to joke. Seeing anger flare in her eyes as she sprung apart from him and stood up, he realised his mistake and tried to take her hand again. She turned to him and brushed his hand away.

'I won't be manipulated into doing what you want, Zack. I know you've been hurt before, but I'm not her. I won't drop you the moment you think I'm bored and I won't desert you and Emmie. I need my own space and time to get used to being with someone again.'

Zack tried to control his fear and anger, but he was so fed up with tiptoeing around her in case he scared her away. He was a strong man and he wanted his woman with him. He hated hiding the fact he was visiting her and abhorred sleeping alone. He'd done it for years and enough was enough.

'Leo and Emmie love spending time together and he's here

so much he might as well move in anyway,' he ground out, a bit more forcefully than he would have liked.

'Why do you have to rush me all the time? It's not up to you where Leo sleeps and I'm not about to drag him out of his home because I like spending time with a man.' Zack saw red at this comment and clearly Skye realised she might have pushed him too far, but seemed so angry with him too that she didn't back down as he'd hoped.

'It's not his home, though, is it? It's mine,' said Zack bitterly. Skye swung round at that comment and, eyes blazing, she moved in closer to him.

'I've just checked on Leo. He's asleep and I won't move him tonight, but I am going back to the cottage. If it pains you so much to have us there, I'll start packing tomorrow.'

'Skye,' he pleaded to her retreating back. 'You know that's not what I meant. I want you both here with me!' He slumped down on the bench seat and held his head in his hands. He had managed to mess up his big display of affection completely.

Chapter Thirty-Eight

Skye angrily brushed tears from her eyes and grabbed a pair of trainers from behind her desk at the CloudClimb office. The door was still ajar after she'd grabbed some more promotional leaflets earlier. She had been so happy a mere few hours before; now she was ready to throttle someone! Why couldn't Zack let them enjoy each other's company for now? She'd told him something of her past, omitting her old job and details of her real marriage to keep Zack safe, but he now knew she'd lost her own parents at a young age and had married soon afterwards. He'd said he understood that she had been alone for a long time and had been grieving for many years. He knew loss from his own marriage breakdown, and Skye had lost her husband in the most horrific way, an accident at work, so Zack should realise that it would take time for her to let love back into her life. He could see how much she cared for him, surely?

She'd spent most of the evening wining and dining clients and it had reminded her of her old life, not in a good way. She used to dress in such finery and pretend to be someone she wasn't for her work. She would engage the target and elicit valuable information from them without arousing suspicion. Tonight, she'd done the same with their new customers, although she'd been finding out how they could improve their service and what the clients were looking for in an activity centre. It had actually been a fun way to utilise her skills in some small way, at first, and she'd begun to feel like she could change and become the woman Zack wanted her to be, the woman she wanted to be.

Then her hands began shaking and tears threatened to flow, so she clamped her eyes tightly shut for a second. She felt like she'd been winded, as those memories of Zack's declarations of love intertwined with images of her past and pushed her over the edge of reason. It hurt like hell to be reminded of Reece and how she was letting him down by finally beginning to move on. She could picture Zack's dark eyes, too, and hated herself for hurting him, but he shouldn't have said what he did about owning her house. It made her want to throw her few meagre belongings into a bag and run again.

She swung her hoodie down from behind the door and pulled it on over her dress. It was so dark now no one would see her, and most people were either wandering the grounds in the moonlight or dancing in the marquee. Slamming the office door shut and hearing the lock click securely, she didn't hang around to see if Zack was looking for her, but grabbed handfuls of the skirt of her dress and ran around the edge of the estate to her little cottage door. She was properly crying by now, which was something she rarely let herself indulge in, but she felt thoroughly misunderstood and miserable. Stepping through the dark front door, she reached for the light switch, as an arm shot out and grabbed her, pulling her into the house. She was so shocked she fleetingly thought about Leo, who was safely sleeping at the estate, before her instincts kicked in and she swung her arm up to connect with her attacker's face.

Chapter Thirty-Nine

Zack was striding across the grass towards the entrance of the marquee and Thea was surprised to see his face creased with worry. 'What's up?' she asked, reaching out to touch his arm to grab his attention, as he was about to walk straight past her.

'I can't find Skye. Have you seen her?' he asked. Thea hid a giggle behind her hand about the fact that he was worried if Skye was out of his sight for more than a second. She could pretty much beat the crap out of most men, so Thea wasn't concerned by the fact that he couldn't find her right now.

'She's probably dancing with Marlo somewhere. Do you want me to help you look for her? It's been an amazing night,' she gazed up at him before realising that something actually was wrong.

'We had a row. I asked her to move in and she stormed off. Now I can't find her,' he said, craning his neck to see if he could catch a glimpse of her midnight blue dress.

'You asked her to move in!' exclaimed Thea.

'What's wrong with that?' he asked, stomping around. 'It's what normal people do when they love each other.' Thea jolted in surprise at his candour, but she wasn't even sure he knew what he had just said, as he was so agitated.

'Skye's not like normal people,' explained Thea. 'She's only herself to rely on for years and it scares her to need people.' She patted Zack on the arm for reassurance and looked around to see where Skye was.

'She said she was going home,' he explained, looking tired and old suddenly. Thea felt sorry for him as this day hadn't turned out quite how he had expected it to.

'Home to your house?' Seeing him flinch, Thea continued,

feeling her stomach turn over suddenly. 'To the cottage? She wouldn't go there in the dark on her own, though, would she?' Thea tried not to look as worried as she suddenly felt. She remembered Skye talking about seeing men following her and she was sure she'd glimpsed someone at the estate entrance the other day. Her stomach clenched in panic and she grabbed Zack's arm. 'Are all of the children asleep?'

'Yes,' he said impatiently. 'Mike and Marlo have just gone in to see them.'

'We need to check she's not gone to the cottage alone. She's mentioned someone loitering in the fields a few times and I'm sure I saw a man standing looking at your house the other day. It was fleeting, but he was there.'

'I told Skye it was probably someone walking their dog. She didn't say it had happened more than once!' Zack cried, turning and racing in the direction of the cottage so that Thea had to struggle to keep up. She was glad she'd changed into flat shoes an hour ago, as her feet were hurting from dancing so much. She grabbed Zack's arm again to slow him down, but rushed as fast as she could as she had a really bad feeling about this and hoped that she was wrong.

Thea was out of breath when they got to the cottage, but the door was wide open and the lights were still off. They raced up the path, but stopped in shock as two figures battled in front of them. Zack appeared momentarily stunned and rooted to the spot, observing someone attacking Skye, who was still in her beautiful dress. Thea guessed that what stopped him was the way she was defending herself. The scene looked like something out of a martial arts film, as they flew around the room.

Thea pushed past Zack as he snapped himself out of it and jumped forward to protect Skye. The moon moved up in the sky and shone a light into the room as Zack reached out and swung a punch at Skye's attacker, just as he managed to pin her arms to her sides in front of him.

'Reece!' cried Thea. Zack's fist connected with the attacker's face and he was knocked out cold, as his arms had been holding Skye and he hadn't seen the strike coming. Skye turned and saw who was behind her as he fell. Her face took on a sickening pallor and she looked at the man behind her in shock, then swivelled back to Thea, before she began to fall in a cold faint. Zack reached out and caught her, wrapping his arms around her and gently easing her onto the couch as Thea turned the switch and the room was filled with light.

Zack stood up and went to grab the phone from his pocket to call the police before Thea stopped him. 'What the hell is going on?' he demanded to know, shooting a worried look at Skye and the man slumped on the floor. 'You called him Reece. Skye's Reece? He's dead.'

'He's not dead,' said Thea mournfully. 'That's him.'

Zack stared at Thea as if she had two heads and started pacing the room in confusion. He bent down to Skye who was murmuring, but still not conscious, and wrapped a blanket around her to keep her warm. He eyed the man with suspicion and kicked his foot more gently than he clearly would have liked, to see if he was still out cold. Thea looked at Reece sadly, but drank in his features and bent to touch his hand. Zack looked at her in horror. 'What the hell is going on here, Thea? How do you know him?'

'He's Flo's dad,' she said sadly.

Chapter Forty

Zack's face was as white as Skye's now, but he hadn't called the police. He sat down next to Skye in shock and placed her head gently in his lap while he smoothed his hand over her hair. He didn't know what the hell to do now, but knew he couldn't make any decisions before he knew the whole damn story.

Thea looked like she'd seen a ghost and Zack's stomach dropped at the thought of Skye being hurt. He shouldn't have argued with her or let her walk home alone. This was his fault. He stared at the slumped form on the floor and took in his chiselled features and blonde hair. This was Leo's dad? Flo's dad too, apparently. 'Does Skye know about Flo?' he ground out menacingly.

'No,' said Thea bitterly, shutting the front door, then kneeling down and putting Reece's head in her lap.

'He wasn't fighting her,' she sobbed. 'I'm guessing he broke in and was trying to find out what she was doing here. Skye must have disturbed him and tried to beat the crap out of him,' she said angrily. 'She always has to come out on top.' Zack couldn't believe what he was hearing and was horrified at Thea's tone and censure of Skye.

'What has she ever done to you, Thea?' he asked, genuinely wanting to understand.

'If only you knew,' she cried, wiping her wet face with the back of her hands and smudging her mascara across her cheeks.

'So tell me,' he demanded, gently laying Skye's head down on the couch as he had seen she had woken now, but was staying deadly still, and he knew she would want to hear this too.

'Skye worked for a government agency called LUCAN,' Thea said, as if she was daydreaming and not really all there. Zack started in surprise at finding this out about Skye, but didn't want to stop Thea now. 'She was part of an elite team who kept the country safe. I'd heard of the team as I worked there too, but we'd never met. There was an accident one night and her field team were killed. Skye wasn't there, but Reece was. Everyone thought he died in the explosion.'

Zack looked at her huddled form in confusion. She kept methodically stroking Reece's head as if he was a child.

'But he wasn't dead?' questioned Zack in a steely tone.

'No,' carried on Thea. 'He was thrown clear by the blast. He hid for a while as he thought it was too dangerous to return. He knew there had to be a mole in the team. He came back when it was safe, but by then Skye had disappeared.'

'He left Skye to think he was dead?' gasped Zack, appalled.

'He thought it was for the best,' defended Thea, looking up and then bowing her head again at the anger blazing in Zack's eyes. 'He thought the people who killed his team might go after Skye and Leo. By the time the threat was gone, he knew it was too late. Then he met me,' she said possessively. 'He asked me to help him find her, as I was the best technical tracker they had,' she saw the incredulity on Zack's face and smiled a bitter smile at him.

'I used to be the top of my field. I could hack any system, track anyone and delete whole towns from existence. I wasn't always as useless and pathetic as I am now,' she said defensively, hating the scorn she saw.

'So, you found her?' he said angrily.

'Not for years,' said Thea, taking a deep breath and laying Reece down on the floor so that she could stand up. She looked at her watch to see how long he'd been out for. It had been mere minutes, although it felt like an age to Zack. She walked towards the fridge to get some ice to wake Reece up.

'Thea!' commanded Zack. 'How did you find her?'

'Technology changes, and when I found out I was pregnant I was angry with her. He didn't want kids with me, just with her.' Thea looked over at Skye, who hadn't moved an inch, before turning to put the ice in a tea towel, ready to apply to Reece's forehead.

'I tried something new and bingo! I had a trail from a couple of years ago. I could see she moved around and then I decided to see what all the fuss was about. If she was so perfect, I wanted to know why, so I brought her here.'

'How the hell could you do that?' Zack demanded to know.

'I knew you had a cottage up for rent, so I placed ads where she'd see them. She thought she was so clever, but she still had regular haunts at her old home. I left subliminal messages everywhere. When anyone else called for the cottage I rerouted the call to a contact and he told them it was booked. When she called, he said it was hers and available straight away. I used a photo of your granddad, as I knew your pretty face would scare her away. She hadn't been near a man for years. Then I sent a friend in to spook her a little. Your granddad would have reminded her of her own dad and home. It worked a treat.' She was marching the words out, but Zack felt sick at what she was saying. 'I hated Skye then, but that was before I knew her.' She started to sob, and reached down to place the ice-cold tea towel onto Reece's forehead.

Zack bent down to stop her, although what he really wanted to do was to forcibly pick up this madwoman and eject her from the cottage. 'He might be dangerous.'

'He would never hurt a hair on her head,' she said through her tears. 'He loves her.'

Zack felt like he'd been punched and Skye leant her arm on the couch and tried to sit up, before she fainted again. Zack knew she'd be reeling from what she'd heard. She wouldn't be able to believe what Thea had done. Zack rushed over to help her to sit up. He knew Thea would be aware Skye could have heard some of what she'd just said. She wiped her arm across her face and stood staring at Skye, a completely different person to the one Skye and Zack had thought they knew. Thea couldn't move from the spot.

Skye looked at Reece and a sob broke from her throat. 'Get out!' she screamed at Thea. 'Get out of my sight and if I ever see you again, I swear I will break your neck and dance around your body. Get out!'

Thea fumbled and fell before rushing for the door, tears streaming down her face. She would head back to the estate to get Flo, Zack realised. She wouldn't want to be alone tonight, and would also fear what Skye would do if she came across Flo later.

Chapter Forty-One

Reece groaned and sat up gingerly, rubbing his jaw and focusing immediately on Skye before turning his head to look for Thea. 'She's gone,' sobbed Skye. 'I think you'd better leave too.'

'Skye,' he implored, moving to hold her cold hand before seeing Zack sitting so close to her, looking at him with disdain, and dropping the idea. 'Please let me explain.'

'How can you explain leaving me for years to bring up our son alone, thinking his father was dead?' Skye raged, trying to get up, but blood rushed to her head and she stumbled and sat down again, as Zack jumped up and settled her onto the couch. He then walked to the kitchen to grab the whisky bottle he had seen there a few weeks ago. Keeping his eyes trained on Reece, he picked up the glasses and Scotch and walked back. Placing two glasses on the low table by the couch, he poured two hefty slugs, handed one to Skye and took a deep draught himself, ignoring Reece.

Skye sipped her drink and colour began to flood back into her face. She looked at Reece as if she'd never seen him before. All of the hopes and dreams she'd had with this man, the memories; they shattered before her eyes. He wasn't the prince she'd made him out to be. He was a weak man who put himself before his family.

'Skye,' he said pleadingly. 'I thought you'd be safer without me. I didn't know Marcus had set us up at first, and thought the threat was still out there. I thought I could protect you if they didn't know I was alive.'

'But you didn't think it might be a good idea to stop my suffering by telling me that my husband wasn't dead?' Skye saw Zack flinch, but there wasn't much she could do about that now. She was surprised he hadn't run for the hills, to be honest.

'I couldn't come back until Marcus was dead and the threat had been neutralised. I spent months proving it was him, then he killed himself so he didn't have to face me, the bastard. I came looking for you then,' he explained.

'You'd left it too late. By leaving me to protect our son, without the information that the threat was gone, I spent years and years running, scared for the safety of our child.'

Reece looked aghast and Skye saw a new understanding come to Zack. A few things would start to slot into place. Perhaps he would finally understand that it was no wonder Skye was always so skittish about strange men in the fields and not happy about settling down. She'd endured hell. She knew he hated the lies, but must understand a parent's need to protect their child. She could even sympathise with the other man before him, in a weird kind of way, although the route he'd taken was wrong and it had almost destroyed her. She certainly wasn't ready to forgive him yet.

Reece rubbed his temples and got up to sit on the armchair opposite them. Skye guessed that he really wanted to wipe the floor with this man who was sitting so close to her. He could take him in seconds, but he probably didn't think that would help his cause and he was right. She bet he was confused about seeing Thea too. Had he discovered the messages Thea said she'd left for Flo's dad, and followed her here months ago? Had he had found he actually missed her, and his curiosity at the clues she'd left made him come and check them out? Did he love her?

Reece spoke in an even tone as if he was trying hard to control his emotions. 'I was so shocked when I first saw you, Skye. Then I saw both you and Thea together and my world blew apart. What the hell has Thea been doing all this time? Has she known where you were all along, and wanted to keep you to herself as a punishment to me? If so, why run away and bring me here?' he sighed. 'I'd originally wanted to confront you both, but I was called in by LUCAN and had to bide my time. I had been on the trail of the people who killed our team

211

and I had to make a choice to stay, or lose them again.' Skye looked horrified that he'd made this decision, but he grimaced and carried on. 'I'd spent years tracking them and couldn't risk them going to ground. I made the decision to follow the lead and prayed that you and Thea would still be here when he returned. I left one of my most trusted people here watching you, but it was still the most challenging decision of my life. It was the right one, though,' he looked into Skye's angry eyes and almost baulked before he continued, 'As the threat had been neutralised and my family would always be safe now. I'm so sorry. I didn't know you were scared.' He looked troubled by the idea that he'd caused so much pain. 'I thought you'd decided to leave when you heard I was gone and chosen a normal life to bring up our son. I hoped it would be safer for you both as far away from me as you could get.'

'That wasn't your choice to make,' yelled Skye, losing all sense of calm and jumping up and swinging for Reece. Zack stood up and reached for her, but Reece was faster and he caught her and pulled her to him, where she broke down and cried as if the world was ending. 'I'm so sorry, Skye,' he soothed, staring directly at Zack over her head, as if silently telling him to leave. Zack stood his ground and waited for Skye to decide what was happening next. Skye glanced his way and understood from his body language that he wanted to drag her from Reece's arms, but knew that could make her push him further away.

She gulped in some air, and couldn't believe she was feeling Reece's arms around her again. It felt so good, but he had broken her trust and, although she was elated that he was alive, he'd crushed her again by lying to her all these years. How would she tell Leo? She pushed him away and started pacing the room, her dress swirling around her legs and creating a pool of stars as she moved.

'What about Thea? You didn't take long to move on to another woman, or several, by the sounds of it?'

Reece took a deep breath and accepted the bullet. 'I met Thea a while after you'd disappeared. I was lonely and I missed you.'

'Not enough to find me,' she said bitterly.

'At first I thought it was safer to leave you alone. Then I thought maybe I'd made a mistake, but it was too late. I asked Thea to find you. We spent so much time together, things just happened. I told her I didn't want anything serious, but she didn't listen.'

'It's pretty serious now Leo has a half-sister!'

'I didn't know about that until recently. I saw you together, but thought maybe she'd left because she'd met someone else. It's why I've been hanging around and trying to work out what was going on here.'

'She was jealous of me,' said Skye, darkly.

'What?' said Reece in confusion, reaching for her glass and taking a gulp of the fiery whisky.

'She wanted to find out why you loved me and not her, so it seems she looked a bit harder for me when she actually wanted to find me, then set me up to come here.'

'Bloody hell,' sighed Reece, putting his head in his hands and cursing the mess he'd inadvertently made. 'She sent me messages to bring me here too.'

'She told me she'd sent messages to Flo's dad, but cleverly omitted who you were. Why would she do that, knowing I was here? It's sick!' Skye wanted to hunt Thea down and demand answers.

Zack looked up at them and his eyes blazed at seeing them so near each other. 'She wanted to see who you'd choose when they both had your child,' he ground out, looking sick, and holding the whisky glass in a death grip as if he was controlling his anger but wanted to throw it at the interloper.

Reece stared dismissively at Zack and squared his shoulders. 'Who are you anyway? I've seen you hanging around Skye and my son. What's his story?' he demanded to know from Skye. Zack straightened his back and stood tall to show he wasn't about to be intimidated by anyone.

Skye stood between them and placed a hand on each of their chests, thinking her heart would break. 'He's the man who has brought me back to life,' she said simply, making Zack smile, tiredly, and Reece look like he'd been kicked in

213

the balls. She wondered if he'd thought about her being with other men over the years, and if the reality of it was quite different. Zack slipped his hand into Skye's and she squeezed it reassuringly. 'I think Reece and I need to sit and talk, though, Zack,' she said gently.

Reece grinned at Zack, clearly letting him know he would make this his victory, but luckily Zack had felt Skye's intent and obviously understood he'd made the mistake earlier that evening of pushing his luck. He would have to rely on his gut instinct and trust her. He bent and softly kissed her lips, and Skye knew he would be enjoying seeing Reece's knuckles go white as he tried to control his anger.

'You sure?' asked Zack, ignoring Reece. When Skye nodded, he whispered into her ear, 'I'll check on the children, then wait to hear from you. Phone me when he's gone.' He gave one last look of warning to Reece, before turning and letting himself out.

Chapter Forty-Two

Zack shut the door quietly behind him and strode back to his house. People were still milling around, and he was surprised to see them as he had completely forgotten about the ball. He nodded a greeting to one or two, but was glad to see that the evening was drawing to a close and taxis were lining the drive to collect the last few revellers. Zack shook hands and chatted with a handful of people as he passed and plastered a smile onto his face while he waited for them to leave. He was glad to have the distraction, to be honest, as it had been a tough night to say the least.

He had tried to stay calm for Skye, but admitted that he had felt betrayed when he learned that Skye had been lying to him all along. Not only was she some kind of secret government agent, retired or not, but the whole background to her life she had given him was probably a pack of lies. He grudgingly admitted that, from what he had heard tonight, she had been scared and protecting her son, but surely she should have started to trust him by now? Would she ever have opened up and told him the truth? He doubted it, hearing how well she had lied to everyone since she had arrived. No-one had suspected a thing and he should have had an inkling by the way she, so expertly, set up Skye-Safe. Seeing her fight off her attacker tonight had shocked him to the core. It had looked like two assassins fighting in a television programme and he had ploughed in without a thought for his own safety. He suddenly worried if Emmie would be safe with people like Skye, Reece and Thea around. What the hell was the world coming to, when a little country village like this had three combat agents amongst them? What if there were more? He rubbed his tired eyes and turned to walk to the house. His prevalent thought was to see his daughter's face and be by her side. He wanted to check on Leo too, and make sure he was sleeping soundly.

After sitting for a while with Emmie and Leo, then checking Mike and Marlo were asleep in one of the spare rooms, Zack decided he wouldn't be able to sleep that night and he might as well go and sober up with a strong coffee.

He felt exhausted and really hated the idea of leaving Skye with Reece. He sounded like a complete lothario and the fact that he was probably still legally Skye's husband made his shoulders sag in defeat as he pushed open the kitchen door. He started in surprise when he saw Thea asleep with her head on her arms on the kitchen table. She must have waited for him but couldn't stay awake. His gut wrenched and he didn't know what he would say to her. He felt angry at what she'd put Skye through, and let down that she hadn't confided in him about Skye's background.

Zack had thought Thea would be too ashamed to stick around, but she must have not wanted to disturb Flo, or maybe she was scared of Reece and didn't want to be alone? The thought struck him and he started to panic about leaving him with Skye. He walked around the big wooden table that stood in the middle of the huge state-of-the-art kitchen and, none too gently, roused Thea from her sleep. She jumped in alarm, her eyes foggy before they focused on him. She slumped back into her chair.

'Is he dangerous?' Zack asked, levelly.

'Not to Skye,' Thea said bitterly. 'Like I said, he loves her.'

Zack went to the cupboard and got out two mugs. He then switched on the coffee machine and filled it with water, trying to give himself time to calm down. 'What about you? Does he love you?'

Thea sighed and wrung her hands together. 'I really don't know. I'm not sure he let himself care about anyone after Skye. Back then I thought he used the accident as an excuse to get her out of his life. He kept saying how he never wanted kids and I wondered if the commitment of a child made him

216

push her away. He changed his mind, though, and tried to find her. When she disappeared, he made me try everything, but she was gone. He'd left it too late to decide that he wanted his family and ruined his own life. In time, he came to accept it and seemed to have concluded that he was right and they were safer without him.'

'That's when he started the affair with you?' Zack wanted to know. He placed a steaming mug of coffee in front of Thea and sat down opposite her, but she still couldn't look him in the eye.

'No, that came later.'

Thea rubbed her tired eyes. 'Reece had flings with women, including my boss, but eventually he turned to me. I think it was because he could talk freely about his past with me. He led me to believe the other women were out of the picture by then, but it seems I was wrong. My boss had set her sights on him for years, apparently, and when she finally got her claws in him, she revelled at letting me know. It was the same day I found out I was pregnant. I wonder now if she had anything to do with Skye once hurting herself on a job. Skye told me the safety checks failed, but knowing Skye now, she wouldn't let that happen.' Tears slipped down Thea's nose and she brushed them angrily away, although it looked like the coffee was seeping into her veins and gradually giving her a burst of energy as she appeared more awake. He thought she must be completely drained from the night's events and possibly wished she had kept Reece away. Who cared if he hadn't a clue about his daughter? Zack knew this was harsh coming from a father, but Reece had given up the rights to his child by abandoning him years ago. He'd let his wife and child run scared for years, not telling them they were safe. The thought of Skye being his wife, while Thea herself was only a mistress, probably made bile rise up in her throat. 'My family are right about me; I'm a complete waste of space. I expect Reece hates me now, too, as I knew he had a daughter and didn't say anything.'

Zack tried to feel sympathy for Thea as he saw a glimmer of the woman he had known for a while now trying to break free, but the creature in front of him had turned into something he didn't understand, and the pain she'd brought to others was hard to fathom.

'You also knew he had a wife,' Zack ground out, making Thea glance up and meet his eye.

'He doesn't,' she said simply. 'My job was to wipe all record of them both. That's how we met. I gave him a new surname and both of them ceased to exist. The marriage they had died with their old identities.'

Zack was dumbfounded that things like this actually went on, but couldn't help a flicker of elation that Skye was no longer Reece's wife.

Chapter Forty-Three

Skye's bones were heavy and she wanted to crawl under her bedcovers and sleep for a week. She felt like she'd been hit by a bus. Every part of her ached and felt broken. Reece sat opposite her and implored her to give him another chance, but she still couldn't get past the fact that he'd abandoned her and their son, scared and without a safe place to hide. He had left her to cope alone, believing him dead, because he felt bad about their team dying while he had survived. She understood that he believed he was still in danger, but what about her? Surely if he was in peril at that time, so would she have been? If anyone on the inside knew he was alive, they would have known about her too. He had left her to fend for herself, however he tried to justify it by saying he was protecting them. What planet did he live on, if he thought it was safer for her to believe he was dead and people were still chasing her? She had run for years, looking over her shoulder at every turn, because she didn't know the threat from Marcus had been neutralised.

She hadn't moved on in her life at all until recently, and wondered if Reece would ever have come back if he hadn't seen her with Zack. She was bitter that she had put her own life on hold for so long, yearning for a man who was living happily somewhere else. The man she had idolised for all those years had really died on the day of the explosion. The man in front of her felt like a complete stranger and it made her soul weary. Her heart was shattering with the loss of him all over again.

'Skye, please,' Reece begged, taking hold of her hand and turning it over to kiss her pulse. She closed her eyes at the intimate gesture, but then slipped her hand from his and put space between them.

'I thought you would both be better off without me. I was useless at protecting our team. Seeing them all die was horrific. I managed to drag myself to safety, but should have been blown up, too. I felt I'd let them down and would ruin your life as well.'

'You were right,' Skye said bitterly, turning on him. 'You did annihilate me by leaving us,' she spat at him. 'What about protecting the mother of your child and your own son? I had to be both parents to our child, while you were alive somewhere screwing God knows how many women to help appease your guilt and fill your mind! Now you have two children who don't know you. Is that what you want?'

'Of course not!' Reece said furiously, visibly trying, but failing, to curb his temper. 'I haven't forgotten how good it felt to hold my wife and I don't intend to let you go now I've found you again. I don't want that other man bringing up my child or screwing my wife! For years I've blocked out all thoughts of you and Leo but, now you're here, I'm going to get you both back. I need you in my life, Skye; our son too.'

Skye raised her head to the heavens and sighed in exasperation at the man before her. She was completely wrung out and didn't want to look at him any more. She needed some breathing space and couldn't have that with him here. 'You need to go and see Thea and meet Flo. Not tonight. I don't think that's a good idea, but go back to wherever you've been staying and we can talk again tomorrow.'

'Skye, please…' Reece pleaded. 'Let me stay here tonight and we can try and sort out this mess.'

'You made this chaos, Reece,' Skye felt a bit sick at using his name again as surely it would be different now? Maybe he had kept it, or maybe it was now a pet name between him and Thea. The thought made her run to the sink and be sick. Holding her stomach, she looked over to him and felt the pain of losing him all over again. It had hurt so much last time, but she had then had to contend with looking after Leo and moving around from country to country. She ran a glass under the tap and gulped down some water, before filling the glass with the whisky Zack had left on the kitchen counter and swallowing down a huge mouthful, gasping as the alcohol hit her empty stomach.

Skye turned to the man she had loved so deeply. 'Thea wanted you to come here.' She saw his face register the comment in surprise and he frowned in confusion. 'She probably wanted you to meet Flo and find me with Zack.' She saw him flinch and was glad he felt her pain. 'She befriended me and then set out to destroy my life. She set me up to come here so she could get to know me, then drew you here to destroy the last traces of what we had.'

'Why would she do that? You and I hadn't seen each other in years.'

'She wanted to see what the real competition was,' said Skye mockingly. Reece grabbed her hands, pulled her to him and kissed her with such passion that she crumbled and melted into his familiar embrace. How she had missed this! He hugged her to him and inhaled the familiar scent of her hair. She sighed and let him hold her for a moment, her pulse racing and her heart almost beating out of her chest. This is what she had dreamed about. She had cried herself to sleep remembering how it felt to be held in his arms, knowing she would never see him again, but now she sighed and gently pushed him away. Too many things had happened in the last few hours for her to be able to think clearly. She was overjoyed that Reece was alive, but he wasn't who she had built him up to be. He was just a regular man who made mistakes like the rest of them. His inadequacy had cost her years of her life to grief and fear, though. She didn't know if it was something she could forgive him for.

'I still love you...' he said forlornly, 'I know things have changed and I pray you can forgive my weakness. You're such a strong woman and I desperately hope you'll come to realise what I did seemed like the right decision at the time.' Looking at the home she had made, with the occasional photo of her and Leo smiling into the camera, he faced his own loss. He evidently realised now that he had missed spending time with an amazing woman and sharing in his son growing up. She could see him steel his nerve and decide he wouldn't miss any more of his son's life. Skye was watching the thoughts flit across his face and waited for him to remember his other child. When the thought registered, he looked guiltily at her.

'I didn't know about the baby,' he implored her to understand.

'I know.' Skye thought that Thea had been truthful about that, but she'd doubted it until she saw his face when he realised there was another child involved. 'You have to take responsibility this time,' said Skye. 'Go and see Thea tomorrow and find out what the hell that deranged witch has been doing with our lives this whole time,' she said tiredly.

Chapter Forty-Four

It was two weeks since the ball and Zack had barely seen Skye. He put his sunglasses on to cover his eyes, exhausted from lack of sleep, and tried to smile as Emmie chattered away on the journey to school.

Skye had arrived looking washed out and enervated the morning after the ball and had found him slumped by the phone asleep. She had been upset about Reece and had completely forgotten to call Zack. He had waited by the phone all night. She'd wearily sat down beside him and touched his arm to wake him, then started talking in a low voice about her past and the scars it had left behind.

Zack noticed Belle at the school gates and she gave him a jaunty wave now they were all 'such good friends', but he ignored her and bent down to hug his daughter, making her squirm in embarrassment.

The school had been awash with gossip about his and Skye's blossoming relationship and he knew Belle wanted to get the inside track on what was happening, as he'd heard that she had been bragging that she knew them both terribly well.

Zack glanced up as Thea pushed the pram up to the school gates and Allie gave her a quick kiss and ran to meet her friends. She nodded to Zack, but his body language was telling her to back off. He wondered if she was happy at the way her life had turned out lately. She would know Leo was already at school in early morning club, but she wasn't used to walking alone and was probably terrified she'd bump into Skye now. She had thought she was being clever by bringing Skye here, but she had been stupid. She had been a jealous harridan and now she had destroyed all of their lives. She should have told Reece where Skye was, but she wanted to find out what was so special about her for herself first. She had bitterly said to Zack that surely, no one could be that perfect, but she was asking the wrong man, as to him, she was.

Thea had mentioned that after meeting Skye, she could see it wasn't really her looks that men fell for; it was something about her personality that drew them in. Thea herself had fallen for it, too. Much as she had passionately wanted to hate Skye, she didn't. Thea had planned revenge on the woman whom Reece desired above all others, but she had made a terrible mistake. Skye could have been her loving and loyal friend and Thea missed her crazy moods and grumpy face. Zack hadn't really wanted to listen to Thea's self pity, but she seemed to be waiting for him by the school most mornings now, as if he would solve all her problems. He wouldn't.

She'd explained that it had been tearing her apart, knowing Reece was alive, and she had been a nervous wreck seeing Skye fall for Zack, unaware of the truth about Reece. She'd had to act, even if it meant losing Reece and Skye forever and them being a family again. Skye deserved to know the truth. Seeing Zack walk around like he wanted to punch anyone who came within ten feet of him made her feel even worse. She had started this as a way to make them pay, but now they were all suffering, herself included. She apologised to Zack practically every day, but he wasn't ready to listen.

Zack walked back up the road and headed towards home. As he got near the house, he changed direction and aimed for the cottage. He couldn't keep away from Skye any longer and decided that he had to know one way or the other if Reece was back to stay. He couldn't believe it when Thea had tearfully told them what they all did. Seeing Skye and Reece fight had nearly given him a heart attack. Thea had explained that she and Skye were no longer working for LUCAN and he had just had to face up to his own insecurities. Skye was an asset to the business and her other skills and knowledge would only benefit them, too. He remembered that he'd worried about Belle frightening Skye and laughed bitterly at his own naivety. He wondered if she was scared of anything. Then he remembered her coming to him when she had thought someone was in the field. She had let him comfort her. He realised it had probably been Reece in the field and he wondered if he would have tried to head him off, if he had known who he was. Zack was sure Reece was pretty resourceful when he wanted to be and he wouldn't have stayed away any longer than he had to, once he'd found his wife and son again.

Knocking on the door and waiting for someone to answer it, Zack felt like grabbing his keys and letting himself into his own house. Skye had gently asked for a little space to decide what to do, but he couldn't stand back any longer.

The door opened and Reece stood in front of him, half-naked and towelling himself dry with one of Zack's towels. Skye reached out to pull Reece indoors and he stepped back with a big grin on his face as he realised who was there. 'Oh, for God's sake, Reece,' said Skye in exasperation.

'Did he stay overnight?' said Zack in a deathly quiet tone, his fists bunching at his sides.

'Of course he didn't, you idiot,' yelled Skye, trying to shove Reece indoors and step outside to speak to Zack.

Reece ambled inside looking pleased with himself and flexing his wet muscles. He'd just got out of the shower, having lied to Skye that the one at his hotel had broken the night before. Evidently he thought it had worked a treat, but she'd called Zack and told him Reece was there and why. Zack hadn't expected to find him half naked and still here though. How many showers did one man need?

Reece had been to see Thea the previous night for a couple of hours and met Flo, too. He wouldn't be able to think about that now, though, as Zack was threatening his position with Skye. Zack understood from Thea that it would take minutes to destroy his business, with Recce's contacts. The way Skye was shouting at him suggested that she would side with Zack, so Reece would be more of an idiot to cause extra friction.

Reece would have to bide his time and wait this one out if he had any sense. Undoubtedly he was banking on the fact that the more time she spent with him, the more she would remember how things used to be. Not a chance, thought Zack. Reece smiled tightly at Zack, who was still standing outside, and gave him a patronising little wave to wind him up.

Zack's muscles knotted up in annoyance. He wanted to plough in and slap the stupid smile from Reece's face. He didn't know what game he was playing, but he'd soon learn that he had left it too late to fix things with Skye. Now that Zack was cooling down and thinking more rationally, he realised he had got to know Skye pretty well over the last few months and she wouldn't take Reece's, or Thea's, betrayal lightly. She would be devastated and hurting, but she had mastered how to be strong over the last eight years on her own. She would survive this and come out tougher than ever.

Zack leant in, his eyes never leaving Reece's, and took Skye by surprise by kissing her on the lips, making her jump slightly, then sink into him and kiss him gently back. She'd been so confused these last few days, she'd forgotten how good it felt to be kissed by Zack. Zack smiled in triumph as he watched Reece walk away in disgust.

'Are you back together?' was all he asked, breaking away from her and taking a deep breath, ready for a deathly blow, but needing to know the truth.

'It's more complicated than that.' Skye looked into Zack's eyes and seemed shocked to see how run-down he looked.

'You haven't been at the site. It's due to open to the public officially in a few weeks. I need your help to get it ready.' Zack knew he sounded desperate and she wouldn't know what to do to make him feel better. This situation was hard on all of them. So far, she hadn't let Reece meet Leo. She didn't know how the hell she would break it to her son that his dad had returned from the dead and he didn't know what to advise her, either.

'Are you okay?' she asked, tears of frustration filling her eyes, taking his hand in her own.

'I miss you,' he said simply, gently turning her wrist over so that he could kiss her pulse, which was racing erratically at his touch.

'I miss you, too,' she said quietly, not pulling her hand away and resting her other hand on his arm, making him tense up and then draw her to him, while shielding her from prying eyes with his body.

'Are you back together?' Zack asked again, his voice cracking with emotion.

'No. That part of my life is over.' Skye seemed to realise that it was true as she said it and she suddenly looked like a weight had been lifted from her shoulders.

'Does he know that?' Zack ground out, hugging Skye even harder, before she squealed slightly and he let go.

'We kind of talked about it. He's not happy, but he's coming to understand that he's too late,' she smiled gently up at him and he swooped down and captured her lips with his, uncaring who saw them now. She pulled the door shut, leaving them standing on the doorstep, and melted into his arms. The relief of holding her near again made him weak with happiness. Whatever happened now, they would get through it – together.

Chapter Forty-Five

It had been a few weeks since Reece's reappearance. Leo was so delirious with joy at meeting his father, he had very quickly forgotten that he hadn't been around for the first eight years of his life, much to Skye's disgust. Although she was happy that Leo was excited and hadn't made a scene, she wasn't sure Leo really understood where his dad had been. They had kind of explained that something awful had happened with their work that had kept them apart all this time. Leo had looked to her for reassurance and, with a nod of her head, he had flown into his father's arms. Seeing them together broke Skye's heart, but filled it with joy too. Sitting in her usual place behind the school gates, tucked behind the bike shed, she sat in a world of her own, glad she'd managed to avoid seeing Thea so far. Zack had just given her a chaste kiss and left to talk to Mike and Marlo, so she had some time with her own thoughts.

Reece had met with her a few times and explained that Thea had been eaten up with jealousy, and Skye could grudgingly admit that maybe Thea had tried to turn things around at the end, but she wasn't ready to forgive her yet.

Skye spotted Thea not far away and she looked up from her position in the playground. Their eyes clashed. Skye wondered if she had decided to face up to her part in this and approach her. Had she seen Zack quickly kiss her before walking away? A few other parents had noticed and they were whispering about it, not being very subtle, as they kept looking her way. The school playground soon started to buzz with excitement at this fantastic bit of gossip about the new couple snogging behind the school bike sheds, of all places. She knew a few of them had seen Reece coming out of her cottage too, so the school was awash with scandalous glee. She bet they wondered how a boring and unglamorous woman like Skye could have such an exciting love life.

Thea had stepped back to give her some space and was glaring at anyone who was staring, until they turned away and left them alone. The school bell rang and Skye turned to see Thea had changed her mind and was behind her on the grass. She sucked in some air and stood up, brushing her jean shorts down and preparing for battle. This wasn't really the place to talk, but it seemed that the universe had other ideas.

Leo and Allie came bounding out of school together and then stopped short when they saw Thea and Skye looking at each other. They had both spoken openly about the arrival of Leo's dad and had mentioned to Skye that they couldn't work out why this would cause problems between Allie's aunt and Skye. Skye felt bad for them, but didn't want to elaborate. Allie had seemed excited to meet Leo's dad, who they explained had been working away. Leo had originally said to Allie his dad was dead but he had been found alive and well and had been looking for them for a very long time, Skye explained. She had held her breath and waited for the barrage of questions, but they hadn't materialised. For once she was glad at the simplified view some children had of the world.

Leo was so happy and couldn't stop talking about Reece, but she'd overheard him confiding in Allie that he thought his mum had been missing Zack. His dad had told him that, for now, his mum and he were just friends, but he had a feeling that there was more to it than that. Thea had stopped coming round and his mum had said it was because the assault course would be up and running soon, so the after school club at their house was on hold for now. He wasn't stupid, though, and could tell his mum was tense when his dad was around, which made him a bit nervous too. Skye felt like her heart was in her throat as she'd listened, knowing she should move away, but finding her limbs were frozen to the spot.

Leo continued solemnly that his mum had been alone for so long now. It had taken him a while to accept that she might like Zack, but he was getting on really well with Emmie and they had played together with Allie a lot while the new business was being set up. The adults had included them and asked for their help with the design, and they'd had great fun exploring the area and deciding what other kids would like to play with. Now his dad had arrived, things had changed and they didn't go to the estate as much. Skye had berated herself for being such a useless mum and for letting her son feel this way. She felt tears sting the back of her eyes and had been about to turn back down the stairs when Leo spoke again. 'I only get to play with Emmie and you at school now and haven't seen Flo for days; even though she's a baby, I've got used to having her and Thea around. We had one big mixed-up family, and I'd been enjoying not being alone with mum all the time, much as I love her. Now dad's back, I feel a bit weird. I love having a real dad, as I've never had one before, but there is tension in the house. Mum says dad is still going to be travelling a lot, and will only be around from time to time.' Allie didn't say anything, but Skye had heard her get up and go to give Leo a hug. Skye had quickly turned around and run back down the stairs before they realised she'd heard every word.

'Kids,' said Skye. 'How would you like to go to the park for an ice cream?' The kids looked a bit uneasy at first, glancing from Skye to Thea, then jumped for joy at the thought that they were allowed to play together after school again, and they grabbed each other's hands and ran along the school path before the women had a chance to change their minds.

Thea looked like she had spent the night in a field, as her hair was sticking out in every direction, and Skye could almost have felt sorry for her if she didn't hate her so much. Skye nodded towards the park and Thea walked alongside her in silence, her shoulders hunched over as she pushed the pram in front of her like a kind of shield. Skye could see by the look on Thea's face that she couldn't believe Skye wanted to talk to her after all she'd done, but she knew she would have to hear what Skye wanted to say and couldn't run and lick her wounds even if she wanted to. Skye could crush her if she chose to and Thea couldn't blame her if she never spoke to her again. She should be ashamed of what she'd done, and Skye didn't care if she had her reasons and no one cared about how she felt in all this. Skye had only relented slightly as Flo had only just met her dad too and, although she was a baby, she was just as important as Leo.

As they neared the park, the kids saw the ice cream van and squealed in delight. Skye reached into her pocket and realised she'd lost weight as the waistband of her shorts was hanging around her hips. She dug around until she found a couple of pound coins and sent the children to get ice cream and play. Seeing how happy they were to be together again broke Skye's heart. She wondered how they would feel when they found out they were now related, and hated Thea and Reece for putting her in this position.

Thea slumped into the seat they had sat on months ago, when they first met beside the big oak tree, and watched the children run to the play area with huge, melting ice creams that dripped over their fingers as they ran.

'They must have spent the whole pound each. Little monkeys!' exclaimed Thea without thinking.

'You lied to me,' said Skye levelly, not taking her eyes off her son as he licked the side of his ice cream while trying to climb onto the swings.

Thea trembled at Skye's tone and stared at the floor, gently rocking the pram to lull Flo to sleep. 'I know I did. I'm sorry.'

'Why?'

'Hasn't Reece, or Zack, told you?' Thea asked bitterly. Daring to look up, Skye gave her one of her 'are you kidding me?' stares and Thea blushed at her own outburst.

'You love him?' asked Skye simply.

'Do you?' Thea parried, wringing her hands in her lap. Skye watched Thea's body language and could see she was flustered. She really wanted to know who this woman was. The woman who had befriended her and wormed her way into her life, who had used years of training to break down barriers and get information from her. Skye really had been suckered. It was a good job she wasn't working for LUCAN any more or she would have been thrown to the wolves for mistakes like

231

this.

Skye thought carefully about her answer. 'Yes,' she admitted, making Thea cringe. Skye saw her mark hit home and felt a small sense of victory. 'You want him back? Is that why you brought him here? You pushed me towards Zack and then brought the knife down?'

'That's not why I brought him here,' said Thea angrily, kicking out at a tuft of grass and sending mud flying. 'I wanted to know if you still loved him.'

'Why bring me here? Why not just tell him about Flo?' asked Skye in exasperation. 'He would have come and you could have had him to yourself. He wouldn't have known about me, nor I him.'

'I would have always felt like second best. I did anyway,' Thea said sadly.

Chapter Forty-Six

'He saw other women,' said Thea. She watched Skye flinch, but carried on regardless. It all had to be out in the open now, and she wanted Skye to know he wasn't the perfect man she made him out to be. He didn't treat women that well and Thea was finally seeing the light herself. Maybe Reece wasn't all she needed to get a life of her own and move on. It would be ironic if Skye and Reece settled here and she had to move away. Then she remembered Skye kissing Zack and felt a flicker of hope flare in her heart.

'Reece did try to find you at the beginning. You were too well hidden,' Thea admitted. 'Then new technology came to light and I found a way. I wanted to meet you, to meet Leo,' she admitted. 'I wanted to see what all the fuss was about.' She couldn't help herself from sneering slightly.

'So you plotted to bring me here. How?'

'I sent a team to track you. They found out where you went, what your daily routines were, although, with your training, you made it pretty hard for them. I told them you were a potential recruit. They were new and hadn't heard of you before. I then set you up to come here. I put posters of the estate with Zack's granddad all around you. How you missed all of them except for the one in the library is beyond me. I thought you'd be drawn to his eccentric style as he'd remind you of your dad.'

Skye winced. 'You knew about my dad all along, but said nothing as I poured my heart out to you? All the times I confided in you?' she stood up and almost spat at Thea in her rage.

'I didn't know much,' protested Thea, tears dropping from her eyes at the betrayal in Skye's. 'I knew Zack had cottages to

233

let and the timing was perfect. I rerouted the calls to one of my team.'

'The old guy? I knew it didn't sound like Zack.'

'I put off other people who called the ad and set you up to move here. I dropped messages into the papers and magazines you bought and put ads on your computer to draw you in.'

'I can't believe I didn't see it. I didn't see how you were setting me up. I finally let my guard down and you manipulated our friendship from the start for your own end. My God, you are such a bitch!'

'You could never have seen my deception, Skye. I keep telling you. I'm as well trained as you are and I know how to recruit, delete the history of, or track someone. I wanted to see what I was up against before I told Reece about Flo. He said he didn't want a child with me, but he wanted yours.' Skye didn't look convinced. Thea could tell she thought this was another lie, as why wouldn't Reece want another Leo?

'You should have been in my team,' said Skye sarcastically. 'You could have lied with the best of them. They would have given you a gold star.' Thea took the verbal hit, but didn't flinch this time. Skye deserved the truth, however much it hurt.

'I was going to tell Reece. I just didn't expect to like you. I wanted to get you here to cause him as much pain as he'd caused me. I wanted him to see us as friends and despair about what to do. I didn't really care how it would affect you or Leo. I didn't know you then,' she said quietly, her eyes misting in shame.

Skye stared at the woman before her as if considering if she was telling the truth. She looked around to check that the children were still happily playing and saw that Flo was starting to wake.

'I wish now that I hadn't brought him here as I realised, too late, that maybe I was just infatuated and he would never love me like he loved you. Then when I started to like you, I wanted to keep you for myself and not involve him.'

Skye looked flabbergasted and as though she couldn't believe what she was hearing.

234

'I hadn't had a real friend in years and you understood me,' Thea continued. 'Whatever you believe, our friendship was real. When I saw how involved you were becoming with Zack, I couldn't keep Reece away any longer. Suppose you fell in love without knowing Reece was alive?'

'So you decided to interfere and mess up my life again?' accused Skye. 'Do you know how difficult it is, having my son's dead father practically living with me, while the man I've just started dating lives just round the corner?' Thea giggled a bit at this and Skye raised a small smile too. Before they knew it, they were both laughing.

'I haven't forgiven you,' said Skye, when she caught her breath.

'I know,' sighed Thea. 'But it's a start.' The children ran over to see them, hopeful of another ice cream, but Skye beckoned them closer and they all walked home together, the children chatting noisily and Skye and Thea walking side by side in an uneasy silence. At the top of the road the women half smiled at each other, before turning towards their separate homes.

Chapter Forty-Seven

Finally, the day had arrived and they were officially opening Skye-Safe. Skye sighed with joy and smiled at Reece, swatting his hand away from her backside and kicking him in the shins for his efforts. He'd been popping in a bit more lately and Zack, although uncomfortable with it, had little choice but to accept it for now. After the debacle of the ball, they had decided that a small party with all the children from Leo's and Emmie's class would be appropriate to open the site.

So far, there had been loads of smiles and squeals of delight from the children as they explored the new climbing apparatus. The parents who had been at Skye's club had been invited an hour early and given six months' free membership to use the course, which had made them super-excited. They had all hugged Skye, which she had taken good-naturedly before backing away, as soon as politely possible, to hide in the staff room.

She had found Zack sitting staring morosely at his computer and had swung herself into his lap, giving him a fright, before he locked his arms around her in case she decided to escape. He had barely seen her since their kiss at the school and he was getting more and more agitated, observing Reece around the place so much.

'How is it out there?' he asked, nuzzling her neck and she squirmed in his lap, hoping she was making his muscles go hard and his insides begin to boil with lust.

'Zack!' she chided playfully. 'Anyone could come into your office.'

'I don't care!' he growled, doubtless enjoying the feeling of her in his arms. He'd been remarkably patient, but she could see it was wearing thin.

'What about Leo and Emmie?' she gasped between kisses, enjoying the way he kept his arms locked around her.

'They both spoke to me last night,' he said into her neck while trailing kisses down to the soft neckline of her corporate T-shirt.

'What?'

'They said they realised that Reece was here, but Leo said you seemed sad without me.' Skye's mouth hung open in shock, as Zack ran his hands around her backside and then up and into her hair before capturing her mouth in a searing kiss.

Skye revelled in the heat of it before gently breaking away. 'I don't know how we are going to work this out.'

'Me neither,' he agreed, 'but what I do know is that Reece may have come back for you, but you're my girlfriend now.' Skye looked at Zack in admiration for this open declaration from such a private man. 'I think he's realised that he came back too late, whatever the circumstances. He might think there's a chance for you, or he might move on or back to Thea, I don't really care. What I do care about is you, and me, and the kids. We make a good team, not just here at work, but as a family.' Skye sat there in shock, not knowing what to say. It had been just her and Leo for so long and Zack had only ever spoken to her like this once before, on the fateful night of the party. This time she was ready to listen.

'I don't expect you to have all the answers right now, I sure as hell don't have them, but I do know that it's you and me now. I've fallen for you and I don't fall easily. If you'll have me, I'm yours.'

Leo and Emmie poked their heads round the door then turned away in disgust at seeing the adults cuddling in a chair. 'You really are gross,' they called after them, 'especially when there's a party and mountains of gooey cake outside.' Skye smiled into Zack's neck and he hugged her tighter. Poor Leo never did know what was going to happen next with his mum. She knew he thought she was a bit eccentric. He'd told her he felt kind of okay about his dad going back home soon, too. He would see him when he wasn't away working. Leo's lip had wobbled a little and she'd pulled him into a fast hug and rested her chin on his head like she had when he was a baby. Skye peeked out of the door just as Emmie poked Leo in the shoulder and pointed out that they needed to get a plate of the cakes before everyone else ate them all. She raced off suddenly and he grinned and ran after her, probably hoping that the strawberry doughnut he'd pointed out earlier was still hiding under a pile of cupcakes.

Seeing Skye and Zack come out of the staff room holding hands, Reece's step faltered, before he straightened his shoulders and carried on walking. Skye glanced his way and a bit of her earlier happiness dimmed. Reece had promised he would here to support her and she was glad to see him, but she had spoken with him earlier that day and he had just heard from his boss that he was urgently needed back at work. Reece had been alerted that there was another connection who had links to those that killed their team, meaning he would be away for some months. He'd thought they had solved this problem, but it now seemed that it was a bigger sting operation than had first appeared, and other teams had been targeted. For now, he said he would have to accept that Skye and Zack were together and walk away, which ripped his insides to shreds. Skye had flinched when he'd said this, as she knew how it felt to be apart from everything you'd ever loved. It did mean that Skye would finally be able to stop running and their son would be safe, as there was officially no trace of them, with a little technical magic from Thea.

Skye got the impression that Reece had made an uneasy truce with Thea too, but accepted they still had a long way to go. He knew he'd hurt both women badly, but his connection to Skye was too great for him to ignore, now that he'd found her again. He'd told her she'd done an amazing job raising their son and, although he couldn't be around all the time, Reece fully intended to return and make his family his own again soon. Where Thea and Flo fitted into this she was unsure, but he had a few months away to work on a plan and she understood he intended to get his wife back. Not a chance in hell.

Skye noticed Reece was now standing to one side of the course and saw some of the school mums glance his way and start gossiping. They were looking between her, Zack, and Reece, waiting to see how this would all play out. Skye grinned to herself about what they would do if they knew Reece was an elite spy, as was she. Zack smiled at Skye's happy face and asked to be let in on the joke.

'I was just thinking about all the gossip circulating about us,' she giggled. 'If only they knew what Reece and I really did for a living, and that little old Thea is a technical whiz who could destroy their lives at the click of a mouse! Not only that, but Emmie's runaway mum is a supermodel and you come from one of the most aristocratic and eccentric families in the UK.' She bent over laughing, as all the tension of the last few months expelled itself and drifted away. Zack grabbed Skye's hand and pulled her towards their guests, grinning widely and looking like he was finally enjoying himself. 'Let's go and introduce you to them as a ninja school mum,' he laughed. 'Shall we place bets on how fast they can run?'

THE END

Fantastic Books
Great Authors

CROOKED
CAT

Meet our authors and discover
our exciting range:

- Gripping Thrillers
- Cosy Mysteries
- Romantic Chick-Lit
- Fascinating Historicals
- Exciting Fantasy
- Young Adult and Children's
  Adventures
- Non-Fiction

Visit us at:
www.crookedcatbooks.com

Join us on facebook:
www.facebook.com/crookedcatbooks